Price .50

Miss Madelyn Lister
598 Berwyn St.
Devon, Conn.
Phone 974-5

Freshman
Room 11

Sir Walter Scott

The Academy Classics

SIR WALTER SCOTT'S

LADY OF THE LAKE

EDITED BY

GEORGE B. AITON

FORMERLY STATE INSPECTOR OF HIGH SCHOOLS
FOR MINNESOTA

ALLYN AND BACON

BOSTON   NEW YORK   CHICAGO
ATLANTA   SAN FRANCISCO   DALLAS

Norwood Press
J. S. Cushing Co. — Berwick & Smith Co.
Norwood, Mass., U.S.A.

PREFACE

THIS edition of *The Lady of the Lake* blazes a new trail. It rejects the purely academic treatment of text and author for a personal, friendly spirit of communion with the folk and scenes that Scott describes. Mr. Aiton, perhaps because of his Scotch ancestry, has linked the pulse of the poem with the heart of every reader who revels in brave act or valiant sacrifice.

A special feature is the unusual number of happily chosen illustrations. They provide a splendid supplement to Scott's wonderful word-pictures and give the pupil a feeling of actual contact with the scene of the story.

Teachers, especially, will enjoy the assistance of the editor's suggestions for study, the brief discussion of prosody, and the interesting account of Scott's life. They will appreciate also the meatiness of the notes, the vigorous exercises, and the thought-provoking questions.

ALLYN AND BACON

ACKNOWLEDGMENT

VALENTINE & SONS, Ltd., of Dundee and London, furnished the illustrations in this book, with the exception of the frontispiece, the map, "Monarch of the Glen," "Abbotsford and the River Tweed," "The Library at Abbotsford," "The Armory at Abbotsford," and "The Monument to Scott at Edinburgh."

CONTENTS

		PAGE
INTRODUCTION	. . . .	ix

THE LADY OF THE LAKE

CANTO FIRST: THE CHASE	. . . . . .	1
CANTO SECOND: THE ISLAND	. . . .	33
CANTO THIRD: THE GATHERING	. . . .	68
CANTO FOURTH: THE PROPHECY	. . . .	102
CANTO FIFTH: THE COMBAT	. . . .	133
CANTO SIXTH: THE GUARD-ROOM	. . .	169

APPENDIX

NOTES	. . . .	205
EXERCISES	. . . .	261
A FINAL EXAMINATION	. . . . . .	264
THE STORY OF THE POEM	. . . . .	266
THE GEOGRAPHY OF SCOTLAND	. . . .	269
THE HIGHLANDERS	. . . . . .	272
THE HISTORICAL BACKGROUND	. . . .	277
LIFE OF WALTER SCOTT	. . . . .	279

ILLUSTRATIONS

Sir Walter Scott . . . . *Frontispiece*

PAGE

Map to illustrate *The Lady of the Lake* . . *facing* 1

Ellen's Isle 1

Glenartney 3

Monarch of the Glen 5

Echo Rock, Lochard 7

Teith and Benledi, Callander 8

Loch Katrine, seen from near the Goblin Cave . . 14

Silver Strand, Loch Katrine 17

Ellen's Isle and Benvenue 21

Path by Loch Katrine 33

Glengyle, Loch Katrine 46

Glen Fruin 49

Loch Lomond and Ben Lomond, from Inverhullen near
    Tarbet 54

The Teviot 58

Windings of the Forth and Abbey Craig, Stirling . . 60

Lanrick Mead and Loch Vennachar 68

Otter Island and Ben-an, Loch Lomond . . . 76

Duncraggan's Huts, Glenfinlas 82

Strath-Ire 86

Chapel of Saint Bride 87

Loch Lubnaig 90

Loch Voil, Balquidder 92

Lake of Menteith 94

                                                            PAGE
Pass of Beal-nam-bo   96

Bochastle seen from Coilantogle Ford   100

Pass of Beal 'maha, Loch Lomond   102

Loch Earn and Benvoirlich   108

Stirling Castle from the Back Walk   134

Doune Castle   138

Blair-Drummond   152

Cambus-kenneth Abbey and Tomb of James III   .   .   154

Stirling Castle   168

Loch Achray and Benvenue   183

Trosachs and Ben-an   184

Bracklinn Falls, Callander   187

The Rivers Tweed and Ettrick   269

Brigg of Turk, Trosachs   271

In the Trosachs   275

Abbotsford and the River Tweed   288

The Library at Abbotsford   289

The Armory at Abbotsford   291

The Braes of Yarrow   293

The Monument to Scott at Edinburgh   301

INTRODUCTION

SUGGESTIONS FOR STUDY

The Lady of the Lake is an open-air poem. To get into the full swing of it one should be off by himself and read it aloud to the great out-of-doors. But *The Lady of the Lake* may be brought into the schoolroom successfully. The verses linger long and delightfully in the memory and repay close study.

This is a poem of action. The first oral reading must get on rapidly. The chase, the glorious climb, the oncoming sweep of Roderick's flotilla, the haste of the Fiery Cross, the breathless duel, the surging battle of the pass, and the final scene in the audience room require spirit and speed. This reading should be accomplished, preferably by the instructor and better readers of the class, in not to exceed ten days. This may be done by generous omissions of minor passages, — the teacher bridging the gaps. An active young mind cannot bear (thole, the Scotch say) to wait seemingly forever to learn how the story comes out. To begin line by line and plod along weeks on end after the style of translating a foreign text is to kill interest in the poem for all time to come, but, if the plot be fixed in mind by a rapid reading so that allusions may have meaning and incidents fall into sequence, the study of detail may be made enjoyable.

The student of Scott needs a few books at hand for constant reference. Lockhart's *Life of Sir Walter Scott* should be in every school library. Valuable articles on Scott may be found in the various encyclopædias. Those in the Britannica are naturally the best, as Scott was closely associated with its publisher. For a critical study of Scott's descriptive power, consult the third volume of Ruskin's *Modern Painters*. A good dictionary like the Century is indispensable. Of essays and reviews, Jeffrey's criticism of *The Lady of the Lake* in the *Edinburgh Review* is valuable, but not usually accessible. Carlyle's essay on Scott is able and appreciative. Stephen's *Hours in a Library* (First Series) and Leslie's *Autobiographical Recollections* are not expensive. No American student should fail to read Irving's *Visit to Abbotsford*. Buy the Globe Edition of Scott's poetical works in one volume, which contains Scott's own notes.

PROSODY

The structure of *The Lady of the Lake* is simple. Like *The Lay of the Last Minstrel* and *Marmion*, the poem consists of six cantos each preceded by an introduction. The cantos are divided into stanzas of varying length corresponding to the paragraphs of prose. The lines or verses are coupled two and two by rhymes. This gives each stanza an even number of lines except the seventh stanza of the first canto.

Each line (verse) consists of eight syllables. With occasional exceptions introduced with excellent effect, the accents fall on the second, fourth, sixth, and eighth syllables. Now and then to retard the movement or to lay emphasis, the accent falls on the first syllable instead of the second. The accents divide the line into four feet, each consisting usually of an unaccented syllable followed by an accented syllable.

Couplets chosen almost at random illustrate the musical structure of the lines.

> The rock-y sum-mits, split and rent
> Formed tur-ret, dome, or bat-tle-ment.

> And creep-ing shrubs of thou-sand dyes
> Waved in the west wind's sum-mer sighs.

> And si-lence set-tled wide and still
> On the lone wood and might-y hill.

Too much should not be made of the meter. Avoid sing-song tones. If the verses be read smoothly and intelligently in such a way as to bring out the meaning, the meter will take care of itself. Once in a while a word like *Roderick*, *whimpering*, or *whispering* requires compression into two syllables, but ordinarily a fair reader complies with the requirements of the verse without knowing it.

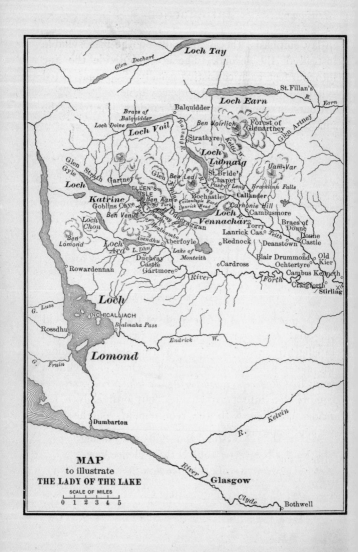

MAP
to illustrate
THE LADY OF THE LAKE

SCALE OF MILES
0 1 2 3 4 5

ELLEN'S ISLE

THE LADY OF THE LAKE

CANTO FIRST

THE CHASE

HARP of the North! that mouldering long hast hung
  On the witch-elm that shades Saint Fillan's spring,
And down the fitful breeze thy numbers flung,
  Till envious ivy did around thee cling,
  Muffling with verdant ringlet every string,—   5
O Minstrel Harp, still must thine accents sleep?
  Mid rustling leaves and fountains murmuring,
Still must thy sweeter sounds their silence keep,
Nor bid a warrior smile, nor teach a maid to weep?

Not thus, in ancient days of Caledon,   10
  Was thy voice mute amid the festal crowd,

When lay of hopeless love, or glory won,
   Aroused the fearful or subdued the proud.
   At each according pause was heard aloud
15 Thine ardent symphony sublime and high!
     Fair dames and crested chiefs attention bowed;
For still the burden of thy minstrelsy
Was Knighthood's dauntless deed, and Beauty's match-
     less eye.

O, wake once more! how rude soe'er the hand
20   That ventures o'er thy magic maze to stray;
  O, wake once more! though scarce my skill command
   Some feeble echoing of thine earlier lay:
   Though harsh and faint, and soon to die away,
And all unworthy of thy nobler strain,
25   Yet, if one heart throb higher at its sway,
The wizard note has not been touched in vain.
Then silent be no more! Enchantress, wake again!

I

   The stag at eve had drunk his fill,
   Where danced the moon on Monan's rill,
30   And deep his midnight lair had made
   In lone Glenartney's hazel shade;
   But, when the sun his beacon red
   Had kindled on Benvoirlich's head,
   The deep-mouthed bloodhound's heavy bay
35   Resounded up the rocky way,
   And faint, from farther distance borne,
   Were heard the clanging hoof and horn.

II

As Chief, who hears his warder call,
"To arms! the foemen storm the wall,"
The antlered monarch of the waste
Sprung from his heathery couch in haste.   40

GLENARTNEY

But, ere his fleet career he took,
The dew-drops from his flanks he shook;
Like crested leader proud and high
Tossed his beamed frontlet to the sky;   45
A moment gazed adown the dale,
A moment snuffed the tainted gale,
A moment listened to the cry,
That thickened as the chase drew nigh;

50　　Then, as the headmost foes appeared,
　　　With one brave bound the copse he cleared,
　　　And, stretching forward free and far,
　　　Sought the wild heaths of Uam-Var.

III

　　　Yelled on the view the opening pack;
55　　Rock, glen, and cavern paid them back;
　　　To many a mingled sound at once
　　　The awakened mountain gave response.
　　　A hundred dogs bayed deep and strong,
　　　Clattered a hundred steeds along,
60　　Their peal the merry horns rung out,
　　　A hundred voices joined the shout;
　　　With hark and whoop and wild halloo,
　　　No rest Benvoirlich's echoes knew.
　　　Far from the tumult fled the roe,
65　　Close in her covert cowered the doe,
　　　The falcon, from her cairn on high,
　　　Cast on the rout a wondering eye,
　　　Till far beyond her piercing ken
　　　The hurricane had swept the glen.
70　　Faint, and more faint, its failing din
　　　Returned from cavern, cliff, and linn,
　　　And silence settled, wide and still,
　　　On the lone wood and mighty hill.

IV

　　　Less loud the sounds of sylvan war
75　　Disturbed the heights of Uam-Var,

And roused the cavern where, 't is told,
A giant made his den of old;
For, ere that steep ascent was won,
High in his pathway hung the sun,

MONARCH OF THE GLEN

And many a gallant, stayed perforce,　　80
Was fain to breathe his faltering horse,
And of the trackers of the deer
Scarce half the lessening pack was near;
So shrewdly on the mountain-side
Had the bold burst their mettle tried.　　85

V

The noble stag was pausing now
Upon the mountain's southern brow,
Where broad extended, far beneath,
The varied realms of fair Menteith.
90   With anxious eye he wandered o'er
Mountain and meadow, moss and moor,
And pondered refuge from his toil,
By far Lochard or Aberfoyle,
But nearer was the copsewood gray
95   That waved and wept on Loch Achray,
And mingled with the pine-trees blue
On the bold cliffs of Benvenue.
Fresh vigor with the hope returned,
With flying foot the heath he spurned,
100   Held westward with unwearied race,
And left behind the panting chase.

VI

'T were long to tell what steeds gave o'er,
As swept the hunt through Cambusmore;
What reins were tightened in despair,
105   When rose Benledi's ridge in air;
Who flagged upon Bochastle's heath,
Who shunned to stem the flooded Teith, —
For twice that day, from shore to shore,
The gallant stag swam stoutly o'er.
110   Few were the stragglers, following far,
That reached the lake of Vennachar,

Echo Rock, Lochard

7

And, when the Brigg of Turk was won,
The headmost horseman rode alone.

VII

Alone, but with unbated zeal,
That horseman plied the scourge and steel;
For jaded now, and spent with toil,
Embossed with foam, and dark with soil,

TEITH AND BENLEDI, CALLANDER

While every gasp with sobs he drew,
The laboring stag strained full in view.
Two dogs of black Saint Hubert's breed,
Unmatched for courage, breath, and speed,
Fast on his flying traces came,
And all but won that desperate game;

For, scarce a spear's length from his haunch,
Vindictive toiled the bloodhounds stanch; 125
Nor nearer might the dogs attain,
Nor farther might the quarry strain.
Thus up the margin of the lake,
Between the precipice and brake,
O'er stock and rock their race they take. 130

VIII

The Hunter marked that mountain high,
The lone lake's western boundary,
And deemed the stag must turn to bay,
Where that huge rampart barred the way;
Already glorying in the prize, 135
Measured his antlers with his eyes;
For the death-wound and death-halloo
Mustered his breath, his whinyard drew: —
But thundering as he came prepared,
With ready arm and weapon bared, 140
The wily quarry shunned the shock,
And turned him from the opposing rock;
Then, dashing down a darksome glen,
Soon lost to hound and Hunter's ken,
In the deep Trosachs' wildest nook 145
His solitary refuge took.
There, while close couched the thicket shed
Cold dews and wild flowers on his head,
He heard the baffled dogs in vain
Rave through the hollow pass amain, 150
Chiding the rocks that yelled again.

IX

Close on the hounds the Hunter came,
To cheer them on the vanished game;
But, stumbling in the rugged dell,
155 The gallant horse exhausted fell.
The impatient rider strove in vain
To rouse him with the spur and rein,
For the good steed, his labors o'er,
Stretched his stiff limbs, to rise no more;
160 Then, touched with pity and remorse,
He sorrowed o'er the expiring horse.
"I little thought, when first thy rein
I slacked upon the banks of Seine,
That Highland eagle e'er should feed
165 On thy fleet limbs, my matchless steed!
Woe worth the chase, woe worth the day,
That costs thy life, my gallant gray!"

X

Then through the dell his horn resounds,
From vain pursuit to call the hounds.
170 Back limped, with slow and crippled pace,
The sulky leaders of the chase;
Close to their master's side they pressed,
With drooping tail and humbled crest;
But still the dingle's hollow throat
175 Prolonged the swelling bugle-note.
The owlets started from their dream,
The eagles answered with their scream,

Round and around the sounds were cast,
Till echo seemed an answering blast;
And on the Hunter hied his way,　　　　　180
To join some comrades of the day,
Yet often paused, so strange the road,
So wondrous were the scenes it showed.

XI

The western waves of ebbing day
Rolled o'er the glen their level way;　　　185
Each purple peak, each flinty spire,
Was bathed in floods of living fire.
But not a setting beam could glow
Within the dark ravines below,
Where twined the path, in shadow hid,　　190
Round many a rocky pyramid,
Shooting abruptly from the dell
Its thunder-splintered pinnacle;
Round many an insulated mass,
The native bulwarks of the pass,　　　　195
Huge as the tower which builders vain
Presumptuous piled on Shinar's plain.
The rocky summits, split and rent,
Formed turret, dome, or battlement,
Or seemed fantastically set　　　　　　200
With cupola or minaret,
Wild crests as pagod ever decked,
Or mosque of Eastern architect.
Nor were these earth-born castles bare,
Nor lacked they many a banner fair;　　205

For, from their shivered brows displayed,
Far o'er the unfathomable glade,
All twinkling with the dewdrop sheen,
The brier-rose fell in streamers green,
210   And creeping shrubs of thousand dyes
Waved in the west-wind's summer sighs.

XII

Boon nature scattered, free and wild,
Each plant or flower, the mountain's child.
Here eglantine embalmed the air,
215   Hawthorn and hazel mingled there;
The primrose pale and violet flower
Found in each clift a narrow bower;
Foxglove and nightshade, side by side,
Emblems of punishment and pride,
220   Grouped their dark hues with every stain
The weather-beaten crags retain.
With boughs, that quaked at every breath,
Gray birch and aspen wept beneath;
Aloft, the ash and warrior oak
225   Cast anchor in the rifted rock;
And, higher yet, the pine-tree hung
His shattered trunk, and frequent flung,
Where seemed the cliffs to meet on high,
His boughs athwart the narrowed sky.
230   Highest of all, where white peaks glanced,
Where glistening streamers waved and danced,
The wanderer's eye could barely view
The summer heaven's delicious blue;

So wondrous wild, the whole might seem
The scenery of a fairy dream.   235

XIII

Onward, amid the copse 'gan peep
A narrow inlet, still and deep,
Affording scarce such breadth of brim
As served the wild duck's brood to swim.
Lost for a space, through thickets veering,   240
But broader when again appearing,
Tall rocks and tufted knolls their face
Could on the dark-blue mirror trace;
And, farther as the Hunter strayed,
Still broader sweep its channels made.   245
The shaggy mounds no longer stood,
Emerging from entangled wood,
But, wave-encircled, seemed to float,
Like castle girdled with its moat;
Yet broader floods extending still   250
Divide them from their parent hill,
Till each, retiring, claims to be
An islet in an inland sea.

XIV

And now, to issue from the glen,
No pathway meets the wanderer's ken,   255
Unless he climb with footing nice
A far-projecting precipice.
The broom's tough roots his ladder made,
The hazel saplings lent their aid;

260   And thus an airy point he won,
         Where, gleaming with the setting sun,
         One burnished sheet of living gold,
         Loch Katrine lay beneath him rolled,
         In all her length far winding lay,
265   With promontory, creek, and bay,
         And islands that, empurpled bright,
         Floated amid the livelier light,

LOCH KATRINE, SEEN FROM NEAR THE GOBLIN CAVE

         And mountains that like giants stand
         To sentinel enchanted land.
270   High on the south, huge Benvenue
         Down on the lake in masses threw
         Crags, knolls, and mounds, confusedly hurled,
         The fragments of an earlier world;
         A wildering forest feathered o'er
275   His ruined sides and summit hoar,

While on the north, through middle air,
Ben-an heaved high his forehead bare.

XV

From the steep promontory gazed
The stranger, raptured and amazed,
And, "What a scene were here," he cried,   280
"For princely pomp or churchman's pride!
On this bold brow, a lordly tower;
In that soft vale, a lady's bower;
On yonder meadow far away,
The turrets of a cloister gray;   285
How blithely might the bugle-horn
Chide on the lake the lingering morn!
How sweet at eve the lover's lute
Chime when the groves were still and mute!
And, when the midnight moon should lave   290
Her forehead in the silver wave,
How solemn on the ear would come
The holy matins' distant hum,
While the deep peal's commanding tone
Should wake, in yonder islet lone,   295
A sainted hermit from his cell,
To drop a bead with every knell!
And bugle, lute, and bell, and all,
Should each bewildered stranger call
To friendly feast and lighted hall.   300

XVI ·

"Blithe were it then to wander here!
But now — beshrew yon nimble deer —

Like that same hermit's, thin and spare,
The copse must give my evening fare;
305   Some mossy bank my couch must be,
Some rustling oak my canopy.
Yet pass we that; the war and chase
Give little choice of resting-place;—
A summer night in greenwood spent
310   Were but to-morrow's merriment:
But hosts may in these wilds abound,
Such as are better missed than found;
To meet with Highland plunderers here
Were worse than loss of steed or deer.—
315   I am alone;— my bugle-strain
May call some straggler of the train;
Or, fall the worst that may betide,
Ere now this falchion has been tried."

XVII

But scarce again his horn he wound,
320   When lo! forth starting at the sound,
From underneath an aged oak
That slanted from the islet rock,
A damsel guider of its way,
A little skiff shot to the bay,
325   That round the promontory steep
Led its deep line in graceful sweep,
Eddying, in almost viewless wave,
The weeping willow twig to lave,
And kiss, with whispering sound and slow,
330   The beach of pebbles bright as snow.

The boat had touched this silver strand
Just as the Hunter left his stand,
And stood concealed amid the brake,
To view this Lady of the Lake.
The maiden paused, as if again   335
She thought to catch the distant strain.

SILVER STRAND, LOCH KATRINE

With head upraised, and look intent,
And eye and ear attentive bent,
And locks flung back, and lips apart,
Like monument of Grecian art,   340
In listening mood, she seemed to stand,
The guardian Naiad of the strand.

XVIII

And ne'er did Grecian chisel trace
A Nymph, a Naiad, or a Grace,

345 Of finer form or lovelier face!
     What though the sun, with ardent frown,
     Had slightly tinged her cheek with brown, —
     The sportive toil, which, short and light,
     Had dyed her glowing hue so bright,
350 Served too in hastier swell to show
     Short glimpses of a breast of snow:
     What though no rule of courtly grace
     To measured mood had trained her pace, —
     A foot more light, a step more true,
355 Ne'er from the heath-flower dashed the dew;
     E'en the slight harebell raised its head,
     Elastic from her airy tread:
     What though upon her speech there hung
     The accents of the mountain tongue, —
360 Those silver sounds, so soft, so dear,
     The listener held his breath to hear!

                    XIX

     A chieftain's daughter seemed the maid;
     Her satin snood, her silken plaid,
     Her golden brooch, such birth betrayed.
365 And seldom was a snood amid
     Such wild luxuriant ringlets hid,
     Whose glossy black to shame might bring
     The plumage of the raven's wing;
     And seldom o'er a breast so fair
370 Mantled a plaid with modest care,
     And never brooch the folds combined
     Above a heart more good and kind.

And, when a space was gained between,
Closer she drew her bosom's screen; —
So forth the startled swan would swing,
So turn to prune his ruffled wing.
Then safe, though fluttered and amazed,
She paused, and on the stranger gazed.
Not his the form, nor his the eye,
That youthful maidens wont to fly.

XXI

On his bold visage middle age
Had slightly pressed its signet sage,
Yet had not quenched the open truth
And fiery vehemence of youth;
Forward and frolic glee was there,
The will to do, the soul to dare,
The sparkling glance, soon blown to fire,
Of hasty love or headlong ire.
His limbs were cast in manly mould
For hardy sports or contest bold;
And, though in peaceful garb arrayed,
And weaponless except his blade,
His stately mien as well implied
A high-born heart, a martial pride,
As if a baron's crest he wore,
And sheathed in armor trode the shore.
Slighting the petty need he showed,
He told of his benighted road;
His ready speech flowed fair and free,
In phrase of gentlest courtesy,

Her kindness and her worth to spy,
You need but gaze on Ellen's eye;
Not Katrine in her mirror blue
Gives back the shaggy banks more true,
Than every free-born glance confessed
The guileless movements of her breast;
Whether joy danced in her dark eye,
Or woe or pity claimed a sigh,
Or filial love was glowing there,
Or meek devotion poured a prayer,
Or tale of injury called forth
The indignant spirit of the North.
One only passion unrevealed
With maiden pride the maid concealed,
Yet not less purely felt the flame; —
O, need I tell that passion's name?

XX

Impatient of the silent horn,
Now on the gale her voice was borne: —   390
"Father!" she cried; the rocks around
Loved to prolong the gentle sound.
Awhile she paused, no answer came; —
"Malcolm, was thine the blast?" the name
Less resolutely uttered fell,   395
The echoes could not catch the swell.
"A stranger I," the Huntsman said,
Advancing from the hazel shade.
The maid, alarmed, with hasty oar
Pushed her light shallop from the shore,   400

Yet seemed that tone and gesture bland
Less used to sue than to command. 430

XXII

Awhile the maid the stranger eyed,
And, reassured, at length replied
That Highland halls were open still
To wildered wanderers of the hill.

ELLEN'S ISLE AND BENVENUE

"Nor think you unexpected come 435
To yon lone isle, our desert home;
Before the heath had lost the dew,
This morn, a couch was pulled for you;
On yonder mountain's purple head
Have ptarmigan and heath-cock bled, 440

And our broad nets have swept the mere,
To furnish forth your evening cheer." —
"Now, by the rood, my lovely maid,
Your courtesy has erred," he said;
445　　"No right have I to claim, misplaced,
The welcome of expected guest.
A wanderer, here by fortune tost,
My way, my friends, my courser lost,
I ne'er before, believe me, fair,
450　　Have ever drawn your mountain air,
Till on this lake's romantic strand
I found a fay in fairy land!" —

XXIII

"I well believe," the maid replied,
As her light skiff approached the side, —
455　　"I well believe, that ne'er before
Your foot has trod Loch Katrine's shore;
But yet, as far as yesternight,
Old Allan-bane foretold your plight, —
A gray-haired sire, whose eye intent
460　　Was on the visioned future bent,
He saw your steed, a dappled gray,
Lie dead beneath the birchen way;
Painted exact your form and mien,
Your hunting-suit of Lincoln green,
465　　That tasselled horn so gaily gilt,
That falchion's crooked blade and hilt,
That cap with heron plumage trim,
And yon two hounds so dark and grim.

He bade that all should ready be
To grace a guest of fair degree;　　　　　470
But light I held his prophecy,
And deemed it was my father's horn
Whose echoes o'er the lake were borne."

XXIV

The stranger smiled: "Since to your home
A destined errant-knight I come,　　　　　475
Announced by prophet sooth and old,
Doomed, doubtless, for achievement bold,
I'll lightly front each high emprise
For one kind glance of those bright eyes.
Permit me first the task to guide　　　　　480
Your fairy frigate o'er the tide."
The maid, with smile suppressed and sly,
The toil unwonted saw him try;
For seldom, sure, if e'er before,
His noble hand had grasped an oar:　　　　485
Yet with main strength his strokes he drew,
And o'er the lake the shallop flew;
With heads erect and whimpering cry,
The hounds behind their passage ply.
Nor frequent does the bright oar break　　490
The darkening mirror of the lake,
Until the rocky isle they reach,
And moor their shallop on the beach.

XXV

The stranger viewed the shore around;
'T was all so close with copsewood bound,　　495

Nor track nor pathway might declare
That human foot frequented there,
Until the mountain maiden showed
A clambering unsuspected road,
500   That winded through the tangled screen,
And opened on a narrow green,
Where weeping birch and willow round
With their long fibres swept the ground.
Here, for retreat in dangerous hour,
505   Some chief had framed a rustic bower.

XXVI

It was a lodge of ample size,
But strange of structure and device;
Of such materials as around
The workman's hand had readiest found.
510   Lopped of their boughs, their hoar trunks bared,
And by the hatchet rudely squared,
To give the walls their destined height,
The sturdy oak and ash unite;
While moss and clay and leaves combined
515   To fence each crevice from the wind.
The lighter pine-trees overhead
Their slender length for rafters spread,
And withered heath and rushes dry
Supplied a russet canopy.
520   Due westward, fronting to the green,
A rural portico was seen,
Aloft on native pillars borne,
Of mountain fir with bark unshorn,

Where Ellen's hand had taught to twine
The ivy and Idæan vine,　　　　　　　　　525
The clematis, the favored flower
Which boasts the name of virgin-bower,
And every hardy plant could bear
Loch Katrine's keen and searching air.
An instant in this porch she stayed,　　　530
And gaily to the stranger said:
"On heaven and on thy lady call,
And enter the enchanted hall!"

XXVII

"My hope, my heaven, my trust must be,
My gentle guide, in following thee!" —　　535
He crossed the threshold, — and a clang
Of angry steel that instant rang.
To his bold brow his spirit rushed,
But soon for vain alarm he blushed,
When on the floor he saw displayed,　　　540
Cause of the din, a naked blade
Dropped from the sheath, that careless flung
Upon a stag's huge antlers swung;
For all around, the walls to grace,
Hung trophies of the fight or chase:　　　545
A target there, a bugle here,
A battle-axe, a hunting-spear,
And broadswords, bows, and arrows store,
With the tusked trophies of the boar.
Here grins the wolf as when he died,　　　550
And there the wild-cat's brindled hide

The frontlet of the elk adorns,
Or mantles o'er the bison's horns;
Pennons and flags defaced and stained,
555   That blackening streaks of blood retained,
And deer-skins, dappled, dun, and white,
With otter's fur and seal's unite,
In rude and uncouth tapestry all,
To garnish forth the sylvan hall.

XXVIII

560   The wondering stranger round him gazed,
And next the fallen weapon raised: —
Few were the arms whose sinewy strength
Sufficed to stretch it forth at length.
And as the brand he poised and swayed,
565   "I never knew but one," he said,
"Whose stalwart arm might brook to wield
A blade like this in battle-field."
She sighed, then smiled and took the word:
"You see the guardian champion's sword;
570   As light it trembles in his hand
As in my grasp a hazel wand:
My sire's tall form might grace the part
Of Ferragus or Ascabart,
But in the absent giant's hold
575   Are women now, and menials old."

XXIX

The mistress of the mansion came,
Mature of age, a graceful dame,

Whose easy step and stately port
Had well become a princely court,
To whom, though more than kindred knew,   580
Young Ellen gave a mother's due.
Meet welcome to her guest she made,
And every courteous rite was paid
That hospitality could claim,
Though all unasked his birth and name.   585
Such then the reverence to a guest,
That fellest foe might join the feast,
And from his deadliest foeman's door
Unquestioned turn, the banquet o'er.
At length his rank the stranger names,   590
"The Knight of Snowdoun, James Fitz-James;
Lord of a barren heritage,
Which his brave sires, from age to age,
By their good swords had held with toil;
His sire had fallen in such turmoil,   595
And he, God wot, was forced to stand
Oft for his right with blade in hand.
This morning with Lord Moray's train
He chased a stalwart stag in vain,
Outstripped his comrades, missed the deer,   600
Lost his good steed, and wandered here."

                    XXX

Fain would the Knight in turn require
The name and state of Ellen's sire.
Well showed the elder lady's mien
That courts and cities she had seen;   605

Ellen, though more her looks displayed
The simple grace of sylvan maid,
In speech and gesture, form and face,
Showed she was come of gentle race.
610 'T were strange in ruder rank to find
Such looks, such manners, and such mind.
Each hint the Knight of Snowdoun gave
Dame Margaret heard with silence grave;
Or Ellen, innocently gay,
615 Turned all inquiry light away: —
"Weird women we! by dale and down
We dwell, afar from tower and town.
We stem the flood, we ride the blast,
On wandering knights our spells we cast.
620 While viewless minstrels touch the string,
'T is thus our charmed rhymes we sing."
She sung, and still a harp unseen
Filled up the symphony between.

XXXI

Song

Soldier, rest! thy warfare o'er,
625 　Sleep the sleep that knows not breaking;
Dream of battled fields no more,
　Days of danger, nights of waking.
In our isle's enchanted hall,
　Hands unseen thy couch are strewing,
630 Fairy strains of music fall,
　Every sense in slumber dewing.
Soldier, rest! thy warfare o'er,
Dream of fighting fields no more;

Sleep the sleep that knows not breaking,
Morn of toil, nor night of waking.　　　　635

No rude sound shall reach thine ear,
　　Armor's clang or war-steed champing,
Trump nor pibroch summon here
　　Mustering clan or squadron tramping.
Yet the lark's shrill fife may come　　　　640
　　At the daybreak from the fallow,
And the bittern sound his drum,
　　Booming from the sedgy shallow.
Ruder sounds shall none be near,
Guards nor warders challenge here,　　　　645
Here's no war-steed's neigh and champing,
Shouting clans or squadrons stamping.

XXXII

She paused, — then, blushing, led the lay,
To grace the stranger of the day.
Her mellow notes awhile prolong　　　　650
The cadence of the flowing song,
Till to her lips in measured frame
The minstrel verse spontaneous came.

Song Continued

Huntsman, rest! thy chase is done;
　　While our slumbrous spells assail ye,　　655
Dream not, with the rising sun,
　　Bugles here shall sound reveille.
Sleep! the deer is in his den;
　　Sleep! thy hounds are by thee lying;

660   Sleep! nor dream in yonder glen
            How thy gallant steed lay dying.
        Huntsman, rest! thy chase is done;
        Think not of the rising sun,
        For at dawning to assail ye
665   Here no bugles sound reveille.

                    XXXIII

        The hall was cleared, — the stranger's bed
        Was there of mountain heather spread,
        Where oft a hundred guests had lain,
        And dreamed their forest sports again.
670   But vainly did the heath-flower shed
        Its moorland fragrance round his head;
        Not Ellen's spell had lulled to rest
        The fever of his troubled breast.
        In broken dreams the image rose
675   Of varied perils, pains, and woes:
        His steed now flounders in the brake,
        Now sinks his barge upon the lake;
        Now leader of a broken host,
        His standard falls, his honor 's lost.
680   Then, — from my couch may heavenly might
        Chase that worst phantom of the night! —
        Again returned the scenes of youth,
        Of confident, undoubting truth;
        Again his soul he interchanged
685   With friends whose hearts were long estranged.
        They come, in dim procession led,
        The cold, the faithless, and the dead;
        As warm each hand, each brow as gay,

As if they parted yesterday.
And doubt distracts him at the view, —   690
O, were his senses false or true?
Dreamed he of death or broken vow,
Or is it all a vision now?

XXXIV

At length, with Ellen in a grove
He seemed to walk and speak of love;   695
She listened with a blush and sigh,
His suit was warm, his hopes were high.
He sought her yielded hand to clasp,
And a cold gauntlet met his grasp:
The phantom's sex was changed and gone,   700
Upon its head a helmet shone;
Slowly enlarged to giant size,
With darkened cheek and threatening eyes,
The grisly visage, stern and hoar,
To Ellen still a likeness bore. —   705
He woke, and, panting with affright,
Recalled the vision of the night.
The hearth's decaying brands were red,
And deep and dusky lustre shed,
Half showing, half concealing, all   710
The uncouth trophies of the hall.
Mid those the stranger fixed his eye
Where that huge falchion hung on high,
And thoughts on thoughts, a countless throng,
Rushed, chasing countless thoughts along,   715
Until, the giddy whirl to cure,
He rose and sought the moonshine pure.

XXXV

The wild rose, eglantine, and broom
Wasted around their rich perfume;
720 The birch-trees wept in fragrant balm;
The aspens slept beneath the calm;
The silver light, with quivering glance,
Played on the water's still expanse, —
Wild were the heart whose passion's sway
725 Could rage beneath the sober ray!
He felt its calm, that warrior guest,
While thus he communed with his breast: —
"Why is it, at each turn I trace
Some memory of that exiled race?
730 Can I not mountain maiden spy,
But she must bear the Douglas eye?
Can I not view a Highland brand,
But it must match the Douglas hand?
Can I not frame a fevered dream,
735 But still the Douglas is the theme?
I 'll dream no more, — by manly mind
Not even in sleep is will resigned.
My midnight orisons said o'er,
I 'll turn to rest, and dream no more."
740 His midnight orisons he told,
A prayer with every bead of gold,
Consigned to heaven his cares and woes,
And sunk in undisturbed repose,
Until the heath-cock shrilly crew,
745 And morning dawned on Benvenue.

PATH BY LOCH KATRINE

CANTO SECOND

THE ISLAND

I

At morn the black-cock trims his jetty wing,
  'T is morning prompts the linnet's blithest lay,
All Nature's children feel the matin spring
  Of life reviving, with reviving day;
  And, while yon little bark glides down the bay, 5
Wafting the stranger on his way again,
  Morn's genial influence roused a minstrel gray,
And sweetly o'er the lake was heard thy strain,
Mixed with the sounding harp, O white-haired Allan-
    bane!

33

II

Song

Not faster yonder rowers' might
    Flings from their oars the spray,
Not faster yonder rippling bright,
That tracks the shallop's course in light,
    Melts in the lake away,
Than men from memory erase
The benefits of former days;
Then, stranger, go! good speed the while,
Nor think again of the lonely isle.

High place to thee in royal court,
    High place in battled line,
Good hawk and hound for sylvan sport,
Where beauty sees the brave resort,
    The honored meed be thine!
True be thy sword, thy friend sincere,
Thy lady constant, kind, and dear,
And lost in love's and friendship's smile
Be memory of the lonely isle!

III

Song Continued

But if beneath yon southern sky
    A plaided stranger roam,
Whose drooping crest and stifled sigh,
And sunken cheek and heavy eye
    Pine for his Highland home;
Then, warrior, then be thine to show
The care that soothes a wanderer's woe;

Remember then thy hap erewhile, 35
A stranger in the lonely isle.

Or if on life's uncertain main
    Mishap shall mar thy sail;
If faithful, wise, and brave in vain,
Woe, want, and exile thou sustain 40
    Beneath the fickle gale;
Waste not a sigh on fortune changed,
On thankless courts, or friends estranged,
But come where kindred worth shall smile,
To greet thee in the lonely isle. 45

IV

As died the sounds upon the tide,
The shallop reached the mainland side,
And, ere his onward way he took,
The stranger cast a lingering look,
Where easily his eye might reach 50
The Harper on the islet beach,
Reclined against a blighted tree,
As wasted, gray, and worn as he.
To minstrel meditation given,
His reverend brow was raised to heaven, 55
As from the rising sun to claim
A sparkle of inspiring flame.
His hand, reclined upon the wire,
Seemed watching the awakening fire,
So still he sat as those who wait 60
Till judgment speak the doom of fate;

So still, as if no breeze might dare
To lift one lock of hoary hair;
So still, as life itself were fled
In the last sound his harp had sped.

V

Upon a rock with lichens wild,
Beside him Ellen sat and smiled. —
Smiled she to see the stately drake
Lead forth his fleet upon the lake,
While her vexed spaniel from the beach
Bayed at the prize beyond his reach?
Yet tell me, then, the maid who knows,
Why deepened on her cheek the rose? —
Forgive, forgive, Fidelity!
Perchance the maiden smiled to see
Yon parting lingerer wave adieu,
And stop and turn to wave anew;
And, lovely ladies, ere your ire
Condemn the heroine of my lyre,
Show me the fair would scorn to spy
And prize such conquest of her eye!

VI

While yet he loitered on the spot,
It seemed as Ellen marked him not;
But, when he turned him to the glade,
One courteous parting sign she made;
And after, oft the knight would say
That not, when prize of festal day

Was dealt him by the brightest fair
Who e'er wore jewel in her hair,
So highly did his bosom swell　　　　　　　90
As at that simple mute farewell.
Now with a trusty mountain-guide,
And his dark stag-hounds by his side,
He parts, — the maid, unconscious still,
Watched him wind slowly round the hill;　　95
But, when his stately form was hid,
The guardian in her bosom chid, —
"Thy Malcolm! vain and selfish maid!"
'T was thus upbraiding conscience said, —
"Not so had Malcolm idly hung　　　　　　100
On the smooth phrase of Southern tongue;
Not so had Malcolm strained his eye
Another step than thine to spy." —
"Wake, Allan-bane," aloud she cried
To the old minstrel by her side, —　　　　105
"Arouse thee from thy moody dream!
I 'll give thy harp heroic theme,
And warm thee with a noble name;
Pour forth the glory of the Græme!"
Scarce from her lip the word had rushed,　　110
When deep the conscious maiden blushed;
For of his clan, in hall and bower,
Young Malcolm Græme was held the flower.

VII

The minstrel waked his harp, — three times
Arose the well-known martial chimes,　　　　115

And thrice their high heroic pride
In melancholy murmurs died.
"Vainly thou bidst, O noble maid,"
Clasping his withered hands, he said,
120   "Vainly thou bidst me wake the strain,
Though all unwont to bid in vain.
Alas! than mine a mightier hand
Has tuned my harp, my strings has spanned!
I touch the chords of joy, but low
125   And mournful answer notes of woe;
And the proud march which victors tread
Sinks in the wailing for the dead.
O, well for me, if mine alone
That dirge's deep prophetic tone!
130   If, as my tuneful fathers said,
This harp, which erst Saint Modan swayed,
Can thus its master's fate foretell,
Then welcome be the minstrel's knell!

VIII

"But ah! dear lady, thus it sighed,
135   The eve thy sainted mother died;
And such the sounds which, while I strove
To wake a lay of war or love,
Came marring all the festal mirth,
Appalling me who gave them birth,
140   And, disobedient to my call,
Wailed loud through Bothwell's bannered hall,
Ere Douglases, to ruin driven,
Were exiled from their native heaven. —

O! if yet worse mishap and woe
My master's house must undergo,   145
Or aught but weal to Ellen fair
Brood in these accents of despair,
No future bard, sad Harp! shall fling
Triumph or rapture from thy string;
One short, one final strain shall flow,   150
Fraught with unutterable woe,
Then shivered shall thy fragments lie,
Thy master cast him down and die!"

IX

Soothing she answered him: "Assuage,
Mine honored friend, the fears of age;   155
All melodies to thee are known
That harp has rung or pipe has blown,
In Lowland vale or Highland glen,
From Tweed to Spey, — what marvel, then,
At times unbidden notes should rise,   160
Confusedly bound in memory's ties,
Entangling, as they rush along,
The war-march with the funeral song? —
Small ground is now for boding fear;
Obscure, but safe, we rest us here.   165
My sire, in native virtue great,
Resigning lordship, lands, and state,
Not then to fortune more resigned
Than yonder oak might give the wind;
The graceful foliage storms may reave,   170
The noble stem they cannot grieve.

For me," — she stooped, and, looking round,
Plucked a blue harebell from the ground, —
"For me, whose memory scarce conveys
175   An image of more splendid days,
This little flower that loves the lea
May well my simple emblem be;
It drinks heaven's dew as blithe as rose
That in the King's own garden grows;
180   And, when I place it in my hair,
Allan, a bard is bound to swear
He ne'er saw coronet so fair."
Then playfully the chaplet wild
She wreathed in her dark locks, and smiled.

X

185   Her smile, her speech, with winning sway,
Wiled the old Harper's mood away.
With such a look as hermits throw;
When angels stoop to soothe their woe,
He gazed till fond regret and pride
190   Thrilled to a tear, then thus replied:
"Loveliest and best! thou little know'st
The rank, the honors, thou hast lost!
O, might I live to see thee grace,
In Scotland's court, thy birthright place,
195   To see my favorite's step advance
The lightest in the courtly dance,
The cause of every gallant's sigh,
And leading star of every eye,
And theme of every minstrel's art,
200   The Lady of the Bleeding Heart!"

XI

"Fair dreams are these," the maiden cried, —
Light was her accent, yet she sighed, —
"Yet is this mossy rock to me
Worth splendid chair and canopy;
Nor would my footstep spring more gay　　　　205
In courtly dance than blithe strathspey,
Nor half so pleased mine ear incline
To royal minstrel's lay as thine.
And then for suitors proud and high,
To bend before my conquering eye, —　　　　210
Thou, flattering bard! thyself wilt say
That grim Sir Roderick owns its sway.
The Saxon scourge, Clan-Alpine's pride,
The terror of Loch Lomond's side,
Would, at my suit, thou know'st, delay　　　　215
A Lennox foray — for a day." —

XII

The ancient bard her glee repressed:
"Ill hast thou chosen theme for jest!
For who, through all this western wild,
Named Black Sir Roderick e'er and smiled?　　　　220
In Holy-Rood a knight he slew;
I saw, when back the dirk he drew,
Courtiers give place before the stride
Of the undaunted homicide;
And since, though outlawed, hath his hand　　　　225
Full sternly kept his mountain land.
Who else dared give — ah! woe the day,
That I such hated truth should say! —

The Douglas, like a stricken deer,
230   Disowned by every noble peer,
Even the rude refuge we have here?
Alas, this wild marauding Chief
Alone might hazard our relief,
And, now thy maiden charms expand,
235   Looks for his guerdon in thy hand;
Full soon may dispensation sought,
To back his suit, from Rome be brought.
Then, though an exile on the hill,
Thy father, as the Douglas, still
240   Be held in reverence and fear;
And, though to Roderick thou 'rt so dear
That thou mightst guide with silken thread,
Slave of thy will, this chieftain dread,
Yet, O loved maid, thy mirth refrain!
245   Thy hand is on a lion's mane." —

XIII

" Minstrel," the maid replied, and high
Her father's soul glanced from her eye,
"My debts to Roderick's house I know:
All that a mother could bestow
250   To Lady Margaret's care I owe,
Since first an orphan in the wild
She sorrowed o'er her sister's child;
To her brave chieftain son, from ire
Of Scotland's king who shrouds my sire,
255   A deeper, holier debt is owed;
And, could I pay it with my blood,

Allan! Sir Roderick should command
My blood, my life, — but not my hand.
Rather will Ellen Douglas dwell
A votaress in Maronnon's cell;   260
Rather through realms beyond the sea,
Seeking the world's cold charity,
Where ne'er was spoke a Scottish word,
And ne'er the name of Douglas heard,
An outcast pilgrim will she rove,   265
Than wed the man she cannot love.

XIV

"Thou shak'st, good friend, thy tresses gray, —
That pleading look, what can it say
But what I own? — I grant him brave,
But wild as Bracklinn's thundering wave;   270
And generous, — save vindictive mood
Or jealous transport chafe his blood:
I grant him true to friendly band,
As his claymore is to his hand;
But oh! that very blade of steel   275
More mercy for a foe would feel:
I grant him liberal, to fling
Among his clan the wealth they bring,
When back by lake and glen they wind,
And in the Lowland leave behind,   280
Where once some pleasant hamlet stood
A mass of ashes slaked with blood.
The hand that for my father fought
I honor, as his daughter ought;

285   But can I clasp it reeking red
       From peasants slaughtered in their shed?
       No! wildly while his virtues gleam,
       They make his passions darker seem,
       And flash along his spirit high,
290   Like lightning o'er the midnight sky.
       While yet a child, — and children know,
       Instinctive taught, the friend and foe, —
       I shuddered at his brow of gloom,
       His shadowy plaid and sable plume;
295   A maiden grown, I ill could bear
       His haughty mien and lordly air:
       But, if thou join'st a suitor's claim,
       In serious mood, to Roderick's name,
       I thrill with anguish! or, if e'er
300   A Douglas knew the word, with fear.
       To change such odious theme were best, —
       What think'st thou of our stranger guest?" —

XV

       "What think I of him? — woe the while
       That brought such wanderer to our isle!
305   Thy father's battle-brand, of yore
       For Tine-man forged by fairy lore,
       What time he leagued, no longer foes,
       His Border spears with Hotspur's bows,
       Did, self-unscabbarded, foreshow
310   The footsteps of a secret foe.
       If courtly spy hath harbored here,
       What may we for the Douglas fear?

What for this island, deemed of old
Clan-Alpine's last and surest hold?
If neither spy nor foe, I pray   315
What yet may jealous Roderick say? —
Nay, wave not thy disdainful head,
Bethink thee of the discord dread
That kindled when at Beltane game
Thou ledst the dance with Malcolm Græme;   320
Still, though thy sire the peace renewed,
Smoulders in Roderick's breast the feud:
Beware! — But hark! what sounds are these?
My dull ears catch no faltering breeze,
No weeping birch nor aspens wake,   325
Nor breath is dimpling in the lake;
Still is the canna's hoary beard,
Yet, by my minstrel faith, I heard —
And hark again! some pipe of war
Sends the bold pibroch from afar."   330

                        XVI

Far up the lengthened lake were spied
Four darkening specks upon the tide,
That, slow enlarging on the view,
Four manned and masted barges grew,
And, bearing downwards from Glengyle,   335
Steered full upon the lonely isle;
The point of Brianchoil they passed,
And, to the windward as they cast,
Against the sun they gave to shine
The bold Sir Roderick's bannered Pine.   340

Nearer and nearer as they bear,
Spears, pikes, and axes flash in air.
Now might you see the tartans brave,
And plaids and plumage dance and wave:
345 Now see the bonnets sink and rise,
As his tough oar the rower plies;

GLENGYLE, LOCH KATRINE

See, flashing at each sturdy stroke,
The wave ascending into smoke;
See the proud pipers on the bow,
350 And mark the gaudy streamers flow
From their loud chanters down, and sweep
The furrowed bosom of the deep,
As, rushing through the lake amain,
They plied the ancient Highland strain.

XVII

Ever, as on they bore, more loud   355
And louder rung the pibroch proud.
At first the sounds, by distance tame,
Mellowed along the waters came,
And, lingering long by cape and bay,
Wailed every harsher note away,   360
Then, bursting bolder on the ear,
The clan's shrill Gathering they could hear,
Those thrilling sounds that call the might
Of old Clan-Alpine to the fight.
Thick beat the rapid notes, as when   365
The mustering hundreds shake the glen,
And, hurrying at the signal dread,
The battered earth returns their tread.
Then prelude light, of livelier tone,
Expressed their merry marching on,   370
Ere peal of closing battle rose,
With mingled outcry, shrieks, and blows;
And mimic din of stroke and ward,
As broadsword upon target jarred;
And groaning pause, ere yet again,   375
Condensed, the battle yelled amain:
The rapid charge, the rallying shout,
Retreat borne headlong into rout,
And bursts of triumph, to declare
Clan-Alpine's conquest — all were there.   380
Nor ended thus the strain, but slow
Sunk in a moan prolonged and low,
And changed the conquering clarion swell
For wild lament o'er those that fell.

XVIII

385 The war-pipes ceased, but lake and hill
Were busy with their echoes still;
And, when they slept, a vocal strain
Bade their hoarse chorus wake again,
While loud a hundred clansmen raise
390 Their voices in their Chieftain's praise.
Each boatman, bending to his oar,
With measured sweep the burden bore,
In such wild cadence as the breeze
Makes through December's leafless trees.
395 The chorus first could Allan know,
"Roderick Vich Alpine, ho! iro!"
And near, and nearer as they rowed,
Distinct the martial ditty flowed.

XIX

Boat Song

Hail to the Chief who in triumph advances!
400 Honored and blessed be the ever-green Pine!
Long may the tree, in his banner that glances,
Flourish, the shelter and grace of our line!
Heaven send it happy dew,
Earth lend it sap anew,
405 Gaily to bourgeon and broadly to grow,
While every Highland glen
Sends our shout back again,
"Roderigh Vich Alpine dhu, ho! ieroe!"

Ours is no sapling, chance-sown by the fountain,
410 Blooming at Beltane, in winter to fade;

When the whirlwind has stripped every leaf on the
    mountain
  The more shall Clan-Alpine exult in her shade.
      Moored in the rifted rock,
      Proof to the tempest's shock,
  Firmer he roots him the ruder it blow;   415
      Menteith and Breadalbane, then,
      Echo his praise again,
  "Roderigh Vich Alpine dhu, ho! ieroe!"

GLEN FRUIN

XX

Boat Song Continued

Proudly our pibroch has thrilled in Glen Fruin,
  And Bannochar's groans to our slogan replied;   420
Glen Luss and Ross-dhu, they are smoking in ruin,
  And the best of Loch Lomond lie dead on her side.

Widow and Saxon maid
Long shall lament our raid,
425   Think of Clan-Alpine with fear and with woe;
Lennox and Leven-glen
Shake when they hear again,
"Roderigh Vich Alpine dhu, ho! ieroe!"

Row, vassals, row, for the pride of the Highlands!
430   Stretch to your oars for the ever-green Pine!
O, that the rosebud that graces yon islands
Were wreathed in a garland around him to twine!
O, that some seedling gem,
Worthy such noble stem,
435   Honored and blest in their shadow might grow!
Loud from Clan-Alpine then
Ring from her deepmost glen,
"Roderigh Vich Alpine dhu, ho! ieroe!"

XXI

With all her joyful female band
440   Had Lady Margaret sought the strand,
Loose on the breeze their tresses flew,
And high their snowy arms they threw,
As echoing back with shrill acclaim,
And chorus wild, the Chieftain's name;
445   While, prompt to please, with mother's art,
The darling passion of his heart,
The Dame called Ellen to the strand,
To greet her kinsman ere he land:
"Come, loiterer, come! a Douglas thou,
450   And shun to wreathe a victor's brow?"

Reluctantly and slow, the maid
The unwelcome summoning obeyed,
And, when a distant bugle rung,
In the mid-path aside she sprung: —
"List, Allan-bane! From mainland cast   455
I hear my father's signal blast.
Be ours," she cried, "the skiff to guide,
And waft him from the mountain-side."
Then, like a sunbeam swift and bright,
She darted to her shallop light,   460
And, eagerly while Roderick scanned,
For her dear form, his mother's band,
The islet far behind her lay,
And she had landed in the bay.

XXII

Some feelings are to mortals given   465
With less of earth in them than heaven;
And, if there be a human tear
From passion's dross refined and clear,
A tear so limpid and so meek
It would not stain an angel's cheek,   470
'T is that which pious fathers shed
Upon a duteous daughter's head!
And, as the Douglas to his breast
His darling Ellen closely pressed,
Such holy drops her tresses steeped,   475
Though 't was an hero's eye that weeped.
Nor, while on Ellen's faltering tongue
Her filial welcomes crowded hung,

Marked she that fear — affection's proof —
480   Still held a graceful youth aloof;
No! not till Douglas named his name,
Although the youth was Malcolm Græme.

XXIII

Allan, with wistful look the while,
Marked Roderick landing on the isle;
485   His master piteously he eyed,
Then gazed upon the Chieftain's pride,
Then dashed with hasty hand away
From his dimmed eye the gathering spray;
And Douglas, as his hand he laid
490   On Malcolm's shoulder, kindly said:
"Canst thou, young friend, no meaning spy
In my poor follower's glistening eye?
I'll tell thee: — he recalls the day
When in my praise he led the lay
495   O'er the arched gate of Bothwell proud,
While many a minstrel answered loud,
When Percy's Norman pennon, won
In bloody field, before me shone,
And twice ten knights, the least a name
500   As mighty as yon Chief may claim,
Gracing my pomp, behind me came.
Yet trust me, Malcolm, not so proud
Was I of all that marshalled crowd,
Though the waned crescent owned my might,
505   And in my train trooped lord and knight,
Though Blantyre hymned her holiest lays,

And Bothwell's bard flung back my praise,
As when this old man's silent tear
And this poor maid's affection dear
A welcome give more kind and true   510
Than aught my better fortunes knew.
Forgive, my friend, a father's boast, —
O, it out-beggars all I lost!"

XXIV

Delightful praise! — like summer rose,
That brighter in the dew-drop glows,   515
The bashful maiden's cheek appeared,
For Douglas spoke, and Malcolm heard.
The flush of shame-faced joy to hide,
The hounds, the hawk, her cares divide;
The loved caresses of the maid   520
The dog with crouch and whimper paid;
And, at her whistle, on her hand
The falcon took his favorite stand,
Closed his dark wing, relaxed his eye,
Nor, though unhooded, sought to fly.   525
And, trust, while in such guise she stood,
Like fabled Goddess of the wood,
That, if a father's partial thought
O'erweighed her worth and beauty aught,
Well might the lover's judgment fail   530
To balance with a juster scale;
For, with each secret glance he stole,
The fond enthusiast sent his soul.

XXV

Of stature fair, and slender frame,
535 But firmly knit, was Malcolm Græme.
The belted plaid and tartan hose
Did ne'er more graceful limbs disclose;
His flaxen hair, of sunny hue,
Curled closely round his bonnet blue.

LOCH LOMOND AND BEN LOMOND, FROM INVERHULLEN NEAR
TARBET

540 Trained to the chase, his eagle eye
The ptarmigan in snow could spy;
Each pass, by mountain, lake, and heath,
He knew, through Lennox and Menteith;
Vain was the bound of dark-brown doe
545 When Malcolm bent his sounding bow,

And scarce that doe, though winged with fear,
Outstripped in speed the mountaineer:
Right up Ben Lomond could he press,
And not a sob his toil confess.
His form accorded with a mind　　　　　　　550
Lively and ardent, frank and kind;
A blither heart, till Ellen came,
Did never love nor sorrow tame;
It danced as lightsome in his breast
As played the feather on his crest.　　　　555
Yet friends, who nearest knew the youth,
His scorn of wrong, his zeal for truth,
And bards, who saw his features bold
When kindled by the tales of old,
Said, were that youth to manhood grown,　　560
Not long should Roderick Dhu's renown,
Be foremost voiced by mountain fame,
But quail to that of Malcolm Græme.

XXVI

Now back they wend their watery way,
And, "O my sire!" did Ellen say,　　　　　565
"Why urge thy chase so far astray?
And why so late returned?　And why" —
The rest was in her speaking eye.
"My child, the chase I follow far,
'T is mimicry of noble war;　　　　　　570
And with that gallant pastime reft
Were all of Douglas I have left.
I met young Malcolm as I strayed
Far eastward, in Glenfinlas' shade;

575 Nor strayed I safe, for all around
Hunters and horsemen scoured the ground.
This youth, though still a royal ward,
Risked life and land to be my guard,
And through the passes of the wood
580 Guided my steps, not unpursued;
And Roderick shall his welcome make,
Despite old spleen, for Douglas' sake.
Then must he seek Strath-Endrick glen,
Nor peril aught for me again."

XXVII

585 Sir Roderick, who to meet them came,
Reddened at sight of Malcolm Græme,
Yet, not in action, word, or eye,
Failed aught in hospitality.
In talk and sport they whiled away
590 The morning of that summer day;
But at high noon a courier light
Held secret parley with the knight,
Whose moody aspect soon declared
That evil was the news he heard.
595 Deep thought seemed toiling in his head;
Yet was the evening banquet made
Ere he assembled round the flame
His mother, Douglas, and the Græme,
And Ellen too; then cast around
600 His eyes, then fixed them on the ground,
As studying phrase that might avail
Best to convey unpleasant tale.

Long with his dagger's hilt he played,
Then raised his haughty brow and said: —

XXVIII

"Short be my speech; — nor time affords,   605
Nor my plain temper, glozing words.
Kinsman and father, — if such a name
Douglas vouchsafe to Roderick's claim;
Mine honored mother; — Ellen, — why,
My cousin, turn away thine eye? —   610
And Græme, in whom I hope to know
Full soon a noble friend or foe,
When age shall give thee thy command,
And leading in thy native land, —
List all! — the King's vindictive pride   615
Boasts to have tamed the Border-side,
Where chiefs, with hound and hawk who came
To share their monarch's sylvan game,
Themselves in bloody toils were snared,
And, when the banquet they prepared,   620
And wide their loyal portals flung,
O'er their own gateway struggling hung.
Loud cries their blood from Meggat's mead,
From Yarrow braes and banks of Tweed,
Where the lone streams of Ettrick glide,   625
And from the silver Teviot's side;
The dales, where martial clans did ride,
Are now one sheep-walk, waste and wide.
This tyrant of the Scottish throne,
So faithless and so ruthless known,   630

Now hither comes; his end the same,
The same pretext of sylvan game.
What grace for Highland Chiefs, judge ye
By fate of Border chivalry.
635   Yet more; amid Glenfinlas' green,
Douglas, thy stately form was seen.
This by espial sure I know:
Your counsel in the streight I show."

THE TEVIOT

XXIX

Ellen and Margaret fearfully
640   Sought comfort in each other's eye,
Then turned their ghastly look, each one,
This to her sire, that to her son.

The hasty color went and came
In the bold cheek of Malcolm Græme,
But from his glance it well appeared   645
'T was but for Ellen that he feared;
While, sorrowful, but undismayed,
The Douglas thus his counsel said:
"Brave Roderick, though the tempest roar,
It may but thunder and pass o'er;   650
Nor will I here remain an hour,
To draw the lightning on thy bower;
For well thou know'st, at this gray head
The royal bolt were fiercest sped.
For thee, who, at thy King's command,   655
Canst aid him with a gallant band,
Submission, homage, humbled pride
Shall turn the Monarch's wrath aside.
Poor remnants of the Bleeding Heart,
Ellen and I will seek apart   660
The refuge of some forest cell,
There, like the hunted quarry, dwell,
Till on the mountain and the moor
The stern pursuit be passed and o'er," —

XXX

"No, by mine honor," Roderick said,   665
"So help me Heaven, and my good blade!
No, never! Blasted be yon Pine,
My fathers' ancient crest and mine,
If from its shade in danger part
The lineage of the Bleeding Heart!   670

Hear my blunt speech: grant me this maid
To wife, thy counsel to mine aid;
To Douglas, leagued with Roderick Dhu,
Will friends and allies flock enow;
675   Like cause of doubt, distrust, and grief,
Will bind to us each Western chief.

WINDINGS OF THE FORTH AND ABBEY CRAIG, STIRLING

When the loud pipes my bridal tell,
The Links of Forth shall hear the knell,
The guards shall start in Stirling's porch;
680   And when I light the nuptial torch,
A thousand villages in flames
Shall scare the slumbers of King James!
Nay, Ellen, blench not thus away,
And, mother, cease these signs, I pray;

I meant not all my heat might say. —   685
Small need of inroad or of fight,
When the sage Douglas may unite
Each mountain clan in friendly band,
To guard the passes of their land,
Till the foiled King from pathless glen   690
Shall bootless turn him home again."

XXXI

There are who have, at midnight hour,
In slumber scaled a dizzy tower,
And, on the verge that beetled o'er
The ocean tide's incessant roar,   695
Dreamed calmly out their dangerous dream,
Till wakened by the morning beam;
When, dazzled by the eastern glow,
Such startler cast his glance below,
And saw unmeasured depth around,   700
And heard unintermitted sound,
And thought the battled fence so frail,
It waved like cobweb in the gale; —
Amid his senses' giddy wheel,
Did he not desperate impulse feel,   705
Headlong to plunge himself below,
And meet the worst his fears foreshow? —
Thus Ellen, dizzy and astound,
As sudden ruin yawned around,
By crossing terrors wildly tossed,   710
Still for the Douglas fearing most,
Could scarce the desperate thought withstand,
To buy his safety with her hand.

XXXII

Such purpose dread could Malcolm spy
715 In Ellen's quivering lip and eye,
And eager rose to speak, — but ere
His tongue could hurry forth his fear,
Had Douglas marked the hectic strife,
Where death seemed combating with life;
720 For to her cheek, in feverish flood,
One instant rushed the throbbing blood,
Then ebbing back, with sudden sway,
Left its domain as wan as clay.
"Roderick, enough! enough!" he cried,
725 "My daughter cannot be thy bride;
Not that the blush to wooer dear,
Nor paleness that of maiden fear.
It may not be, — forgive her, Chief,
Nor hazard aught for our relief.
730 Against his sovereign, Douglas ne'er
Will level a rebellious spear.
'T was I that taught his youthful hand
To rein a steed and wield a brand;
I see him yet, the princely boy!
735 Not Ellen more my pride and joy;
I love him still, despite my wrongs
By hasty wrath and slanderous tongues.
O, seek the grace you well may find,
Without a cause to mine combined!"

XXXIII

740 Twice through the hall the Chieftain strode;
The waving of his tartans broad,

And darkened brow, where wounded pride
With ire and disappointment vied,
Seemed, by the torch's gloomy light,
Like the ill Demon of the night,   745
Stooping his pinions' shadowy sway
Upon the nighted pilgrim's way:
But, unrequited Love! thy dart
Plunged deepest its envenomed smart,
And Roderick, with thine anguish stung,   750
At length the hand of Douglas wrung,
While eyes that mocked at tears before
With bitter drops were running o'er.
The death-pangs of long-cherished hope
Scarce in that ample breast had scope,   755
But, struggling with his spirit proud,
Convulsive heaved its checkered shroud,
While every sob — so mute were all —
Was heard distinctly through the hall.
The son's despair, the mother's look,   760
Ill might the gentle Ellen brook;
She rose, and to her side there came,
To aid her parting steps, the Græme.

                    XXXIV

Then Roderick from the Douglas broke —
As flashes flame through sable smoke,   765
Kindling its wreaths, long, dark, and low,
To one broad blaze of ruddy glow,
So the deep anguish of despair
Burst, in fierce jealousy, to air.

770 With stalwart grasp his hand he laid
     On Malcolm's breast and belted plaid:
     "Back, beardless boy!" he sternly said,
     "Back, minion! holdst thou thus at naught
     The lesson I so lately taught?
775 This roof, the Douglas, and that maid,
     Thank thou for punishment delayed."
     Eager as greyhound on his game,
     Fiercely with Roderick grappled Græme.
     "Perish my name, if aught afford
780 Its Chieftain safety save his sword!"
     Thus as they strove, their desperate hand
     Gripped to the dagger or the brand,
     And death had been — but Douglas rose,
     And thrust between the struggling foes
785 His giant strength: — "Chieftains, forego!
     I hold the first who strikes my foe. —
     Madmen, forbear your frantic jar!
     What! is the Douglas fallen so far,
     His daughter's hand is deemed the spoil
790 Of such dishonorable broil?"
     Sullen and slowly they unclasp,
     As struck with shame, their desperate grasp,
     And each upon his rival glared,
     With foot advanced and blade half bared.

XXXV

795 Ere yet the brands aloft were flung,
     Margaret on Roderick's mantle hung,
     And Malcolm heard his Ellen's scream,
     As faltered through terrific dream.

Then Roderick plunged in sheath his sword,
And veiled his wrath in scornful word: 800
"Rest safe till morning; pity 't were
Such cheek should feel the midnight air!
Then mayst thou to James Stuart tell,
Roderick will keep the lake and fell,
Nor lackey with his freeborn clan   805
The pageant pomp of earthly man.
More would he of Clan-Alpine know,
Thou canst our strength and passes show. —
Malise, what ho!" — his henchman came:
"Give our safe-conduct to the Græme."   810
Young Malcolm answered, calm and bold:
"Fear nothing for thy favorite hold;
The spot an angel deigned to grace
Is blessed, though robbers haunt the place.
Thy churlish courtesy for those   815
Reserve, who fear to be thy foes.
As safe to me the mountain way
At midnight as in blaze of day,
Though with his boldest at his back
Even Roderick Dhu beset the track. —   820
Brave Douglas, — lovely Ellen, — nay,
Naught here of parting will I say.
Earth does not hold a lonesome glen
So secret but we meet again. —
Chieftain! we too shall find an hour," —   825
He said, and left the sylvan bower.

XXXVI

Old Allan followed to the strand —
Such was the Douglas's command —
And anxious told, how, on the morn,
830 The stern Sir Roderick deep had sworn
The Fiery Cross should circle o'er
Dale, glen, and valley, down and moor.
Much were the peril to the Græme
From those who to the signal came;
835 Far up the lake 't were safest land,
Himself would row him to the strand.
He gave his counsel to the wind,
While Malcolm did, unheeding, bind,
Round dirk and pouch and broadsword rolled,
840 His ample plaid in tightened fold,
And stripped his limbs to such array
As best might suit the watery way, —

XXXVII

Then spoke abrupt: "Farewell to thee,
Pattern of old fidelity!"
845 The Minstrel's hand he kindly pressed, —
"Oh, could I point a place of rest!
My sovereign holds in ward my land,
My uncle leads my vassal band;
To tame his foes, his friends to aid,
850 Poor Malcolm has but heart and blade.
Yet, if there be one faithful Græme
Who loves the chieftain of his name,
Not long shall honored Douglas dwell
Like hunted stag in mountain cell;

Nor, ere yon pride-swollen robber dare, —   855
I may not give the rest to air!
Tell Roderick Dhu I owed him naught,
Not the poor service of a boat,
To waft me to yon mountain-side."
Then plunged he in the flashing tide.   860
Bold o'er the flood his head he bore,
And stoutly steered him from the shore;
And Allan strained his anxious eye,
Far mid the lake his form to spy,
Darkening across each puny wave,   865
To which the moon her silver gave.
Fast as the cormorant could swim,
The swimmer plied each active limb;
Then landing in the moonlight dell,
Loud shouted of his weal to tell.   870
The Minstrel heard the far halloo,
And joyful from the shore withdrew.

CANTO THIRD

THE GATHERING

I

TIME rolls his ceaseless course.   The race of yore,
   Who danced our infancy upon their knee,
And told our marvelling boyhood legends store
   Of their strange ventures happed by land or sea,
5   How are they blotted from the things that be!
How few, all weak and withered of their force,
   Wait on the verge of dark eternity,
Like stranded wrecks, the tide returning hoarse,
To sweep them from our sight!   Time rolls his ceaseless
     course.

10 Yet live there still who can remember well,
   How, when a mountain chief his bugle blew,

Both field and forest, dingle, cliff, and dell,
   And solitary heath, the signal knew;
   And fast the faithful clan around him drew,
What time the warning note was keenly wound,   15
   What time aloft their kindred banner flew,
While clamorous war-pipes yelled the gathering sound,
And while the Fiery Cross glanced, like a meteor, round.

II

   The Summer dawn's reflected hue
   To purple changed Loch Katrine blue;   20
   Mildly and soft the western breeze
   Just kissed the lake, just stirred the trees,
   And the pleased lake, like maiden coy,
   Trembled but dimpled not for joy:
   The mountain-shadows on her breast   25
   Were neither broken nor at rest;
   In bright uncertainty they lie,
   Like future joys to Fancy's eye.
   The water-lily to the light
   Her chalice reared of silver bright;   30
   The doe awoke, and to the lawn,
   Begemmed with dew-drops, led her fawn;
   The gray mist left the mountain-side,
   The torrent showed its glistening pride;
   Invisible in flecked sky   35
   The lark sent down her revelry;
   The blackbird and the speckled thrush
   Good-morrow gave from brake and brush;
   In answer cooed the cushat dove
   Her notes of peace and rest and love.   40

III

No thought of peace, no thought of rest
Assuaged the storm in Roderick's breast.
With sheathed broadsword in his hand,
Abrupt he paced the islet strand,
45 And eyed the rising sun, and laid
His hand on his impatient blade.
Beneath a rock, his vassals' care
Was prompt the ritual to prepare,
With deep and deathful meaning fraught;
50 For such Antiquity had taught
Was preface meet, ere yet abroad
The Cross of Fire should take its road.
The shrinking band stood oft aghast
At the impatient glance he cast; —
55 Such glance the mountain eagle threw,
As, from the cliffs of Benvenue,
She spread her dark sails on the wind,
And, high in middle heaven reclined,
With her broad shadow on the lake,
60 Silenced the warblers of the brake.

IV

A heap of withered boughs was piled,
Of juniper and rowan wild,
Mingled with shivers from the oak,
Rent by the lightning's recent stroke.
65 Brian the Hermit by it stood,
Barefooted, in his frock and hood.

His grizzled beard and matted hair
Obscured a visage of despair;
His naked arms and legs, seamed o'er,
The scars of frantic penance bore.　　　　70
That monk, of savage form and face,
The impending danger of his race
Had drawn from deepest solitude,
Far in Benharrow's bosom rude.
Not his the mien of Christian priest,　　75
But Druid's, from the grave released,
Whose hardened heart and eye might brook
On human sacrifice to look;
And much, 't was said, of heathen lore
Mixed in the charms he muttered o'er.　　80
The hallowed creed gave only worse
And deadlier emphasis of curse.
No peasant sought that Hermit's prayer,
His cave the pilgrim shunned with care;
The eager huntsman knew his bound,　　85
And in mid chase called off his hound;
Or, if, in lonely glen or strath,
The desert-dweller met his path,
He prayed, and signed the cross between,
While terror took devotion's mien.　　90

v

Of Brian's birth strange tales were told.
His mother watched a midnight fold,
Built deep within a dreary glen,
Where scattered lay the bones of men

95 In some forgotten battle slain,
And bleached by drifting wind and rain.
It might have tamed a warrior's heart
To view such mockery of his art!
The knot-grass fettered there the hand
100 Which once could burst an iron band;
Beneath the broad and ample bone,
That bucklered heart to fear unknown,
A feeble and a timorous guest,
The fieldfare framed her lowly nest;
105 There the slow blindworm left his slime
On the fleet limbs that mocked at time;
And there, too, lay the leader's skull,
Still wreathed with chaplet, flushed and full,
For heath-bell with her purple bloom
110 Supplied the bonnet and the plume.
All night, in this sad glen, the maid
Sat shrouded in her mantle's shade:
She said no shepherd sought her side,
No hunter's hand her snood untied,
115 Yet ne'er again to braid her hair
The virgin snood did Alice wear;
Gone was her maiden guile and sport,
Her maiden girdle all too short,
Nor sought she, from that fatal night,
120 Or holy church or blessed rite,
But locked her secret in her breast,
And died in travail, unconfessed.

VI

Alone, among his young compeers,
Was Brian from his infant years;
A moody and heart-broken boy,   125
Estranged from sympathy and joy,
Bearing each taunt which careless tongue
On his mysterious lineage flung.
Whole nights he spent by moonlight pale,
To wood and stream his hap to wail,   130
Till, frantic, he as truth received
What of his birth the crowd believed,
And sought, in mist and meteor fire,
To meet and know his Phantom Sire!
In vain, to soothe his wayward fate,   135
The cloister oped her pitying gate;
In vain the learning of the age
Unclasped the sable-lettered page;
Even in its treasures he could find
Food for the fever of his mind.   140
Eager he read whatever tells
Of magic, cabala, and spells,
And every dark pursuit allied
To curious and presumptuous pride;
Till, with fired brain and nerves o'erstrung   145
And heart with mystic horrors wrung,
Desperate he sought Benharrow's den,
And hid him from the haunts of men.

VII

The desert gave him visions wild,
Such as might suit the spectre's child.   150

Where with black cliffs the torrents toil,
He watched the wheeling eddies boil,
Till from their foam his dazzled eyes
Beheld the River Demon rise:
155 The mountain mist took form and limb
Of noontide hag or goblin grim;
The midnight wind came wild and dread,
Swelled with the voices of the dead;
Far on the future battle-heath
160 His eye beheld the ranks of death:
Thus the lone Seer, from mankind hurled,
Shaped forth a disembodied world.
One lingering sympathy of mind
Still bound him to the mortal kind;
165 The only parent he could claim
Of ancient Alpine's lineage came.
Late had he heard, in prophet's dream,
The fatal Ben-Shie's boding scream;
Sounds, too, had come in midnight blast
170 Of charging steeds, careering fast
Along Benharrow's shingly side,
Where mortal horseman ne'er might ride;
The thunderbolt had split the pine, —
All augured ill to Alpine's line.
175 He girt his loins, and came to show
The signals of impending woe,
And now stood prompt to bless or ban,
As bade the Chieftain of his clan.

VIII

'T was all prepared; — and from the rock
A goat, the patriarch of the flock,   180
Before the kindling pile was laid,
And pierced by Roderick's ready blade.
Patient the sickening victim eyed
The life-blood ebb in crimson tide
Down his clogged beard and shaggy limb,   185
Till darkness glazed his eyeballs dim.
The grisly priest, with murmuring prayer,
A slender crosslet framed with care,
A cubit's length in measure due;
The shaft and limbs were rods of yew,   190
Whose parents in Inch-Calliach wave
Their shadows o'er Clan-Alpine's grave,
And, answering Lomond's breezes deep,
Soothe many a chieftain's endless sleep.
The Cross thus formed he held on high   195
With wasted hand and haggard eye,
And strange and mingled feelings woke,
While his anathema he spoke: —

IX

"Woe to the clansman who shall view
This symbol of sepulchral yew,   200
Forgetful that its branches grew
Where weep the heavens their holiest dew
    On Alpine's dwelling low!
Deserter of his Chieftain's trust,
He ne'er shall mingle with their dust,   205

But, from his sires and kindred thrust,
Each clansman's execration just
   Shall doom him wrath and woe."
He paused; — the word the vassals took,
210 With forward step and fiery look,
On high their naked brands they shook,
Their clattering targets wildly strook;

OTTER ISLAND AND BEN-AN, LOCH LOMOND

   And first in murmur low,
Then, like the billow in his course,
215 That far to seaward finds his source,
And flings to shore his mustered force,
Burst with loud roar their answer hoarse,
   "Woe to the traitor, woe!"
Ben-an's gray scalp the accents knew,
220 The joyous wolf from covert drew,

The exulting eagle screamed afar, —
They knew the voice of Alpine's war.

X

The shout was hushed on lake and fell,
The Monk resumed his muttered spell:
Dismal and low its accents came,   225
The while he scathed the Cross with flame;
And the few words that reached the air,
Although the holiest name was there,
Had more of blasphemy than prayer.
But when he shook above the crowd   230
Its kindled points, he spoke aloud: —
"Woe to the wretch who fails to rear
At this dread sign the ready spear!
For, as the flames this symbol sear,
His home, the refuge of his fear,   235
    A kindred fate shall know;
Far o'er its roof the volumed flame
Clan-Alpine's vengeance shall proclaim,
While maids and matrons on his name
Shall call down wretchedness and shame,   240
    And infamy and woe."
Then rose the cry of females, shrill
As goshawk's whistle on the hill,
Denouncing misery and ill,
Mingled with childhood's babbling trill   245
    Of curses stammered slow;
Answering with imprecation dread,
"Sunk be his home in embers red!

And cursed be the meanest shed
250   That e'er shall hide the houseless head
        We doom to want and woe!"
A sharp and shrieking echo gave,
Coir-Uriskin, thy goblin cave!
And the gray pass where birches wave
255   On Beala-nam-bo.

XI

Then deeper paused the priest anew,
And hard his laboring breath he drew,
While, with set teeth and clenched hand,
And eyes that glowed like fiery brand,
260   He meditated curse more dread,
And deadlier, on the clansman's head
Who, summoned to his chieftain's aid,
The signal saw and disobeyed.
The crosslet's points of sparkling wood
265   He quenched among the bubbling blood,
And, as again the sign he reared,
Hollow and hoarse his voice was heard:
"When flits this Cross from man to man,
Vich-Alpine's summons to his clan,
270   Burst be the ear that fails to heed!
Palsied the foot that shuns to speed!
May ravens tear the careless eyes,
Wolves make the coward heart their prize!
As sinks that blood-stream in the earth,
275   So may his heart's-blood drench his hearth!
As dies in hissing gore the spark,
Quench thou his light, Destruction dark!

And be the grace to him denied,
Bought by this sign to all beside!"
He ceased; no echo gave again   280
The murmur of the deep Amen.

XII

Then Roderick with impatient look
From Brian's hand the symbol took:
"Speed, Malise, speed!" he said, and gave
The crosslet to his henchman brave.   285
"The muster-place be Lanrick mead —
Instant the time — speed, Malise, speed!"
Like heath-bird, when the hawks pursue,
A barge across Loch Katrine flew:
High stood the henchman on the prow;   290
So rapidly the barge-men row,
The bubbles, where they launched the boat,
Were all unbroken and afloat,
Dancing in foam and ripple still,
When it had neared the mainland hill;   295
And from the silver beach's side
Still was the prow three fathom wide,
When lightly bounded to the land
The messenger of blood and brand.

XIII

Speed, Malise, speed! the dun deer's hide   300
On fleeter foot was never tied.
Speed, Malise, speed! such cause of haste
Thine active sinews never braced.

Bend 'gainst the steepy hill thy breast,
305   Burst down like torrent from its crest;
With short and springing footstep pass
The trembling bog and false morass;
Across the brook like roebuck bound,
And thread the brake like questing hound;
310   The crag is high, the scaur is deep,
Yet shrink not from the desperate leap:
Parched are thy burning lips and brow,
Yet by the fountain pause not now;
Herald of battle, fate, and fear,
315   Stretch onward in thy fleet career!
The wounded hind thou track'st not now,
Pursuest not maid through greenwood bough,
Nor pliest thou now thy flying pace
With rivals in the mountain race;
320   But danger, death, and warrior deed
Are in thy course — speed, Malise, speed!

XIV

Fast as the fatal symbol flies,
In arms the huts and hamlets rise;
From winding glen, from upland brown,
325   They poured each hardy tenant down.
Nor slacked the messenger his pace;
He showed the sign, he named the place,
And, pressing forward like the wind,
Left clamor and surprise behind.
330   The fisherman forsook the strand,
The swarthy smith took dirk and brand;

With changed cheer, the mower blithe
Left in the half-cut swath his scythe;
The herds without a keeper strayed,
The plough was in mid-furrow stayed,   335
The falconer tossed his hawk away,
The hunter left the stag at bay;
Prompt at the signal of alarms,
Each son of Alpine rushed to arms;
So swept the tumult and affray   340
Along the margin of Achray.
Alas, thou lovely lake! that e'er
Thy banks should echo sounds of fear!
The rocks, the bosky thickets, sleep
So stilly on thy bosom deep,   345
The lark's blithe carol from the cloud
Seems for the scene too gaily loud.

XV

Speed, Malise, speed!   The lake is past,
Duncraggan's huts appear at last,
And peep, like moss-grown rocks, half seen,   350
Half hidden in the copse so green;
There mayst thou rest, thy labor done,
Their lord shall speed the signal on. —
As stoops the hawk upon his prey,
The henchman shot him down the way.   355
What woeful accents load the gale?
The funeral yell, the female wail!
A gallant hunter's sport is o'er,
A valiant warrior fights no more.

360   Who, in the battle or the chase,
       At Roderick's side shall fill his place! —
       Within the hall, where torch's ray
       Supplies the excluded beams of day,
       Lies Duncan on his lonely bier,
365   And o'er him streams his widow's tear.

DUNCRAGGAN'S HUTS, GLENFINLAS

His stripling son stands mournful by,
His youngest weeps, but knows not why;
The village maids and matrons round
The dismal coronach resound.

XVI

Coronach

370   He is gone on the mountain,
          He is lost to the forest,
       Like a summer-dried fountain,
          When our need was the sorest.

The font, reappearing,
　　From the rain-drops shall borrow,　　375
But to us comes no cheering,
　　To Duncan no morrow!

The hand of the reaper
　　Takes the ears that are hoary,
But the voice of the weeper　　380
　　Wails manhood in glory.
The autumn winds rushing
　　Waft the leaves that are searest,
But our flower was in flushing,
　　When blighting was nearest.　　385

Fleet foot on the correi,
　　Sage counsel in cumber,
Red hand in the foray,
　　How sound is thy slumber!
Like the dew on the mountain,　　390
　　Like the foam on the river,
Like the bubble on the fountain,
　　Thou art gone, and forever!

XVII

Duncan's hound

See Stumah, who, the bier beside,
His master's corpse with wonder eyed,　　395
Poor Stumah! whom his least halloo
Could send like lightning o'er the dew,
Bristles his crest, and points his ears,
As if some stranger step he hears.

400   'T is not a mourner's muffled tread,
      Who comes to sorrow o'er the dead,
      But headlong haste or deadly fear
      Urge the precipitate career.
      All stand aghast : — unheeding all,
405   The henchman bursts into the hall ;
      Before the dead man's bier he stood,
      Held forth the Cross besmeared with blood ;
      "The muster-place is Lanrick mead ;
      Speed forth the signal ! clansmen, speed !"

                    XVIII

410   Angus, the heir of Duncan's line,
      Sprung forth and seized the fatal sign.
      In haste the stripling to his side
      His father's dirk and broadsword tied ;
      But, when he saw his mother's eye
415   Watch him in speechless agony,
      Back to her opened arms he flew,
      Pressed on her lips a fond adieu, —
      "Alas !" she sobbed, — "and yet be gone,
      And speed thee forth like Duncan's son !"
420   One look he cast upon the bier,
      Dashed from his eye the gathering tear,
      Breathed deep to clear his laboring breast,
      And tossed aloft his bonnet crest,
      Then, like the high-bred colt when, freed,
425   First he essays his fire and speed,
      He vanished, and o'er moor and moss
      Sped forward with the Fiery Cross.

Suspended was the widow's tear
While yet his footsteps she could hear;
And when she marked the henchman's eye   430
Wet with unwonted sympathy,
"Kinsman," she said, "his race is run
That should have sped thine errand on;
The oak has fallen, — the sapling bough
Is all Duncraggan's shelter now.   435
Yet trust I well, his duty done,
The orphan's God will guard my son. —
And you, in many a danger true,
At Duncan's hest your blades that drew,
To arms, and guard that orphan's head!   440
Let babes and women wail the dead."
Then weapon-clang and martial call
Resounded through the funeral hall,
While from the walls the attendant band
Snatched sword and targe with hurried hand;   445
And short and flitting energy
Glanced from the mourner's sunken eye,
As if the sounds to warrior dear
Might rouse her Duncan from his bier.
But faded soon that borrowed force;   450
Grief claimed his right, and tears their course.

                    XIX

Benledi saw the Cross of Fire,
It glanced like lightning up Strath-Ire.
O'er dale and hill the summons flew,
Nor rest nor pause young Angus knew;   455

The tear that gathered in his eye
He left the mountain-breeze to dry;
Until, where Teith's young waters roll
Betwixt him and a wooded knoll
460   That graced the sable strath with green,
The chapel of Saint Bride was seen.

STRATH-IRE

Swoln was the stream, remote the bridge,
But Angus paused not on the edge;
Though the dark waves danced dizzily,
465   Though reeled his sympathetic eye,
He dashed amid the torrent's roar:
His right hand high the crosslet bore,
His left the pole-axe grasped, to guide
And stay his footing in the tide.

He stumbled twice, — the foam splashed high, 470
With hoarser swell the stream raced by;
And had he fallen, — forever there,
Farewell Duncraggan's orphan heir!
But still, as if in parting life,
Firmer he grasped the Cross of strife, 475
Until the opposing bank he gained,
And up the chapel pathway strained.

CHAPEL OF SAINT BRIDE

XX

A blithesome rout that morning-tide
Had sought the chapel of Saint Bride.
Her troth Tombea's Mary gave 480
To Norman, heir of Armandave,

And, issuing from the Gothic arch,
The bridal now resumed their march.
In rude but glad procession came
485   Bonneted sire and coif-clad dame:
And plaided youth, with jest and jeer,
Which snooded maiden would not hear;
And children, that, unwitting why,
Lent the gay shout their shrilly cry;
490   And minstrels, that in measures vied
Before the youth and bonny bride,
Whose downcast eye and cheek disclose
The tear and blush of morning rose.
With virgin step and bashful hand
495   She held the kerchief's snowy band.
The gallant bridegroom by her side
Beheld his prize with victor's pride,
And the glad mother in her ear
Was closely whispering word of cheer.

XXI

500   Who meets them at the churchyard gate?
The messenger of fear and fate!
Haste in his hurried accent lies,
And grief is swimming in his eyes.
All dripping from the recent flood,
505   Panting and travel-soiled he stood,
The fatal sign of fire and sword
Held forth, and spoke the appointed word:
"The muster-place is Lanrick mead;
Speed forth the signal! Norman, speed!"

And must he change so soon the hand,　　510
Just linked to his by holy band,
For the fell Cross of blood and brand?
And must the day so blithe that rose,
And promised rapture in the close,
Before its setting hour, divide　　　　515
The bridegroom from the plighted bride?
O fatal doom!—it must! it must!
Clan-Alpine's cause, her chieftain's trust,
Her summons dread, brook no delay;
Stretch to the race,—away! away!　　520

XXII

Yet slow he laid his plaid aside,
And lingering eyed his lovely bride,
Until he saw the starting tear
Speak woe he might not stop to cheer;
Then, trusting not a second look,　　　525
In haste he sped him up the brook,
Nor backward glanced till on the heath
Where Lubnaig's lake supplies the Teith.—
What in the racer's bosom stirred?
The sickening pang of hope deferred,　　530
And memory with a torturing train
Of all his morning visions vain.
Mingled with love's impatience, came
The manly thirst for martial fame;
The stormy joy of mountaineers　　　535
Ere yet they rush upon the spears;
And zeal for Clan and Chieftain burning,
And hope, from well-fought field returning,

With war's red honors on his crest,
540   To clasp his Mary to his breast.
Stung by such thoughts, o'er bank and brae,
Like fire from flint he glanced away,
While high resolve and feeling strong
Burst into voluntary song.

LOCH LUBNAIG

XXIII

Song

545   The heath this night must be my bed,
The bracken curtain for my head,
My lullaby the warder's tread,
     Far, far, from love and thee, Mary;

To-morrow eve, more stilly laid,
My couch may be my bloody plaid,   550
My vesper song thy wail, sweet maid!
    It will not waken me, Mary!

I may not, dare not, fancy now
The grief that clouds thy lovely brow,
I dare not think upon thy vow,   555
    And all it promised me, Mary.
No fond regret must Norman know;
When bursts Clan-Alpine on the foe,
His heart must be like bended bow,
    His foot like arrow free, Mary.   560

A time will come with feeling fraught,
For, if I fall in battle fought,
Thy hapless lover's dying thought
    Shall be a thought on thee, Mary.
And, if returned from conquered foes,   565
How blithely will the evening close,
How sweet the linnet sing repose,
    To my young bride and me, Mary!

XXIV

Not faster o'er thy heathery braes,
Balquidder, speeds the midnight blaze,   570
Rushing in conflagration strong
Thy deep ravines and dells along,
Wrapping thy cliffs in purple glow,
And reddening the dark lakes below;

575   Nor faster speeds it, nor so far,
        As o'er thy heaths the voice of war.
        The signal roused to martial coil
        The sullen margin of Loch Voil,
        Waked still Loch Doine, and to the source
580   Alarmed, Balvaig, thy swampy course;

LOCH VOIL, BALQUIDDER

        Thence southward turned its rapid road
        Adown Strath-Gartney's valley broad,
        Till rose in arms each man might claim
        A portion in Clan-Alpine's name,
585   From the gray sire, whose trembling hand
        Could hardly buckle on his brand,
        To the raw boy, whose shaft and bow
        Were yet scarce terror to the crow.

Each valley, each sequestered glen,
Mustered its little horde of men,   590
That met as torrents from the height
In Highland dales their streams unite,
Still gathering, as they pour along,
A voice more loud, a tide more strong,
Till at the rendezvous they stood   595
By hundreds prompt for blows and blood,
Each trained to arms since life began,
Owning no tie but to his clan,
No oath but by his chieftain's hand,
No law but Roderick Dhu's command.   600

                        XXV

That summer morn had Roderick Dhu
Surveyed the skirts of Benvenue,
And sent his scouts o'er hill and heath,
To view the frontiers of Menteith.
All backward came with news of truce;   605
Still lay each martial Græme and Bruce,
In Rednock courts no horsemen wait,
No banner waved at Cardross gate,
On Duchray's towers no beacon shone,
Nor scared the herons from Loch Con;   610
All seemed at peace. — Now wot ye why
The Chieftain with such anxious eye,
Ere to the muster he repair,
This western frontier scanned with care? —
In Benvenue's most darksome cleft,   615
A fair though cruel pledge was left;

For Douglas, to his promise true,
That morning from the isle withdrew,
And in a deep sequestered dell
620   Had sought a low and lonely cell.

LAKE OF MENTEITH

By many a bard in Celtic tongue
Has Coir-nan-Uriskin been sung;
A softer name the Saxons gave,
And called the grot the Goblin Cave.

XXVI

625   It was a wild and strange retreat,
As e'er was trod by outlaw's feet.
The dell, upon the mountain's crest,
Yawned like a gash on warrior's breast;

Its trench had stayed full many a rock,
Hurled by primeval earthquake shock   630
From Benvenue's gray summit wild,
And here, in random ruin piled,
They frowned incumbent o'er the spot,
And formed the rugged sylvan grot.
The oak and birch with mingled shade   635
At noontide there a twilight made,
Unless when short and sudden shone
Some straggling beam on cliff or stone,
With such a glimpse as prophet's eye
Gains on thy depth, Futurity.   640
No murmur waked the solemn still,
Save tinkling of a fountain rill; ·
But, when the wind chafed with the lake,
A sullen sound would upward break,
With dashing hollow voice, that spoke   645
The incessant war of wave and rock.
Suspended cliffs with hideous sway
Seemed nodding o'er the cavern gray.
From such a den the wolf had sprung,
In such the wild-cat leaves her young;   650
Yet Douglas and his daughter fair
Sought for a space their safety there.
Gray Superstition's whisper dread
Debarred the spot to vulgar tread;
For there, she said, did fays resort,   655
And satyrs hold their sylvan court,
By moonlight tread their mystic maze,
And blast the rash beholder's gaze.

XXVII

Now eve, with western shadows long,
Floated on Katrine bright and strong,
When Roderick with a chosen few
Repassed the heights of Benvenue.
Above the Goblin Cave they go,
Through the wild pass of Beal-nam-bo;

PASS OF BEAL-NAM-BO

The prompt retainers speed before,
To launch the shallop from the shore,
For 'cross Loch Katrine lies his way
To view the passes of Achray,
And place his clansmen in array.
Yet lags the Chief in musing mind,
Unwonted sight, his men behind.
A single page, to bear his sword,
Alone attended on his lord;

The rest their way through thickets break,
And soon await him by the lake.   675
It was a fair and gallant sight,
To view them from the neighboring height,
By the low-levelled sunbeam's light!
For strength and stature, from the clan
Each warrior was a chosen man,   680
As even afar might well be seen,
By their proud step and martial mien.
Their feathers dance, their tartans float,
Their targets gleam, as by the boat
A wild and warlike group they stand,   685
That well became such mountain-strand.

XXVIII

Their Chief with step reluctant still
Was lingering on the craggy hill,
Hard by where turned apart the road
To Douglas's obscure abode.   690
It was but with that dawning morn
That Roderick Dhu had proudly sworn
To drown his love in war's wild roar,
Nor think of Ellen Douglas more;
But he who stems a stream with sand,   695
And fetters flame with flaxen band,
Has yet a harder task to prove, —
By firm resolve to conquer love!
Eve finds the Chief, like restless ghost,
Still hovering near his treasure lost;   700
For, though his haughty heart deny
A parting meeting to his eye,

Still fondly strains his anxious ear
The accents of her voice to hear,
705 And inly did he curse the breeze
That waked to sound the rustling trees.
But hark! what mingles in the strain?
It is the harp of Allan-bane,
That wakes its measure slow and high,
710 Attuned to sacred minstrelsy.
What melting voice attends the strings?
'T is Ellen, or an angel, sings.

XXIX

Hymn to the Virgin

Ave Maria! maiden mild!
   Listen to a maiden's prayer!
715 Thou canst hear though from the wild,
   Thou canst save amidst despair.
Safe may we sleep beneath thy care,
   Though banished, outcast, and reviled —
Maiden! hear a maiden's prayer;
720   Mother, hear a suppliant child!
                   Ave Maria!
Ave Maria! undefiled!
   The flinty couch we now must share
Shall seem with down of eider piled,
725   If thy protection hover there.
The murky cavern's heavy air
   Shall breathe of balm if thou hast smiled;
Then, Maiden! hear a maiden's prayer,
   Mother, list a suppliant child!
730   *Ave Maria!*

Ave Maria! stainless styled!
   Foul demons of the earth and air,
From this their wonted haunt exiled,
   Shall flee before thy presence fair.
We bow us to our lot of care,   735
   Beneath thy guidance reconciled:
Hear for a maid a maiden's prayer,
   And for a father hear a child!
            Ave Maria!

XXX

Died on the harp the closing hymn, —   740
Unmoved in attitude and limb,
As listening still, Clan-Alpine's lord
Stood leaning on his heavy sword,
Until the page with humble sign
Twice pointed to the sun's decline.   745
Then while his plaid he round him cast,
"It is the last time — 't is the last,"
He muttered thrice, — "the last time e'er
That angel-voice shall Roderick hear!"
It was a goading thought, — his stride   750
Hied hastier down the mountain-side;
Sullen he flung him in the boat,
An instant 'cross the lake it shot.
They landed in that silvery bay,
And eastward held their hasty way,   755
Till, with the latest beams of light,
The band arrived on Lanrick height,
Where mustered in the vale below
Clan-Alpine's men in martial show.

XXXI

760
A various scene the clansmen made :
Some sat, some stood, some slowly strayed ;
But most, with mantles folded round,
Were couched to rest upon the ground,
Scarce to be known by curious eye

765
From the deep heather where they lie,

BOCHASTLE SEEN FROM COILANTOGLE FORD

So well was matched the tartan screen
With heath-bell dark and brackens green ;
Unless where, here and there, a blade
Or lance's point a glimmer made,

770
Like glow-worm twinkling through the shade.
But, when, advancing through the gloom,
They saw the Chieftain's eagle plume,

Their shout of welcome, shrill and wide,
Shook the steep mountain's steady side.
Thrice it arose, and lake and fell   775
Three times returned the martial yell;
It died upon Bochastle's plain,
And Silence claimed her evening reign.

PASS OF BEAL 'MAHA, LOCH LOMOND

CANTO FOURTH

THE PROPHECY

I

"THE rose is fairest when 't is budding new,
    And hope is brightest when it dawns from fears;
The rose is sweetest washed with morning dew,
    And love is loveliest when embalmed in tears.
5   O wilding rose, whom fancy thus endears,
I bid your blossoms in my bonnet wave,
    Emblem of hope and love through future years!"
Thus spoke young Norman, heir of Armandave,
What time the sun arose on Vennachar's broad wave.

II

10   Such fond conceit, half said, half sung,
     Love prompted to the bridegroom's tongue.

All while he stripped the wild-rose spray,
His axe and bow beside him lay,
For on a pass 'twixt lake and wood
A wakeful sentinel he stood.   15
Hark! — on the rock a footstep rung,
And instant to his arms he sprung.
"Stand, or thou diest! — What, Malise? — soon
Art thou returned from Braes of Doune.
By thy keen step and glance I know,   20
Thou bring'st us tidings of the foe," —
For while the Fiery Cross hied on,
On distant scout had Malise gone. —
"Where sleeps the Chief?" the henchman said.
"Apart, in yonder misty glade;   25
To his lone couch I'll be your guide." —
Then called a slumberer by his side,
And stirred him with his slackened bow, —
"Up, up, Glentarkin! rouse thee, ho!
We seek the Chieftain; on the track   30
Keep eagle watch till I come back."

III

Together up the pass they sped:
"What of the foeman?" Norman said. —
"Varying reports from near and far;
This certain, — that a band of war   35
Has for two days been ready boune,
At prompt command to march from Doune;
King James the while, with princely powers,
Holds revelry in Stirling towers.

40   Soon will this dark and gathering cloud
    Speak on our glens in thunder loud.
    Inured to bide such bitter bout,
    The warrior's plaid may bear it out;
    But, Norman, how wilt thou provide
45   A shelter for thy bonny bride?" —
    "What! know ye not that Roderick's care
    To the lone isle hath caused repair
    Each maid and matron of the clan,
    And every child and aged man
50   Unfit for arms; and given his charge,
    Nor skiff nor shallop, boat nor barge,
    Upon these lakes shall float at large,
    But all beside the islet moor,
    That such dear pledge may rest secure?" —

IV

55   "'T is well advised, — the Chieftain's plan
    Bespeaks the father of his clan.
    But wherefore sleeps Sir Roderick Dhu
    Apart from all his followers true?"
    "It is because last evening-tide
60   Brian an augury hath tried,
    Of that dread kind which must not be
    Unless in dread extremity,
    The Taghairm called; by which, afar,
    Our sires foresaw the events of war.
65   Duncraggan's milk-white bull they slew," —

Malise

    "Ah! well the gallant brute I knew!
    The choicest of the prey we had

When swept our merrymen Gallangad,
His hide was snow, his horns were dark,
His red eye glowed like fiery spark;　　70
So fierce, so tameless, and so fleet,
Sore did he cumber our retreat,
And kept our stoutest kerns in awe,
Even at the pass of Beal 'maha.
But steep and flinty was the road,　　75
And sharp the hurrying pikeman's goad,
And when we came to Dennan's Row
A child might scathless stroke his brow."

V

Norman

"That bull was slain; his reeking hide
They stretched the cataract beside,　　80
Whose waters their wild tumult toss
Adown the black and craggy boss
Of that huge cliff whose ample verge
Tradition calls the Hero's Targe.
Couched on a shelf beneath its brink,　　85
Close where the thundering torrents sink,
Rocking beneath their headlong sway,
And drizzled by the ceaseless spray,
Midst groan of rock and roar of stream,
The wizard waits prophetic dream.　　90
Nor distant rests the Chief; — but hush!
See, gliding slow through mist and bush,
The hermit gains yon rock, and stands
To gaze upon our slumbering bands.

95　Seems he not, Malise, like a ghost,
That hovers o'er a slaughtered host?
Or raven on the blasted oak,
That, watching while the deer is broke,
His morsel claims with sullen croak?"

Malise

100　"Peace! peace! to other than to me
Thy words were evil augury;
But still I hold Sir Roderick's blade
Clan-Alpine's omen and her aid,
Not aught that, gleaned from heaven or hell,
105　Yon fiend-begotten Monk can tell.
The Chieftain joins him, see — and now
Together they descend the brow."

VI

And, as they came, with Alpine's Lord
The Hermit Monk held solemn word: —
110　"Roderick! it is a fearful strife,
For man endowed with mortal life,
Whose shroud of sentient clay can still
Feel feverish pang and fainting chill,
Whose eye can stare in stony trance,
115　Whose hair can rouse like warrior's lance, —
'T is hard for such to view, unfurled,
The curtain of the future world.
Yet, witness every quaking limb,
My sunken pulse, mine eyeballs dim,
120　My soul with harrowing anguish torn,
This for my Chieftain have I borne! —

The shapes that sought my fearful couch
A human tongue may ne'er avouch;
No mortal man — save he, who, bred
Between the living and the dead,   125
Is gifted beyond nature's law —
Had e'er survived to say he saw.
At length the fateful answer came
In characters of living flame!
Nor spoke in word, nor blazed in scroll,   130
But borne and branded on my soul: —
WHICH SPILLS THE FOREMOST FOEMAN'S LIFE
THAT PARTY CONQUERS IN THE STRIFE."

VII

"Thanks, Brian, for thy zeal and care!
Good is thine augury, and fair.   135
Clan-Alpine ne'er in battle stood
But first our broadswords tasted blood.
A surer victim still I know,
Self-offered to the auspicious blow:
A spy has sought my land this morn, —   140
No eve shall witness his return!
My followers guard each pass's mouth,
To east, to westward, and to south;
Red Murdoch, bribed to be his guide,
Has charge to lead his steps aside,   145
Till in deep path or dingle brown
He light on those shall bring him down. —
But see, who comes his news to show!
Malise! what tidings of the foe?"

VIII

150   "At Doune, o'er many a spear and glaive
     Two Barons proud their banners wave.
     I saw the Moray's silver star,
     And marked the sable pale of Mar."
     "By Alpine's soul, high tidings those!
155   I love to hear of worthy foes.

LOCH EARN AND BENVOIRLICH

     When move they on?"   "To-morrow's noon
     Will see them here for battle boune."
     "Then shall it see a meeting stern!
     But, for the place, — say, couldst thou learn
160   Nought of the friendly clans of Earn?
     Strengthened by them, we well might bide
     The battle on Benledi's side.

Thou couldst not? — well! Clan-Alpine's men
Shall man the Trosachs' shaggy glen;
Within Loch Katrine's gorge we'll fight,   165
All in our maids' and matrons' sight,
Each for his hearth and household fire,
Father for child, and son for sire,
Lover for maid beloved! — But why —
Is it the breeze affects mine eye?   170
Or dost thou come, ill-omened tear!
A messenger of doubt or fear?
No! sooner may the Saxon lance
Unfix Benledi from his stance,
Than doubt or terror can pierce through   175
The unyielding heart of Roderick Dhu!
'T is stubborn as his trusty targe.
Each to his post! — all know their charge."
The pibroch sounds, the bands advance,
The broadswords gleam, the banners dance,   180
Obedient to the Chieftain's glance. —
I turn me from the martial roar,
And seek Coir-Uriskin once more.

                         IX

Where is the Douglas? — he is gone;
And Ellen sits on the gray stone   185
Fast by the cave, and makes her moan,
While vainly Allan's words of cheer
Are poured on her unheeding ear.
"He will return — dear lady, trust! —
With joy return; — he will — he must.   190

Well was it time to seek afar
Some refuge from impending war,
When e'en Clan-Alpine's rugged swarm
Are cowed by the approaching storm.
195 I saw their boats with many a light,
Floating the livelong yesternight,
Shifting like flashes darted forth
By the red streamers of the north;
I marked at morn how close they ride,
200 Thick moored by the lone islet's side,
Like wild ducks couching in the fen
When stoops the hawk upon the glen.
Since this rude race dare not abide
The peril on the mainland side,
205 Shall not thy noble father's care
Some safe retreat for thee prepare?"

X

"No, Allan, no! Pretext so kind
My wakeful terrors could not blind.
When in such tender tone, yet grave,
210 Douglas a parting blessing gave,
The tear that glistened in his eye
Drowned not his purpose fixed and high.
My soul, though feminine and weak,
Can image his; e'en as the lake,
215 Itself disturbed by slightest stroke,
Reflects the invulnerable rock.
He hears report of battle rife,
He deems himself the cause of strife.

I saw him redden when the theme
Turned, Allan, on thine idle dream   220
Of Malcolm Græme in fetters bound,
Which I, thou saidst, about him wound.
Think'st thou he trowed thine omen aught?
O no! 't was apprehensive thought
For the kind youth, — for Roderick too —   225
Let me be just — that friend so true;
In danger both, and in our cause!
Minstrel, the Douglas dare not pause.
Why else that solemn warning given,
'If not on earth, we meet in heaven!'   230
Why else, to Cambus-kenneth's fane,
If eve return him not again,
Am I to hie and make me known?
Alas! he goes to Scotland's throne,
Buys his friends' safety with his own;   235
He goes to do — what I had done,
Had Douglas' daughter been his son!"

XI

"Nay, lovely Ellen! — dearest, nay!
If aught should his return delay,
He only named yon holy fane   240
As fitting place to meet again.
Be sure he's safe; and for the Græme, —
Heaven's blessing on his gallant name! —
My visioned sight may yet prove true,
Nor bode of ill to him or you.   245
When did my gifted dream beguile?
Think of the stranger at the isle,

And think upon the harpings slow
That presaged this approaching woe!
250   Sooth was my prophecy of fear;
Believe it when it augurs cheer.
Would we had left this dismal spot!
Ill luck still haunts a fairy grot.
Of such a wondrous tale I know —
255   Dear lady, change that look of woe,
My harp was wont thy grief to cheer."
"Well, be it as thou wilt; I hear,
But cannot stop the bursting tear."
The Minstrel tried his simple art,
260   But distant far was Ellen's heart.

XII

Ballad: Alice Brand

Merry it is in the good greenwood,
    When the mavis and merle are singing,
When the deer sweeps by, and the hounds are in cry,
    And the hunter's horn is ringing.

265   "O Alice Brand, my native land
        Is lost for love of you;
And we must hold by wood and wold,
        As outlaws wont to do.

"O Alice, 't was all for thy locks so bright,
270   And 't was all for thine eyes so blue,
That on the night of our luckless flight
        Thy brother bold I slew.

"Now must I teach to hew the beech
  The hand that held the glaive,
For leaves to spread our lowly bed,
  And stakes to fence our cave.

"And for vest of pall, thy fingers small,
  That wont on harp to stray,
A cloak must shear from the slaughtered deer,
  To keep the cold away."

"O Richard! if my brother died,
  'T was but a fatal chance;
For darkling was the battle tried,
  And fortune sped the lance.

"If pall and vair no more I wear,
  Nor thou the crimson sheen,
As warm, we 'll say, is the russet gray,
  As gay the forest-green.

"And, Richard, if our lot be hard,
  And lost thy native land,
Still Alice has her own Richard,
  And he has Alice Brand."

XIII

Ballad Continued

'T is merry, 't is merry, in good greenwood;
  So blithe Lady Alice is singing;
On the beech's pride, and oak's brown side,
  Lord Richard's axe is ringing.

275

280

285

290

295

Up spoke the moody Elfin King,
   Who woned within the hill, —
Like wind in the porch of a ruined church,
300   His voice was ghostly shrill.

"Why sounds yon stroke on beech and oak,
   Our moonlight circle's screen?
Or who comes here to chase the deer,
   Beloved of our Elfin Queen?
305 Or who may dare on wold to wear
   The fairies' fatal green?

"Up, Urgan, up! to yon mortal hie,
   For thou wert christened man;
For cross or sign thou wilt not fly,
310   For muttered word or ban.

"Lay on him the curse of the withered heart,
   The curse of the sleepless eye;
Till he wish and pray that his life would part,
   Nor yet find leave to die."

XIV

Ballad Continued

315 'T is merry, 't is merry, in good greenwood,
   Though the birds have stilled their singing;
The evening blaze doth Alice raise,
   And Richard is fagots bringing.

Up Urgan starts, that hideous dwarf,
320   Before Lord Richard stands,

And, as he crossed and blessed himself,
"I fear not sign," quoth the grisly elf,
  "That is made with bloody hands."

But out then spoke she, Alice Brand,
  That woman void of fear, —   325
"And if there's blood upon his hand,
  'T is but the blood of deer."

"Now loud thou liest, thou bold of mood!
  It cleaves unto 'his hand,
The stain of thine own kindly blood,   330
  The blood of Ethert Brand."

Then forward stepped she, Alice Brand,
  And made the holy sign, —
"And if there's blood on Richard's hand,
  A spotless hand is mine.   335

"And I conjure thee, demon elf,
  By Him whom demons fear,
To show us whence thou art thyself,
  And what thine errand here?"

XV

Ballad Continued

"'T is merry, 't is merry, in Fairy-land,   340
  When fairy birds are singing,
When the court doth ride by their monarch's side,
  With bit and bridle ringing:

"And gaily shines the Fairy-land —
345   But all is glistening show,
Like the idle gleam that December's beam
    Can dart on ice and snow.

"And fading, like that varied gleam,
    Is our inconstant shape,
350 Who now like knight and lady seem,
    And now like dwarf and ape.

"It was between the night and day,
    When the Fairy King has power,
That I sunk down in a sinful fray,
355 And 'twixt life and death was snatched away
    To the joyless Elfin bower.

"But wist I of a woman bold,
    Who thrice my brow durst sign,
I might regain my mortal mould,
360   As fair a form as thine."

She crossed him once — she crossed him twice —
    That lady was so brave;
The fouler grew his goblin hue,
    The darker grew the cave.

365 She crossed him thrice, that lady bold;
    He rose beneath her hand
The fairest knight on Scottish mould,
    Her brother, Ethert Brand!

Merry it is in good greenwood,
370   When the mavis and merle are singing,

But merrier were they in Dunfermline gray,
　When all the bells were ringing.

XVI

Just as the minstrel sounds were stayed,
A stranger climbed the steepy glade;
His martial step, his stately mien,　　　　375
His hunting-suit of Lincoln green,
His eagle glance, remembrance claims —
'T is Snowdoun's Knight, 't is James Fitz-James
Ellen beheld as in a dream,
Then, starting, scarce suppressed a scream:　　380
"O stranger! in such hour of fear
What evil hap has brought thee here?"
"An evil hap how can it be
That bids me look again on thee?
By promise bound, my former guide　　　　385
Met me betimes this morning-tide,
And marshalled over bank and bourne
The happy path of my return."
"The happy path! — what! said he naught
Of war, of battle to be fought,　　　　390
Of guarded pass?" "No, by my faith!
Nor saw I aught could augur scathe."
"O hasten, Allan, to the kern:
Yonder his tartans I discern;
Learn thou his purpose, and conjure　　　　395
That he will guide the stranger sure! —
What prompted thee, unhappy man?
The meanest serf in Roderick's clan

Had not been bribed, by love or fear,
400   Unknown to him to guide thee here."

XVII

"Sweet Ellen, dear my life must be,
Since it is worthy care from thee;
Yet life I hold but idle breath
When love or honor 's weighed with death.
405   Then let me profit by my chance,
And speak my purpose bold at once.
I come to bear thee from a wild
Where ne'er before such blossom smiled,
By this soft hand to lead thee far
410   From frantic scenes of feud and war.
Near Bochastle my horses wait;
They bear us soon to Stirling gate.
I 'll place thee in a lovely bower,
I 'll guard thee like a tender flower —"
415   "O hush, Sir Knight! 't were female art,
To say I do not read thy heart;
Too much, before, my selfish ear
Was idly soothed my praise to hear.
That fatal bait hath lured thee back,
420   In deathful hour, o'er dangerous track;
And how, O how, can I atone
The wreck my vanity brought on! —
One way remains — I 'll tell him all —
Yes! struggling bosom, forth it shall!
425   Thou, whose light folly bears the blame,
Buy thine own pardon with thy shame!

But first — my father is a man
Outlawed and exiled, under ban;
The price of blood is on his head,
With me 't were infamy to wed,   430
Still wouldst thou speak? — then hear the truth!
Fitz-James, there is a noble youth —
If yet he is! — exposed for me
And mine to dread extremity —
Thou hast the secret of my heart;   435
Forgive, be generous, and depart!"

XVIII

Fitz-James knew every wily train
A lady's fickle heart to gain,
But here he knew and felt them vain.
There shot no glance from Ellen's eye,   440
To give her steadfast speech the lie;
In maiden confidence she stood,
Though mantled in her cheek the blood,
And told her love with such a sigh
Of deep and hopeless agony,   445
As death had sealed her Malcolm's doom
And she sat sorrowing on his tomb.
Hope vanished from Fitz-James's eye,
But not with hope fled sympathy,
He proffered to attend her side,   450
As brother would a sister guide.
"O little know'st thou Roderick's heart!
Safer for both we go apart.
O haste thee, and from Allan learn

455 If thou mayst trust yon wily kern."
     With hand upon his forehead laid,
     The conflict of his mind to shade,
     A parting step or two he made;
     Then, as some thought had crossed his brain,
460 He paused, and turned, and came again.

XIX

     "Hear, lady, yet a parting word! —
     It chanced in fight that my poor sword
     Preserved the life of Scotland's lord.
     This ring the grateful Monarch gave,
465 And bade, when I had boon to crave,
     To bring it back, and boldly claim
     The recompense that I would name.
     Ellen, I am no courtly lord,
     But one who lives by lance and sword,
470 Whose castle is his helm and shield,
     His lordship the embattled field.
     What from a prince can I demand,
     Who neither reck of state nor land?
     Ellen, thy hand — the ring is thine;
475 Each guard and usher knows the sign.
     Seek thou the King without delay;
     This signet shall secure thy way:
     And claim thy suit, whate'er it be,
     As ransom of his pledge to me."
480 He placed the golden circlet on,
     Paused — kissed her hand — and then was gone.
     The aged Minstrel stood aghast,
     So hastily Fitz-James shot past.

He joined his guide, and wending down
The ridges of the mountain brown,　　　　485
Across the stream they took their way
That joins Loch Katrine to Achray.

XX

All in the Trosachs' glen was still,
Noontide was sleeping on the hill:
Sudden his guide whooped loud and high —　　490
"Murdoch! was that a signal cry?" —
He stammered forth, "I shout to scare
Yon raven from his dainty fare."
He looked — he knew the raven's prey,
His own brave steed: "Ah! gallant gray!　　495
For thee — for me, perchance — 't were well
We ne'er had seen the Trosachs' dell. —
Murdoch, move first — but silently;
Whistle or whoop, and thou shalt die!"
Jealous and sullen on they fared,　　　　500
Each silent, each upon his guard.

XXI

Now wound the path its dizzy ledge
Around a precipice's edge,
When lo! a wasted female form,
Blighted by wrath of sun and storm,　　　505
In tattered weeds and wild array,
Stood on a cliff beside the way,
And glancing round her restless eye
Upon the wood, the rock, the sky,
Seemed naught to mark, yet all to spy.　　510

Her brow was wreathed with gaudy broom;
With gesture wild she waved a plume
Of feathers, which the eagles fling
To crag and cliff from dusky wing;
515 Such spoils her desperate step had sought,
Where scarce was footing for the goat.
The tartan plaid she first descried,
And shrieked till all the rocks replied;
As loud she laughed when near they drew,
520 For then the Lowland garb she knew;
And then her hands she wildly wrung,
And then she wept, and then she sung —
She sung! — the voice, in better time,
Perchance to harp or lute might chime;
525 And now, though strained and roughened, still
Rung wildly sweet to dale and hill.

XXII

Song

They bid me sleep, they bid me pray,
    They say my brain is warped and wrung —
I cannot sleep on Highland brae,
530   I cannot pray in Highland tongue.
But were I now where Allan glides,
Or heard my native Devan's tides,
So sweetly would I rest, and pray
That Heaven would close my wintry day!

535 'T was thus my hair they bade me braid,
    They made me to the church repair;

It was my bridal morn they said,
　　And my true love would meet me there.
But woe betide the cruel guile
That drowned in blood the morning smile!　　540
And woe betide the fairy dream!
　　I only waked to sob and scream.

XXIII

"Who is this maid? what means her lay?
She hovers o'er the hollow way,
And flutters wide her mantle gray,　　545
As the lone heron spreads his wing,
By twilight, o'er a haunted spring."
"'T is Blanche of Devan," Murdoch said,
"A crazed and captive Lowland maid,
Ta'en on the morn she was a bride,　　550
When Roderick forayed Devan-side.
The gay bridegroom resistance made,
And felt our Chief's unconquered blade.
I marvel she is now at large,
But oft she 'scapes from Maudlin's charge. —　　555
Hence, brain-sick fool!" — He raised his bow: —
"Now, if thou strik'st her but one blow,
I'll pitch thee from the cliff as far
As ever peasant pitched a bar!"
"Thanks, champion, thanks!" the Maniac cried,　　560
And pressed her to Fitz-James's side.
"See the gray pennons I prepare,
To seek my true love through the air!
I will not lend that savage groom,
To break his fall, one downy plume!　　565

No! — deep amid disjointed stones,
The wolves shall batten on his bones,
And then shall his detested plaid,
By bush and brier in mid-air stayed,
Wave forth a banner fair and free,
Meet signal for their revelry."

XXIV

"Hush thee, poor maiden, and be still!"
"O! thou look'st kindly, and I will.
Mine eye has dried and wasted been,
But still it loves the Lincoln green;
And, though mine ear is all unstrung,
Still, still it loves the Lowland tongue.

"For O, my sweet William was forester true,
    He stole poor Blanche's heart away!
His coat it was all of the greenwood hue,
    And so blithely he trilled the Lowland lay!

"It was not that I meant to tell . . .
But thou art wise and guessest well."
Then, in a low and broken tone,
And hurried note, the song went on.
Still on the Clansman fearfully
She fixed her apprehensive eye,
Then turned it on the Knight, and then
Her look glanced wildly o'er the glen.

XXV

"The toils are pitched, and the stakes are set, —   590
  Ever sing merrily, merrily;
The bows they bend, and the knives they whet,
  Hunters live so cheerily.

"It was a stag, a stag of ten,
  Bearing its branches sturdily;   595
He came stately down the glen, —
  Ever sing hardily, hardily.

"It was there he met with a wounded doe,
  She was bleeding deathfully;
She warned him of the toils below,   600
  O, so faithfully, faithfully!

"He had an eye, and he could heed, —
  Ever sing warily, warily;
He had a foot, and he could speed, —
  Hunters watch so narrowly."   605

XXVI

Fitz-James's mind was passion-tossed,
When Ellen's hints and fears were lost;
But Murdoch's shout suspicion wrought,
And Blanche's song conviction brought.
Not like a stag that spies the snare,   610
But lion of the hunt aware,
He waved at once his blade on high,
"Disclose thy treachery, or die!"

Forth at full speed the Clansman flew,
615   But in his race his bow he drew.
The shaft just grazed Fitz-James's crest,
And thrilled in Blanche's faded breast. —
Murdoch of Alpine! prove thy speed,
For ne'er had Alpine's son such need;
620   With heart of fire, and foot of wind,
The fierce avenger is behind!
Fate judges of the rapid strife —
The forfeit death — the prize is life;
Thy kindred ambush lies before,
625   Close couched upon the heathery moor;
Them couldst thou reach! — it may not be —
Thine ambushed kin thou ne'er shalt see,
The fiery Saxon gains on thee! —
Resistless speeds the deadly thrust,
630   As lightning strikes the pine to dust;
With foot and hand Fitz-James must strain
Ere he can win his blade again.
Bent o'er the fallen with falcon eye,
He grimly smiled to see him die,
635   Then slower wended back his way,
Where the poor maiden bleeding lay.

XXVII

She sat beneath the birchen tree,
Her elbow resting on her knee;
She had withdrawn the fatal shaft,
640   And gazed on it, and feebly laughed;
Her wreath of broom and feathers gray,

Daggled with blood, beside her lay.
The Knight to stanch the life-stream tried, —
"Stranger, it is in vain!" she cried.
"This hour of death has given me more   645
Of reason's power than years before;
For, as these ebbing veins decay,
My frenzied visions fade away.
A helpless injured wretch I die,
And something tells me in thine eye   650
That thou wert mine avenger born.
Seest thou this tress? — O, still I've worn
This little tress of yellow hair,
Through danger, frenzy, and despair!
It once was bright and clear as thine,   655
But blood and tears have dimmed its shine.
I will not tell thee when 't was shred,
Nor from what guiltless victim's head, —
My brain would turn! — but it shall wave
Like plumage on thy helmet brave,   660
Till sun and wind shall bleach the stain,
And thou wilt bring it me again.
I waver still, — O God! more bright
Let reason beam her parting light! — —
O, by thy knighthood's honored sign,   665
And for thy life preserved by mine,
When thou shalt see a darksome man,
Who boasts him Chief of Alpine's Clan,
With tartans broad and shadowy plume,
And hand of blood, and brow of gloom,   670
Be thy heart bold, thy weapon strong,
And wreak poor Blanche of Devan's wrong! —

They watch for thee by pass and fell . . .
Avoid the path . . . O God! . . . farewell."

XXVIII

675   A kindly heart had brave Fitz-James;
Fast poured his eyes at pity's claims;
And now, with mingled grief and ire,
He saw the murdered maid expire.
"God, in my need, be my relief,
680   As I wreak this on yonder Chief!"
A lock from Blanche's tresses fair
He blended with her bridegroom's hair;
The mingled braid in blood he dyed,
And placed it on his bonnet-side:
685   "By Him whose word is truth, I swear,
No other favor will I wear,
Till this sad token I imbrue
In the best blood of Roderick Dhu! —
But hark! what means yon faint halloo?
690   The chase is up, — but they shall know,
The stag at bay's a dangerous foe."
Barred from the known but guarded way,
Through copse and cliffs Fitz-James must stray,
And oft must change his desperate track,
695   By stream and precipice turned back.
Heartless, fatigued, and faint, at length,
From lack of food and loss of strength,
He couched him in a thicket hoar,
And thought his toils and perils o'er: —
700   "Of all my rash adventures past,
This frantic feat must prove the last!

Who e'er so mad but might have guessed
That all this Highland hornet's nest
Would muster up in swarms so soon
As e'er they heard of bands at Doune? —　　705
Like bloodhounds now they search me out, —
Hark, to the whistle and the shout! —
If farther through the wilds I go,
I only fall upon the foe:
I 'll couch me here till evening gray,　　710
Then darkling try my dangerous way."

XXIX

The shades of eve come slowly down,
The woods are wrapt in deeper brown,
The owl awakens from her dell,
The fox is heard upon the fell;　　715
Enough remains of glimmering light
To guide the wanderer's steps aright,
Yet not enough from far to show
His figure to the watchful foe.
With cautious step and ear awake,　　720
He climbs the crag and threads the brake;
And not the summer solstice there
Tempered the midnight mountain air,
But every breeze that swept the wold
Benumbed his drenched limbs with cold.　　725
In dread, in danger, and alone,
Famished and chilled, through ways unknown,
Tangled and steep, he journeyed on;
Till, as a rock's huge point he turned,
A watch-fire close before him burned.　　730

XXX

Beside its embers red and clear,
Basked in his plaid a mountaineer;
And up he sprung with sword in hand, —
"Thy name and purpose! Saxon, stand!"
735   "A stranger." "What dost thou require?"
"Rest and a guide, and food and fire.
My life's beset, my path is lost,
The gale has chilled my limbs with frost."
"Art thou a friend to Roderick?" "No."
740   "Thou dar'st not call thyself a foe?"
"I dare! to him and all the band
He brings to aid his murderous hand."
"Bold words! — but, though the beast of game
The privilege of chase may claim,
745   Though space and law the stag we lend,
Ere hound we slip or bow we bend,
Who ever recked, where, how, or when,
The prowling fox was trapped or slain?
Thus treacherous scouts, — yet sure they lie,
750   Who say thou cam'st a secret spy!" —
"They do, by heaven! — come Roderick Dhu,
And of his clan the boldest two,
And let me but till morning rest,
I write the falsehood on their crest."
755   "If by the blaze I mark aright,
Thou bear'st the belt and spur of Knight."
"Then by these tokens mayst thou know
Each proud oppressor's mortal foe."
"Enough, enough; sit down and share
760   A soldier's couch, a soldier's fare."

XXXI

He gave him of his Highland cheer,
The hardened flesh of mountain deer;
Dry fuel on the fire he laid,
And bade the Saxon share his plaid.
He tended him like welcome guest,   765
Then thus his further speech addressed : —
"Stranger, I am to Roderick Dhu
A clansman born, a kinsman true;
Each word against his honor spoke
Demands of me avenging stroke;   770
Yet more, — upon thy fate, 't is said,
A mighty augury is laid.
It rests with me to wind my horn, —
Thou art with numbers overborne;
It rests with me, here, brand to brand,   775
Worn as thou art, to bid thee stand :
But, not for clan, nor kindred's cause,
Will I depart from honor's laws;
To assail a wearied man were shame,
And stranger is a holy name;   780
Guidance and rest, and food and fire,
In vain he never must require.
Then rest thee here till dawn of day;
Myself will guide thee on the way,
O'er stock and stone, through watch and ward,   785
Till past Clan-Alpine's outmost guard,
As far as Coilantogle's ford;
From thence thy warrant is thy sword."
"I take thy courtesy, by heaven,
As freely as 't is nobly given!"   790

"Well, rest thee; for the bittern's cry
Sings us the lake's wild lullaby."
With that he shook the gathered heath,
And spread his plaid upon the wreath;
And the brave foemen, side by side,
Lay peaceful down like brothers tried,
And slept until the dawning beam
Purpled the mountain and the stream.

CANTO FIFTH

THE COMBAT

I

FAIR as the earliest beam of eastern light,
  When first, by the bewildered pilgrim spied,
It smiles upon the dreary brow of night,
  And silvers o'er the torrent's foaming tide,
  And lights the fearful path on mountain-side, —   5
Fair as that beam, although the fairest far,
  Giving to horror grace, to danger pride,
Shine martial Faith, and Courtesy's bright star,
Through all the wreckful storms that cloud the brow of
    War.

II

That early beam, so fair and sheen,   10
Was twinkling through the hazel screen,
When, rousing at its glimmer red,
The warriors left their lowly bed,
Looked out upon the dappled sky,
Muttered their soldier matins by,   15
And then awaked their fire, to steal,
As short and rude, their soldier meal.
That o'er, the Gael around him threw
His graceful plaid of varied hue,

STIRLING CASTLE FROM THE BACK WALK

And, true to promise, led the way,   20
By thicket green and mountain gray.
A wildering path! — they winded now
Along the precipice's brow,
Commanding the rich scenes beneath,
The windings of the Forth and Teith,   25
And all the vales between that lie,
Till Stirling's turrets melt in sky;
Then, sunk in copse, their farthest glance
Gained not the length of horseman's lance.
'T was oft so steep, the foot was fain   30
Assistance from the hand to gain;
So tangled oft that, bursting through,
Each hawthorn shed her showers of dew, —
That diamond dew, so pure and clear,
It rivals all but Beauty's tear!   35

III

At length they came where, stern and steep,
The hill sinks down upon the deep.
Here Vennachar in silver flows,
There, ridge on ridge, Benledi rose;
Ever the hollow path twined on,   40
Beneath steep bank and threatening stone;
A hundred men might hold the post
With hardihood against a host.
The rugged mountain's scanty cloak
Was dwarfish shrubs of birch and oak,   45
With shingles bare, and cliffs between,
And patches bright of bracken green,

And heather black, that waved so high,
It held the copse in rivalry.
50 But, where the lake slept deep and still,
Dank osiers fringed the swamp and hill;
And oft both path and hill were torn,
Where wintry torrent down had borne,
And heaped upon the cumbered land
55 Its wreck of gravel, rocks, and sand.
So toilsome was the road to trace,
The guide, abating of his pace,
Led slowly through the pass's jaws,
And asked Fitz-James by what strange cause
60 He sought these wilds, traversed by few,
Without a pass from Roderick Dhu.

IV

"Brave Gael, my pass, in danger tried,
Hangs in my belt and by my side;
Yet, sooth to tell," the Saxon said,
65 "I dreamt not now to claim its aid.
When here, but three days since, I came,
Bewildered in pursuit of game,
All seemed as peaceful and as still
As the mist slumbering on yon hill;
70 Thy dangerous Chief was then afar,
Nor soon expected back from war.
Thus said, at least, my mountain-guide,
Though deep perchance the villain lied."
"Yet why a second venture try?"
75 "A warrior thou, and ask me why! —

Moves our free course by such fixed cause
As gives the poor mechanic laws?
Enough, I sought to drive away
The lazy hours of peaceful day;
Slight cause will then suffice to guide   80
A Knight's free footsteps far and wide, —
A falcon flown, a greyhound strayed,
The merry glance of mountain maid;
Or, if a path be dangerous known,
The danger's self is lure alone."   85

V

"Thy secret keep, I urge thee not; —
Yet, ere again ye sought this spot,
Say, heard ye naught of Lowland war,
Against Clan-Alpine, raised by Mar?"
"No, by my word; — of bands prepared   90
To guard King James's sports I heard;
Nor doubt I aught, but, when they hear
This muster of the mountaineer,
Their pennons will abroad be flung,
Which else in Doune had peaceful hung."   95
"Free be they flung! for we were loath
Their silken folds should feast the moth.
Free be they flung! — as free shall wave
Clan-Alpine's pine in banner brave.
But, stranger, peaceful since you came,   100
Bewildered in the mountain-game,
Whence the bold boast by which you show
Vich-Alpine's vowed and mortal foe?"

"Warrior, but yester-morn I knew
105   Naught of thy Chieftain, Roderick Dhu,
Save as an outlawed desperate man,
The chief of a rebellious clan,

DOUNE CASTLE

Who, in the Regent's court and sight,
With ruffian dagger stabbed a knight;
110   Yet this alone might from his part
Sever each true and loyal heart."

VI

Wrathful at such arraignment foul,
Dark lowered the clansman's sable scowl.
A space he paused, then sternly said,
115   "And heardst thou why he drew his blade?

Heardst thou that shameful word and blow
Brought Roderick's vengeance on his foe?
What recked the Chieftain if he stood
On Highland heath or Holy-Rood?
He rights such wrong where it is given,   120
If it were in the court of heaven."
"Still was it outrage; — yet, 't is true,
Not then claimed sovereignty his due;
While Albany with feeble hand
Held borrowed truncheon of command,   125
The Young King, mewed in Stirling tower,
Was stranger to respect and power.
But then, thy Chieftain's robber life! —
Winning mean prey by causeless strife,
Wrenching from ruined Lowland swain   130
His herds and harvest reared in vain, —
Methinks a soul like thine should scorn
The spoils from such foul foray borne!"

VII

The Gael beheld him grim the while,
And answered with disdainful smile: 135
"Saxon, from yonder mountain high,
I marked thee send delighted eye
Far to the south and east, where lay,
Extended in succession gay,
Deep waving fields and pastures green,   140
With gentle slopes and groves between: —
These fertile plains, that softened vale,
Were once the birthright of the Gael;

The stranger came with iron hand,
145   And from our fathers reft the land.
Where dwell we now? See, rudely swell
Crag over crag, and fell o'er fell.
Ask we this savage hill we tread
For fattened steer or household bread,
150   Ask we for flocks these shingles dry,
And well the mountain might reply —
'To you, as to your sires of yore,
Belong the target and claymore!
I give you shelter in my breast,
155   Your own good blades must win the rest.'
Pent in this fortress of the North,
Think'st thou we will not sally forth,
To spoil the spoiler as we may,
And from the robber rend the prey?
160   Ay, by my soul! — While on yon plain
The Saxon rears one shock of grain,
While of ten thousand herds there strays
But one along yon river's maze, —
The Gael, of plain and river heir,
165   Shall with strong hand redeem his share.
Where live the mountain Chiefs who hold
That plundering Lowland field and fold
Is aught but retribution true?
Seek other cause 'gainst Roderick Dhu."

VIII

170   Answered Fitz-James: "And, if I sought,
Think'st thou no other could be brought?

What deem ye of my path waylaid?
My life given o'er to ambuscade?"
"As of a meed to rashness due:
Hadst thou sent warning fair and true, —	175
I seek my hound or falcon strayed,
I seek, good faith, a Highland maid, —
Free hadst thou been to come and go;
But secret path marks secret foe.
Nor yet for this, even as a spy,	180
Hadst thou, unheard, been doomed to die,
Save to fulfil an augury."
"Well, let it pass; nor will I now
Fresh cause of enmity avow,
To chafe thy mood and cloud thy brow.	185
Enough, I am by promise tied
To match me with this man of pride:
Twice have I sought Clan-Alpine's glen
In peace; but, when I come again,
I come with banner, brand, and bow,	190
As leader seeks his mortal foe.
For love-lorn swain in lady's bower
Ne'er panted for the appointed hour,
As I, until before me stand
This rebel Chieftain and his band!"	195

IX

"Have then thy wish!" — He whistled shrill,
And he was answered from the hill;
Wild as the scream of the curlew,
From crag to crag the signal flew.

200   Instant, through copse and heath, arose
       Bonnets and spears and bended bows;
       On right, on left, above, below,
       Sprung up at once the lurking foe;
       From shingles gray their lances start,
205   The bracken bush sends forth the dart,
       The rushes and the willow-wand
       Are bristling into axe and band,
       And every tuft of broom gives life
       To plaided warrior armed for strife.
210   That whistle garrisoned the glen
       At once with full five hundred men,
       As if the yawning hill to heaven
       A subterranean host had given.
       Watching their leader's beck and will,
215   All silent there they stood and still.
       Like the loose crags whose threatening mass
       Lay tottering o'er the hollow pass,
       As if an infant's touch could urge
       Their headlong passage down the verge,
220   With step and weapon forward flung,
       Upon the mountain-side they hung.
       The Mountaineer cast glance of pride
       Along Benledi's living side,
       Then fixed his eye and sable brow
225   Full on Fitz-James: "How say'st thou now?
       These are Clan-Alpine's warriors true;
       And, Saxon, — I am Roderick Dhu!"

X

Fitz-James was brave: — though to his heart
The life-blood thrilled with sudden start,
He manned himself with dauntless air,   230
Returned the Chief his haughty stare,
His back against a rock he bore,
And firmly placed his foot before: —
"Come one, come all! this rock shall fly
From its firm base as soon as I."   235
Sir Roderick marked, — and in his eyes
Respect was mingled with surprise,
And the stern joy which warriors feel
In foeman worthy of their steel.
Short space he stood — then waved his hand: 240
Down sunk the disappearing band;
Each warrior vanished where he stood,
In broom or bracken, heath or wood;
Sunk brand and spear and bended bow,
In osiers pale and copses low;   245
It seemed as if their mother Earth
Had swallowed up her warlike birth.
The wind's last breath had tossed in air
Pennon and plaid and plumage fair, —
The next but swept a lone hill-side,   250
Where heath and fern were waving wide:
The sun's last glance was glinted back
From spear and glaive, from targe and jack, —
The next, all unreflected, shone
On bracken green and cold gray stone.   255

XI

Fitz-James looked round, — yet scarce believed
The witness that his sight received;
Such apparition well might seem
Delusion of a dreadful dream.
260   Sir Roderick in suspense he eyed,
And to his look the Chief replied:
"Fear naught — nay, that I need not say —
But — doubt not aught from mine array.
Thou art my guest; — I pledged my word
265   As far as Coilantogle ford:
Nor would I call a clansman's brand
For aid against one valiant hand,
Though on our strife lay every vale
Rent by the Saxon from the Gael.
270   So move we on; — I only meant
To show the reed on which you leant,
Deeming this path you might pursue
Without a pass from Roderick Dhu."
They moved; — I said Fitz-James was brave
275   As ever knight that belted glaive,
Yet dare not say that now his blood
Kept on its wont and tempered flood,
As, following Roderick's stride, he drew
That seeming lonesome pathway through,
280   Which yet by fearful proof was rife
With lances, that, to take his life,
Waited but signal from a guide,
So late dishonored and defied.
Ever, by stealth, his eye sought round
285   The vanished guardians of the ground,

And still from copse and heather deep
Fancy saw spear and broadsword peep,
And in the plover's shrilly strain
The signal whistle heard again.
Nor breathed he free till far behind　　　　290
The pass was left; for then they wind
Along a wide and level green,
Where neither tree nor tuft was seen,
Nor rush nor bush of broom was near,
To hide a bonnet or a spear.　　　　295

XII

The Chief in silence strode before,
And reached that torrent's sounding shore,
Which, daughter of three mighty lakes
From Vennachar in silver breaks,
Sweeps through the plain, and ceaseless mines　　　　300
On Bochastle the mouldering lines,
Where Rome, the Empress of the world,
Of yore her eagle wings unfurled.
And here his course the Chieftain stayed,
Threw down his target and his plaid,　　　　305
And to the Lowland warrior said:
"Bold Saxon! to his promise just,
Vich-Alpine has discharged his trust.
This murderous Chief, this ruthless man,
This head of a rebellious clan,　　　　310
Hath led thee safe, through watch and ward
Far past Clan-Alpine's outmost guard.
Now, man to man, and steel to steel,
A Chieftain's vengeance thou shalt feel.

315   See, here all vantageless I stand,
       Armed like thyself with single brand;
       For this is Coilantogle ford,
       And thou must keep thee with thy sword."

                    XIII

       The Saxon paused: "I ne'er delayed,
320   When foeman bade me draw my blade;
       Nay more, brave Chief, I vowed thy death;
       Yet sure thy fair and generous faith,
       And my deep debt for life preserved,
       A better meed have well deserved:
325   Can naught but blood our feud atone?
       Are there no means?" — "No, stranger, none!
       And hear, — to fire thy flagging zeal, —
       The Saxon cause rests on thy steel;
       For thus spoke Fate by prophet bred
330   Between the living and the dead:
       'Who spills the foremost foeman's life,
       His party conquers in the strife.'"
       "Then, by my word," the Saxon said,
       "The riddle is already read.
335   Seek yonder brake beneath the cliff, —
       There lies Red Murdoch, stark and stiff.
       Thus Fate had solved her prophecy;
       Then yield to Fate, and not to me.
       To James at Stirling let us go,
340   When, if thou wilt be still his foe,
       Or if the King shall not agree
       To grant thee grace and favor free,

I plight mine honor, oath and word
That, to thy native strengths restored,
With each advantage shalt thou stand　　　345
That aids thee now to guard thy land."

XIV

Dark lightning flashed from Roderick's eye:
"Soars thy presumption, then, so high,
Because a wretched kern ye slew,
Homage to name to Roderick Dhu?　　　350
He yields not, he, to man nor Fate!
Thou add'st but fuel to my hate; —
My clansman's blood demands revenge.
Not yet prepared? — By heaven, I change
My thought, and hold thy valor light　　　355
As that of some vain carpet knight,
Who ill deserved my courteous care,
And whose best boast is but to wear
A braid of his fair lady's hair."
"I thank thee, Roderick, for the word!　　　360
It nerves my heart, it steels my sword;
For I have sworn this braid to stain
In the best blood that warms thy vein.
Now, truce, farewell! and, ruth, begone! —
Yet think not that by thee alone,　　　365
Proud Chief! can courtesy be shown;
Though not from copse, or heath, or cairn,
Start at my whistle clansmen stern,
Of this small horn one feeble blast
Would fearful odds against thee cast.　　　370

But fear not — doubt not — which thou wilt —
We try this quarrel hilt to hilt."
Then each at once his falchion drew,
Each on the ground his scabbard threw,
375 Each looked to sun and stream and plain
As what they ne'er might see again;
Then foot and point and eye opposed,
In dubious strife they darkly closed.

XV

Ill fared it then with Roderick Dhu,
380 That on the field his targe he threw,
Whose brazen studs and tough bull-hide
Had death so often dashed aside;
For, trained abroad his arms to wield,
Fitz-James's blade was sword and shield.
385 He practised every pass and ward,
To thrust, to strike, to feint, to guard;
While less expert, though stronger far,
The Gael maintained unequal war.
Three times in closing strife they stood,
390 And thrice the Saxon blade drank blood;
No stinted draught, no scanty tide,
The gushing flood the tartans dyed.
Fierce Roderick felt the fatal drain,
And showered his blows like wintry rain;
395 And, as firm rock or castle-roof
Against the winter shower is proof,
The foe, invulnerable still,
Foiled his wild rage by steady skill;

Till, at advantage ta'en, his brand
Forced Roderick's weapon from his hand,   400
And backward borne upon the lea,
Brought the proud Chieftain to his knee.

XVI

"Now yield thee, or by Him who made
The world, thy heart's blood dyes my blade!"
"Thy threats, thy mercy, I defy!   405
Let recreant yield, who fears to die."
Like adder darting from his coil,
Like wolf that dashes through the toil,
Like mountain-cat who guards her young,
Full at Fitz-James's throat he sprung;   410
Received, but recked not of a wound,
And locked his arms his foeman round. —
Now, gallant Saxon, hold thine own!
No maiden's hand is round thee thrown!
That desperate grasp thy frame might feel   415
Through bars of brass and triple steel!
They tug, they strain! down, down they go,
The Gael above, Fitz-James below.
The Chieftain's gripe his throat compressed,
His knee was planted on his breast;   420
His clotted locks he backward threw,
Across his brow his hand he drew,
From blood and mist to clear his sight,
Then gleamed aloft his dagger bright!
But hate and fury ill supplied   425
The stream of life's exhausted tide,

And all too late the advantage came,
To turn the odds of deadly game:
For, while the dagger gleamed on high,
430   Reeled soul and sense, reeled brain and eye.
Down came the blow! but in the heath
The erring blade found bloodless sheath.
The struggling foe may now unclasp
The fainting Chief's relaxing grasp;
435   Unwounded from the dreadful close,
But breathless all, Fitz-James arose.

XVII

He faltered thanks to heaven for life,
Redeemed, unhoped, from desperate strife;
Next on his foe his look he cast,
440   Whose every gasp appeared his last;
In Roderick's gore he dipped the braid, —
"Poor Blanche! thy wrongs are dearly paid;
Yet with thy foe must die, or live,
The praise that faith and valor give."
445   With that he blew a bugle note,
Undid the collar from his throat,
Unbonneted, and by the wave
Sat down his brow and hands to lave.
Then faint afar are heard the feet
450   Of rushing steeds in gallop fleet;
The sounds increase, and now are seen
Four mounted squires in Lincoln green;
Two who bear lance, and two who lead
By loosened rein a saddled steed;

Each onward held his headlong course,   455
And by Fitz-James reined up his horse, —
With wonder viewed the bloody spot, —
"Exclaim not, gallants! question not. —
You, Herbert and Luffness, alight,
And bind the wounds of yonder knight;   460
Let the gray palfrey bear his weight,
We destined for a fairer freight,
And bring him on to Stirling straight,
I will before at better speed,
To seek fresh horse and fitting weed.   465
The sun rides high; — I must be boune
To see the archer-game at noon;
But lightly Bayard clears the lea. —
De Vaux and Herries, follow me.

XVIII

"Stand, Bayard, stand!" — the steed obeyed,   470
With arching neck and bended head,
And glancing eye and quivering ear,
As if he loved his lord to hear.
No foot Fitz-James in stirrup stayed,
No grasp upon the saddle laid,   475
But wreathed his left hand in the mane,
And lightly bounded from the plain,
Turned on the horse his armed heel,
And stirred his courage with the steel.
Bounded the fiery steed in air,   480
The rider sat erect and fair,
Then, like a bolt from steel crossbow
Forth launched, along the plain they go.

They dashed that rapid torrent through,
485   And up Carhonie's hill they flew;
Still at the gallop pricked the Knight,
His merrymen followed as they might.
Along thy banks, swift Teith! they ride,
And in the race they mock thy tide;

BLAIR-DRUMMOND

490   Torry and Lendrick now are past,
And Deanstown lies behind them cast;
They rise, the bannered towers of Doune,
They sink in distant woodland soon;
Blair-Drummond sees the hoofs strike fire,
495   They sweep like breeze through Ochtertyre;
They mark just glance and disappear
The lofty brow of ancient Kier;

They bathe their coursers' sweltering sides,
Dark Forth! amid thy sluggish tides,
And on the opposing shore take ground,   500
With plash, with scramble, and with bound.
Right-hand they leave thy cliffs, Craig-Forth!
And soon the bulwark of the North,
Gray Stirling, with her towers and town,
Upon their fleet career looked down.   505

XIX

As up the flinty path they strained,
Sudden his steed the leader reined;
A signal to his squire he flung,
Who instant to his stirrup sprung: —
"Seest thou, De Vaux, yon woodsman gray,   510
Who townward holds the rocky way,
Of stature tall and poor array?
Mark'st thou the firm, yet active stride,
With which he scales the mountain side?
Know'st thou from whence he comes, or whom?"   515
"No, by my word; — a burly groom
He seems, who in the field or chase
A baron's train would nobly grace —"
"Out, out, De Vaux! can fear supply,
And jealousy, no sharper eye?   520
Afar, ere to the hill he drew,
That stately form and step I knew;
Like form in Scotland is not seen,
Treads not such step on Scottish green.
'T is James of Douglas, by Saint Serle!   525
The uncle of the banished Earl.

Away, away, to court to show
The near approach of dreaded foe:
The King must stand upon his guard;
530   Douglas and he must meet prepared."
Then right-hand wheeled their steeds, and straight
They won the Castle's postern gate.

CAMBUS-KENNETH ABBEY AND TOMB OF JAMES III

XX

The Douglas, who had bent his way
From Cambus-kenneth's abbey gray,
535   Now, as he climbed the rocky shelf,
Held sad communion with himself: —
"Yes! all is true my fears could frame;
A prisoner lies the noble Græme,

And fiery Roderick soon will feel
The vengeance of the royal steel.   540
I, only I, can ward their fate, —
God grant the ransom come not late!
The Abbess hath her promise given,
My child shall be the bride of Heaven; —
Be pardoned one repining tear!   545
For He who gave her knows how dear,
How excellent! — but that is by,
And now my business is — to die. —
Ye towers! within whose circuit dread
A Douglas by his sovereign bled;   550
And thou, O sad and fatal mound!
That oft hast heard the death-axe sound,
As on the noblest of the land
Fell the stern headsman's bloody hand, —
The dungeon, block, and nameless tomb   555
Prepare — for Douglas seeks his doom!
But hark! what blithe and jolly peal
Makes the Franciscan steeple reel?
And see! upon the crowded street,
In motley groups what masquers meet!   560
Banner and pageant, pipe and drum,
And merry morrice-dancers come.
I guess, by all this quaint array,
The burghers hold their sports to-day.
James will be there; he loves such show,   565
Where the good yeoman bends his bow,
And the tough wrestler foils his foe,
As well as where, in proud career,
The high-born tilter shivers spear.

570   I'll follow to the Castle-park,
       And play my prize; — King James shall mark
       If age has tamed these sinews stark,
       Whose force so oft in happier days
       His boyish wonder loved to praise."

XXI

575   The Castle gates were open flung,
       The quivering drawbridge rocked and rung,
       And echoed loud the flinty street
       Beneath the coursers' clattering feet,
       As slowly down the steep descent
580   Fair Scotland's King and nobles went,
       While all along the crowded way
       Was jubilee and loud huzza.
       And ever James was bending low
       To his white jennet's saddle-bow,
585   Doffing his cap to city dame,
       Who smiled and blushed for pride and shame.
       And well the simperer might be vain, —
       He chose the fairest of the train.
       Gravely he greets each city sire,
590   Commends each pageant's quaint attire,
       Gives to the dancers thanks aloud,
       And smiles and nods upon the crowd,
       Who rend the heavens with their acclaims, —
       "Long live the Commons' King, King James!"
595   Behind the King thronged peer and knight,
       And noble dame and damsel bright,
       Whose fiery steeds ill brooked the stay
       Of the steep street and crowded way.

But in the train you might discern
Dark lowering brow and visage stern;   600
There nobles mourned their pride restrained,
And the mean burgher's joys disdained;
And chiefs, who, hostage for their clan,
Were each from home a banished man,
There thought upon their own gray tower,   605
Their waving woods, their feudal power,
And deemed themselves a shameful part
Of pageant which they cursed in heart.

XXII

Now, in the Castle-park, drew out
Their checkered bands the joyous rout.   610
There morricers, with bell at heel
And blade in hand, their mazes wheel;
But chief, beside the butts, there stand
Bold Robin Hood and all his band, —
Friar Tuck with quarterstaff and cowl,   615
Old Scathelocke with his surly scowl,
Maid Marian, fair as ivory bone,
Scarlet, and Mutch, and Little John;
Their bugles challenge all that will,
In archery to prove their skill.   620
The Douglas bent a bow of might,
His first shaft centred in the white,
And when in turn he shot again,
His second split the first in twain.
From the King's hand must Douglas take   625
A silver dart, the archer's stake;

Fondly he watched, with watery eye,
Some answering glance of sympathy, —
No kind emotion made reply!
630   Indifferent as to archer wight,
The monarch gave the arrow bright.

XXIII

Now, clear the ring! for, hand to hand,
The manly wrestlers take their stand.
Two o'er the rest superior rose,
635   And proud demanded mightier foes, —
Nor called in vain, for Douglas came. —
For life is Hugh of Larbert lame;
Scarce better John of Alloa's fare,
Whom senseless home his comrades bare.
640   Prize of the wrestling match, the King
To Douglas gave a golden ring,
While coldly glanced his eye of blue,
As frozen drop of wintry dew.
Douglas would speak, but in his breast
645   His struggling soul his words suppressed;
Indignant then he turned him where
Their arms the brawny yeomen bare,
To hurl the massive bar in air.
When each his utmost strength had shown,
650   The Douglas rent an earth-fast stone
From its deep bed, then heaved it high,
And sent the fragment through the sky
A rood beyond the farthest mark;
And still in Stirling's royal park,

The gray-haired sires, who know the past,　　655
To strangers point the Douglas cast,
And moralize on the decay
Of Scottish strength in modern day.

XXIV

The vale with loud applauses rang,
The Ladies' Rock sent back the clang.　　660
The King, with look unmoved, bestowed
A purse well filled with pieces broad.
Indignant smiled the Douglas proud,
And threw the gold among the crowd,
Who now with anxious wonder scan,　　665
And sharper glance, the dark gray man;
Till whispers rose among the throng,
That heart so free, and hand so strong,
Must to the Douglas blood belong.
The old men marked and shook the head,　　670
To see his hair with silver spread,
And winked aside, and told each son
Of feats upon the English done,
Ere Douglas of the stalwart hand
Was exiled from his native land.　　675
The women praised his stately form,
Though wrecked by many a winter's storm;
The youth with awe and wonder saw
His strength surpassing Nature's law.
Thus judged, as is their wont, the crowd,　　680
Till murmurs rose to clamors loud.
But not a glance from that proud ring
Of peers who circled round the King

With Douglas held communion kind,
685   Or called the banished man to mind;
No, not from those who at the chase
Once held his side the honored place,
Begirt his board, and in the field
Found safety underneath his shield;
690   For he whom royal eyes disown,
When was his form to courtiers known!

XXV

The Monarch saw the gambols flag,
And bade let loose a gallant stag,
Whose pride, the holiday to crown,
695   Two favorite greyhounds should pull down.
That venison free and Bourdeaux wine
Might serve the archery to dine.
But Lufra, — whom from Douglas' side
Nor bribe nor threat could e'er divide,
700   The fleetest hound in all the North, —
Brave Lufra saw, and darted forth.
She left the royal hounds midway,
And dashing on the antlered prey,
Sunk her sharp muzzle in his flank,
705   And deep the flowing life-blood drank.
The King's stout huntsman saw the sport
By strange intruder broken short,
Came up, and with his leash unbound,
In anger struck the noble hound.
710   The Douglas had endured, that morn,
The King's cold look, the nobles' scorn,

And last, and worst to spirit proud,
Had borne the pity of the crowd;
But Lufra had been fondly bred,
To share his board, to watch his bed,   715
And oft would Ellen Lufra's neck
In maiden glee with garlands deck;
They were such playmates that with name
Of Lufra Ellen's image came.
His stifled wrath is brimming high,   720
In darkened brow and flashing eye;
As waves before the bark divide,
The crowd gave way before his stride;
Needs but a buffet and no more,
The groom lies senseless in his gore.   725
Such blow no other hand could deal,
Though gauntleted in glove of steel.

XXVI

Then clamored loud the royal train,
And brandished swords and staves amain.
But stern the Baron's warning: "Back!   730
Back, on your lives, ye menial pack!
Beware the Douglas. — Yes! behold,
King James! The Douglas, doomed of old,
And vainly sought for near and far,
A victim to atone the war,   735
A willing victim, now attends,
Nor craves thy grace but for his friends." —
"Thus is my clemency repaid?
Presumptuous Lord!" the Monarch said:

740 "Of thy misproud ambitious clan,
Thou, James of Bothwell, wert the man,
The only man, in whom a foe
My woman-mercy would not know;
But shall a Monarch's presence brook
745 Injurious blow and haughty look? —
What ho! the Captain of our Guard!
Give the offender fitting ward. —
Break off the sports!" — for tumult rose,
And yeomen 'gan to bend their bows, —
750 "Break off the sports!" he said and frowned,
"And bid our horsemen clear the ground."

XXVII

Then uproar wild and misarray
Marred the fair form of festal day.
The horsemen pricked among the crowd,
755 Repelled by threats and insult loud;
To earth are borne the old and weak,
The timorous fly, the women shriek;
With flint, with shaft, with staff, with bar,
The hardier urge tumultuous war.
760 At once round Douglas darkly sweep
The royal spears in circle deep,
And slowly scale the pathway steep,
While on the rear in thunder pour
The rabble with disordered roar.
765 With grief the noble Douglas saw
The Commons rise against the law,
And to the leading soldier said:

"Sir John of Hyndford, 't was my blade
That knighthood on thy shoulder laid;
For that good deed permit me then   770
A word with these misguided men. —

XXVIII

"Hear, gentle friends, ere yet for me
Ye break the bands of fealty.
My life, my honor, and my cause,
I tender free to Scotland's laws.   775
Are these so weak as must require
The aid of your misguided ire?
Or, if I suffer causeless wrong,
Is then my selfish rage so strong,
My sense of public weal so low,   780
That, for mean vengeance on a foe,
Those cords of love I should unbind
Which knit my country and my kind?
O no! Believe, in yonder tower
It will not soothe my captive hour,   785
To know those spears our foe should dread
For me in kindred gore are red:
To know, in fruitless brawl begun,
For me that mother wails her son,
For me that widow's mate expires,   790
For me that orphans weep their sires,
That patriots mourn insulted laws,
And curse the Douglas for the cause.
O, let your patience ward such ill,
And keep your right to love me still!"   795

XXIX

The crowd's wild fury sunk again
In tears, as tempests melt in rain.
With lifted hands and eyes, they prayed
For blessings on his generous head
800   Who for his country felt alone,
And prized her blood beyond his own.
Old men upon the verge of life
Blessed him who stayed the civil strife;
And mothers held their babes on high,
805   The self-devoted Chief to spy,
Triumphant over wrongs and ire,
To whom the prattlers owed a sire.
Even the rough soldier's heart was moved;
As if behind some bier beloved,
810   With trailing arms and drooping head,
The Douglas up the hill he led,
And at the Castle's battled verge,
With sighs resigned his honored charge.

XXX

The offended Monarch rode apart,
815   With bitter thought and swelling heart,
And would not now vouchsafe again
Through Stirling streets to lead his train.
"O Lennox, who would wish to rule
This changeling crowd, this common fool?
820   Hear'st thou," he said, "the loud acclaim
With which they shout the Douglas name?

With like acclaim the vulgar throat
Strained for King James their morning note;
With like acclaim they hailed the day
When first I broke the Douglas sway;   825
And like acclaim would Douglas greet
If he could hurl me from my seat.
Who o'er the herd would wish to reign,
Fantastic, fickle, fierce, and vain?
Vain as the leaf upon the stream,   830
And fickle as a changeful dream;
Fantastic as a woman's mood,
And fierce as Frenzy's fevered blood.
Thou many-headed monster-thing,
O, who would wish to be thy king? —   835

XXXI

"But soft! what messenger of speed
Spurs hitherward his panting steed?
I guess his cognizance afar —
What from our cousin, John of Mar?"
"He prays, my liege, your sports keep bound   840
Within the safe and guarded ground;
For some foul purpose yet unknown, —
Most sure for evil to the throne, —
The outlawed Chieftain, Roderick Dhu,
Has summoned his rebellious crew;   845
'T is said, in James of Bothwell's aid
These loose banditti stand arrayed.
The Earl of Mar this morn from Doune
To break their muster marched, and soon

850   Your grace will hear of battle fought;
        But earnestly the Earl besought,
        Till for such danger he provide,
        With scanty train you will not ride."

                        XXXII

        "Thou warn'st me I have done amiss, —
855   I should have earlier looked to this;
        I lost it in this bustling day. —
        Retrace with speed thy former way;
        Spare not for spoiling of thy steed,
        The best of mine shall be thy meed.
860   Say to our faithful Lord of Mar,
        We do forbid the intended war;
        Roderick this morn in single fight
        Was made our prisoner by a knight,
        And Douglas hath himself and cause
865   Submitted to our kingdom's laws.
        The tidings of their leaders lost
        Will soon dissolve the mountain host,
        Nor would we that the vulgar feel,
        For their Chief's crimes, avenging steel.
870   Bear Mar our message, Braco, fly!"
        He turned his steed, — "My liege, I hie,
        Yet ere I cross this lily lawn
        I fear the broadswords will be drawn."
        The turf the flying courser spurned,
875   And to his towers the King returned.

XXXIII

Ill with King James's mood that day
Suited gay feast and minstrel lay;
Soon were dismissed the courtly throng,
And soon cut short the festal song.
Nor less upon the saddened town　　　　　　880
The evening sank in sorrow down.
The burghers spoke of civil jar,
Of rumored feuds and mountain war,
Of Moray, Mar, and Roderick Dhu,
All up in arms; — the Douglas too,　　　　　885
They mourned him pent within the hold,
"Where stout Earl William was of old." —
And there his word the speaker stayed,
And finger on his lip he laid,
Or pointed to his dagger blade.　　　　　　890
But jaded horsemen from the west
At evening to the Castle pressed,
And busy talkers said they bore
Tidings of fight on Katrine's shore;
At noon the deadly fray begun,　　　　　　895
And lasted till the set of sun.
Thus giddy rumor shook the town,
Till closed the Night her pennons brown.

Stirling Castle

CANTO SIXTH

THE GUARD-ROOM

I

The sun, awakening through the smoky air
   Of the dark city casts a sullen glance,
Rousing each caitiff to his task of care,
   Of sinful man the sad inheritance;
   Summoning revellers from the lagging dance,   5
Scaring the prowling robber to his den;
   Gilding on battled tower the warder's lance,
And warning student pale to leave his pen,
And yield his drowsy eyes to the kind nurse of men.

What various scenes and O, what scenes of woe,   10
   Are witnessed by that red and struggling beam!
The fevered patient from his pallet low,
   Through crowded hospital beholds it stream;
   The ruined maiden trembles at its gleam,
The debtor wakes to thought of gyve and jail,   15
   The love-lorn wretch starts from tormenting dream;
The wakeful mother, by the glimmering pale,
Trims her sick infant's couch, and soothes his feeble wail.

II

   At dawn the towers of Stirling rang
   With soldier-step and weapon-clang,   20
   While drums with rolling note foretell
   Relief to weary sentinel.

Through narrow loop and casement barred,
The sunbeams sought the Court of Guard,
25 And, struggling with the smoky air,
Deadened the torches' yellow glare.
In comfortless alliance shone
The lights through arch of blackened stone,
And showed wild shapes in garb of war,
30 Faces deformed with beard and scar,
All haggard from the midnight watch,
And fevered with the stern debauch;
For the oak table's massive hoard,
Flooded with wine, with fragments stored,
35 And beakers drained, and cups o'erthrown,
Showed in what sport the night had flown.
Some, weary, snored on floor and bench;
Some labored still their thirst to quench;
Some, chilled with watching, spread their hands
40 O'er the huge chimney's dying brands,
While round them, or beside them flung,
At every step their harness rung.

III

These drew not for their fields the sword,
Like tenants of a feudal lord,
45 Nor owned the patriarchal claim
Of Chieftain in their leader's name;
Adventurers they, from far who roved,
To live by battle which they loved.
There the Italian's clouded face,
50 The swarthy Spaniard's there you trace;

The mountain-loving Switzer there
More freely breathed in mountain-air;
The Fleming there despised the soil
That paid so ill the laborer's toil;
Their rolls showed French and German name;   55
And merry England's exiles came,
To share, with ill-concealed disdain,
Of Scotland's pay the scanty gain.
All brave in arms, well trained to wield
The heavy halberd, brand, and shield;   60
In camps licentious, wild, and bold;
In pillage fierce and uncontrolled;
And now, by holytide and feast,
From rules of discipline released.

IV

They held debate of bloody fray,   65
Fought 'twixt Loch Katrine and Achray.
Fierce was their speech, and mid their words
Their hands oft grappled to their swords;
Nor sunk their tone to spare the ear
Of wounded comrades groaning near,   70
Whose mangled limbs and bodies gored
Bore token of the mountain sword.
Though, neighboring to the Court of Guard,
Their prayers and feverish wails were heard, —
Sad burden to the ruffian joke,   75
And savage oath by fury spoke! —
At length up started John of Brent,
A yeoman from the banks of Trent;

A stranger to respect or fear,
80   In peace a chaser of the deer,
In host a hardy mutineer,
But still the boldest of the crew
When deed of danger was to do.
He grieved that day their games cut short,
85   And marred the dicer's brawling sport,
And shouted loud, "Renew the bowl!
And, while a merry catch I troll,
Let each the buxom chorus bear,
Like brethren of the brand and spear."

V

Soldier's Song

90 Our vicar still preaches that Peter and Poule
Laid a swinging long curse on the bonny brown bowl,
That there's wrath and despair in the jolly black-jack,
And the seven deadly sins in a flagon of sack;
Yet whoop, Barnaby! off with thy liquor,
95 Drink upsees out, and a fig for the vicar!

Our vicar he calls it damnation to sip
The ripe ruddy dew of a woman's dear lip,
Says that Beelzebub lurks in her kerchief so sly,
And Apollyon shoots darts from her merry black eye;
100 Yet whoop, Jack! kiss Gillian the quicker,
Till she bloom like a rose, and a fig for the vicar!

Our vicar thus preaches, — and why should he not?
For the dues of his cure are the placket and pot;

And 't is right of his office poor laymen to lurch
Who infringe the domains of our good Mother Church. 105
Yet whoop, bully-boys! off with your liquor,
Sweet Marjorie's the word, and a fig for the vicar!

VI

The warder's challenge, heard without,
Stayed in mid-roar the merry shout.
A soldier to the portal went, —   110
"Here is old Bertram, sirs, of Ghent;
And — beat for jubilee the drum! —
A maid and minstrel with him come."
Bertram, a Fleming, gray and scarred,
Was entering now the Court of Guard,   115
A harper with him, and, in plaid
All muffled close, a mountain maid,
Who backward shrunk to 'scape the view
Of the loose scene and boisterous crew.
"What news?" they roared: — "I only know, 120
From noon till eve we fought with foe,
As wild and as untamable
As the rude mountains where they dwell;
On both sides store of blood is lost,
Nor much success can either boast."   125
"But whence thy captives, friend? such spoil
As theirs must needs reward thy toil.
Old dost thou wax, and wars grow sharp;
Thou now hast glee-maiden and harp!
Get thee an ape, and trudge the land,   130
The leader of a juggler band."

VII

"No, comrade; — no such fortune mine.
After the fight these sought our line,
That aged harper and the girl,
135 And, having audience of the Earl,
Mar bade I should purvey them steed,
And bring them hitherward with speed.
Forbear your mirth and rude alarm,
For none shall do them shame or harm." —
140 "Hear ye his boast?" cried John of Brent,
Ever to strife and jangling bent;
"Shall he strike doe beside our lodge,
And yet the jealous niggard grudge
To pay the forester his fee?
145 I'll have my share howe'er it be,
Despite of Moray, Mar, or thee."
Bertram his forward step withstood;
And, burning in his vengeful mood,
Old Allan, though unfit for strife,
150 Laid hand upon his dagger-knife;
But Ellen boldly stepped between,
And dropped at once the tartan screen: —
So, from his morning cloud, appears
The sun of May through summer tears.
155 The savage soldiery, amazed,
As on descended angel gazed;
Even hardy Brent, abashed and tamed,
Stood half admiring, half ashamed.

VIII

Boldly she spoke: "Soldiers, attend!
My father was the soldier's friend,   160
Cheered him in camps, in marches led,
And with him in the battle bled.
Not from the valiant or the strong
Should exile's daughter suffer wrong."
Answered De Brent, most forward still   165
In every feat or good or ill:
"I shame me of the part I played;
And thou an outlaw's child, poor maid!
An outlaw I by forest laws,
And merry Needwood knows the cause.   170
Poor Rose, — if Rose be living now," —
He wiped his iron eye and brow, —
"Must bear such age, I think, as thou. —
Hear ye, my mates! I go to call
The Captain of our watch to hall: 175
There lies my halberd on the floor;
And he that steps my halberd o'er,
To do the maid injurious part,
My shaft shall quiver in his heart!
Beware rude speech, or jesting rough;   180
Ye all know John de Brent. Enough."

IX

Their Captain came, a gallant young, —
Of Tullibardine's house he sprung,
Nor wore he yet the spurs of knight;
Gay was his mien, his humor light,   185

And, though by courtesy controlled,
Forward his speech, his bearing bold.
The high-born maiden ill could brook
The scanning of his curious look
190 And dauntless eye : — and yet, in sooth,
Young Lewis was a generous youth;
But Ellen's lovely face and mien,
Ill suited to the garb and scene,
Might lightly bear construction strange,
195 And give loose fancy scope to range.
"Welcome to Stirling towers, fair maid!
Come ye to seek a champion's aid,
On palfrey white, with harper hoar,
Like errant damosel of yore?
200 Does thy high quest a knight require,
Or may the venture suit a squire?"
Her dark eye flashed ; — she paused and sighed : —
"O what have I to do with pride ! —
Through scenes of sorrow, shame, and strife,
205 A suppliant for a father's life,
I crave an audience of the King.
Behold, to back my suit, a ring,
The royal pledge of grateful claims,
Given by the Monarch to Fitz-James."

X

210 The signet-ring young Lewis took
With deep respect and altered look,
And said : "This ring our duties own;
And pardon, if to worth unknown,

In semblance mean obscurely veiled,
Lady, in aught my folly failed.   215
Soon as the day flings wide its gates,
The King shall know what suitor waits.
Please you meanwhile in fitting bower
Repose you till his waking hour;
Female attendance shall obey   220
Your hest, for service or array.
Permit I marshal you the way."
But, ere she followed, with the grace
And open bounty of her race,
She bade her slender purse be shared   225
Among the soldiers of the guard.
The rest with thanks their guerdon took,
But Brent, with shy and awkward look,
On the reluctant maiden's hold
Forced bluntly back the proffered gold: —   230
"Forgive a haughty English heart,
And O, forget its ruder part!
The vacant purse shall be my share,
Which in my barret-cap I'll bear,
Perchance, in jeopardy of war,   235
Where gayer crests may keep afar."
With thanks — 't was all she could — the maid
His rugged courtesy repaid.

XI

When Ellen forth with Lewis went,
Allan made suit to John of Brent: —   240
"My lady safe, O, let your grace
Give me to see my master's face!

His minstrel I, — to share his doom
Bound from the cradle to the tomb.
245 Tenth in descent, since first my sires
Waked for his noble house their lyres,
Nor one of all the race was known
But prized its weal above their own.
With the Chief's birth begins our care;
250 Our harp must soothe the infant heir,
Teach the youth tales of fight, and grace
His earliest feat of field or chase;
In peace, in war, our rank we keep,
We cheer his board, we soothe his sleep,
255 Nor leave him till we pour our verse —
A doleful tribute! — o'er his hearse.
Then let me share his captive lot;
It is my right, — deny it not!"
"Little we reck," said John of Brent,
260 "We Southern men, of long descent;
Nor wot we how a name — a word —
Makes clansmen vassals to a lord:
Yet kind my noble landlord's part, —
God bless the house of Beaudesert!
265 And, but I loved to drive the deer
More than to guide the laboring steer,
I had not dwelt an outcast here.
Come, good old Minstrel, follow me;
Thy Lord and Chieftain shalt thou see."

XII

270 Then, from a rusted iron hook,
A bunch of ponderous keys he took,

Lighted a torch, and Allan led
Through grated arch and passage dread.
Portals they passed, where, deep within,
Spoke prisoner's moan and fetters' din;   275
Through rugged vault, where, loosely stored,
Lay wheel, and axe, and headsman's sword,
And many a hideous engine grim,
For wrenching joint and crushing limb,
By artists formed who deemed it shame   280
And sin to give their work a name.
They halted at a low-browed porch,
And Brent to Allan gave the torch, .
While bolt and chain he backward rolled,
And made the bar unhasp its hold.   285
They entered: — 't was a prison-room
Of stern security and gloom,
Yet not a dungeon; for the day
Through lofty gratings found its way,
And rude and antique garniture   290
Decked the sad walls and oaken floor,
Such as the rugged days of old
Deemed fit for captive noble's hold.
"Here," said De Brent, "thou mayst remain
Till the Leech visit him again.   295
Strict is his charge, the warders tell,
To tend the noble prisoner well."
Retiring then the bolt he drew,
And the lock's murmurs growled anew.
Roused at the sound, from lowly bed   300
A captive feebly raised his head;
The wondering Minstrel looked, and knew —

Not his dear lord, but Roderick Dhu!
For, come from where Clan-Alpine fought,
305 They, erring, deemed the Chief he sought.

XIII

As the tall ship whose lofty prore
Shall never stem the billows more,
Deserted by her gallant band,
Amid the breakers lies astrand, —
310 So on his couch lay Roderick Dhu!
And oft his fevered limbs he threw
In toss abrupt, as when her sides
Lie rocking in the advancing tides,
That shake her frame with ceaseless beat,
315 Yet cannot heave her from her seat; —
O, how unlike her course at sea!
Or his free step on hill and lea! —
Soon as the Minstrel he could scan, —
"What of thy lady? — of my clan? —
320 My mother? — Douglas? — tell me all!
Have they been ruined in my fall?
Ah, yes! or wherefore art thou here?
Yet speak, — speak boldly, — do not fear." —
For Allan, who his mood well knew,
325 Was choked with grief and terror too. —
"Who fought? — who fled? — Old man, be brief; —
Some might, — for they have lost their Chief.
Who basely live? — who bravely died?"
"O, calm thee, Chief!" the Minstrel cried,
330 "Ellen is safe!" "For that thank Heaven!"
"And hopes are for the Douglas given; —

The Lady Margaret, too, is well;
And, for thy clan, — on field or fell,
Has never harp of minstrel told
Of combat fought so true and bold.   335
Thy stately Pine is yet unbent,
Though many a goodly bough is rent."

XIV

The Chieftain reared his form on high,
And fever's fire was in his eye;
But ghastly, pale, and livid streaks   340
Checkered his swarthy brow and cheeks.
"Hark, Minstrel!   I have heard thee play,
With measure bold on festal day,
In yon lone isle, — again where ne'er
Shall harper play or warrior hear! —   345
That stirring air that peals on high,
O'er Dermid's race our victory. —
Strike it! — and then, — for well thou canst, —
Free from thy minstrel-spirit glanced,
Fling me the picture of the fight,   350
When met my clan the Saxon might.
I'll listen, till my fancy hears
The clang of swords, the crash of spears!
These grates, these walls, shall vanish then
For the fair field of fighting men,   355
And my free spirit burst away,
As if it soared from battle fray."
The trembling Bard with awe obeyed, —
Slow on the harp his hand he laid;

360 But soon remembrance of the sight
     He witnessed from the mountain height,
     With what old Bertram told at night,
     Awakened the full power of song,
     And bore him in career along; —
365 As shallop launched on river's tide,
     That slow and fearful leaves the side,
     But, when it feels the middle stream,
     Drives downward swift as lightning's beam.

XV

Battle of Beal' an Duine

     "The Minstrel came once more to view
370 The eastern·ridge of Benvenue,
     For ere he parted he would say
     Farewell to lovely Loch Achray —
     Where shall he find, in foreign land,
     So lone a lake, so sweet a strand! —
375   There is no breeze upon the fern,
              No ripple on the lake,
          Upon her eyry nods the erne,
              The deer has sought the brake;
          The small birds will not sing aloud,
380   The springing trout lies still,
          So darkly glooms yon thunder-cloud,
          That swathes, as with a purple shroud,
              Benledi's distant hill.
          Is it the thunder's solemn sound
385   That mutters deep and dread,
          Or echoes from the groaning ground
              The warrior's measured tread?

Is it the lightning's quivering glance
 That on the thicket streams,
Or do they flash on spear and lance,   390
 The sun's retiring beams? —
I see the dagger-crest of Mar,
I see the Moray's silver star,
Wave o'er the cloud of Saxon war,
That up the lake comes winding far!   395

LOCH ACHRAY AND BENVENUE

To hero boune for battle-strife,
 Or bard of martial lay,
'T were worth ten years of peaceful life,
 One glance at their array!

XVI

"Their light-armed archers far and near   400
 Surveyed the tangled ground,

Their centre ranks, with pike and spear,
    A twilight forest frowned,
Their barded horsemen in the rear
405   The stern batalia crowned.
No cymbal clashed, no clarion rang,
    Still were the pipe and drum;
Save heavy tread, and armor's clang,
    The sullen march was dumb.

TROSACHS AND BEN-AN

410   There breathed no wind their crests to shake,
    Or wave their flags abroad;
Scarce the frail aspen seemed to quake,
    That shadowed o'er their road.
Their vaward scouts no tidings bring,
415   Can rouse no lurking foe,
Nor spy a trace of living thing,
    Save when they stirred the roe;

The host moves like a deep-sea wave,
　Where rise no rocks its pride to brave,
　　High-swelling, dark, and slow.　　　　420
The lake is passed, and now they gain
A narrow and a broken plain,
Before the Trosachs' rugged jaws;
And here the horse and spearmen pause,
While, to explore the dangerous glen,　　425
Dive through the pass the archer-men.

XVII

"At once there rose so wild a yell
Within that dark and narrow dell,
As all the fiends from heaven that fell
Had pealed the banner-cry of hell!　　　430
　Forth from the pass in tumult driven,
　Like chaff before the wind of heaven,
　　The archery appear:
　For life! for life! their flight they ply —
　And shriek, and shout, and battle-cry,　435
　And plaids and bonnets waving high,
　And broadswords flashing to the sky,
　　Are maddening in the rear.
　Onward they drive in dreadful race,
　　Pursuers and pursued;　　　　　440
　Before that tide of flight and chase,
　How shall it keep its rooted place,
　　The spearmen's twilight wood? —
　'Down, down,' cried Mar, 'your lances down!
　Bear back both friend and foe!' —　　445

Like reeds before the tempest's frown,
That serried grove of lances brown
    At once lay levelled low;
And closely shouldering side to side,
450   The bristling ranks the onset bide. —
'We 'll quell the savage mountaineer,
    As their Tinchel cows the game!
They come as fleet as forest deer,
    We 'll drive them back as tame.'

XVIII

455   "Bearing before them in their course
The relics of the archer force,
Like wave with crest of sparkling foam,
Right onward did Clan-Alpine come.
    Above the tide, each broadsword bright
460   Was brandishing like beam of light,
        Each targe was dark below;
And with the ocean's mighty swing,
When heaving to the tempest's wing,
    They hurled them on the foe.
465 I heard the lance's shivering crash,
As when the whirlwind rends the ash;
I heard the broadsword's deadly clang,
As if a hundred anvils rang!
But Moray wheeled his rearward rank
470 Of horsemen on Clan-Alpine's flank, —
    'My banner-man, advance!
I see,' he cried, 'their column shake.
Now, gallants! for your ladies' sake,
    Upon them with the lance!' —

Bracklinn Falls, Callander

475   The horsemen dashed among the rout,
          As deer break through the broom;
      Their steeds are stout, their swords are out,
          They soon make lightsome room.
      Clan-Alpine's best are backward borne —
480   Where, where was Roderick then!
      One blast upon his bugle-horn
          Were worth a thousand men.
      And refluent through the pass of fear
          The battle's tide was poured;
485   Vanished the Saxon's struggling spear,
          Vanished the mountain-sword.
      As Bracklinn's chasm, so black and steep,
          Receives her roaring linn,
      As the dark caverns of the deep
490   Suck the whirlpool in,
      So did the deep and darksome pass
      Devour the battle's mingled mass;
      None linger now upon the plain,
      Save those who ne'er shall fight again.

                    XIX

495   "Now westward rolls the battle's din,
      That deep and doubling pass within. —
      Minstrel, away! the work of fate
      Is bearing on; its issues wait,
      Where the rude Trosachs' dread defile
500   Opens on Katrine's lake and isle.
      Gray Benvenue I soon repassed,
      Loch Katrine lay beneath me cast.

The sun is set; — the clouds are met;
　　The lowering scowl of heaven
An inky hue of livid blue　　　　　　　　505
　　To the deep lake has given;
Strange gusts of wind from mountain glen
Swept o'er the lake, then sunk again.
I heeded not the eddying surge,
Mine eye but saw the Trosachs' gorge,　　510
Mine ear but heard that sullen sound,
Which like an earthquake shook the ground,
And spoke the stern and desperate strife
That parts not but with parting life,
Seeming, to minstrel ear, to toll　　　　515
The dirge of many a passing soul.
　　Nearer it comes — the dim-wood glen
　　The martial flood disgorged again,
　　　　But not in mingled tide;
　　The plaided warriors of the North　　520
　　High on the mountain thunder forth
　　　　And overhang its side,
While by the lake below appears
The darkening cloud of Saxon spears.
At weary bay each shattered band,　　　525
Eying their foemen, sternly stand;
Their banners stream like tattered sail,
That flings its fragments to the gale,
And broken arms and disarray
Marked the fell havoc of the day.　　　　530

XX

"Viewing the mountain's ridge askance,
The Saxons stood in sullen trance,
Till Moray pointed with his lance,
  And cried: 'Behold yon isle!
535 See! none are left to guard its strand
But women weak, that wring the hand:
'T is there of yore the robber band
  Their booty wont to pile; —
My purse, with bonnet-pieces store,
540 To him will swim a bow-shot o'er,
And loose a shallop from the shore.
Lightly we 'll tame the war-wolf then,
Lords of his mate, and brood, and den.'
Forth from the ranks a spearman sprung,
545 On earth his casque and corselet rung,
  He plunged him in the wave: —
All saw the deed, — the purpose knew,
And to their clamors Benvenue
  A mingled echo gave;
550 The Saxons shout, their mate to cheer,
The helpless females scream for fear,
And yells for rage the mountaineer.
'T was then, as by the outcry riven,
Poured down at once the lowering heaven.
555 A whirlwind swept Loch Katrine's breast,
Her billows reared their snowy crest.
Well for the swimmer swelled they high,
To mar the Highland marksman's eye;
For round him showered, mid rain and hail,
560 The vengeful arrows of the Gael.

In vain. — He nears the isle — and lo!
His hand is on a shallop's bow.
Just then a flash of lightning came,
It tinged the waves and strand with flame;
I marked Duncraggan's widowed dame,   565
Behind an oak I saw her stand,
A naked dirk gleamed in her hand: —
It darkened, — but amid the moan
Of waves I heard a dying groan; —
Another flash! — the spearman floats   570
A weltering corse beside the boats,
And the stern matron o'er him stood,
Her hand and dagger streaming blood.

XXI

"'Revenge! revenge!' the Saxons cried,
The Gaels' exulting shout replied.   575
Despite the elemental rage,
Again they hurried to engage;
But, ere they closed in desperate fight,
Bloody with spurring came a knight,
Sprung from his horse, and from a crag   580
Waved 'twixt the hosts a milk-white flag.
Clarion and trumpet by his side
Rung forth a truce-note high and wide,
While, in the Monarch's name, afar
A herald's voice forbade the war,   585
For Bothwell's lord and Roderick bold
Were both, he said, in captive hold." —
But here the lay made sudden stand,
The harp escaped the Minstrel's hand!

590 Oft had he stolen a glance, to spy
How Roderick brooked his minstrelsy:
At first, the Chieftain, to the chime,
With lifted hand kept feeble time;
That motion ceased, — yet feeling strong
595 Varied his look as changed the song;
At length, no more his deafened ear
The minstrel melody can hear;
His face grows sharp, — his hands are clenched,
As if some pang his heart-strings wrenched;
600 Set are his teeth, his fading eye
Is sternly fixed on vacancy;
Thus, motionless and moanless, drew
His parting breath stout Roderick Dhu! —
Old Allan-bane looked on aghast,
605 While grim and still his spirit passed;
But when he saw that life was fled,
He poured his wailing o'er the dead.

XXII

Lament

"And art thou cold and lowly laid,
Thy foeman's dread, thy people's aid,
610 Breadalbane's boast, Clan-Alpine's shade!
For thee shall none a requiem say? —
For thee, who loved the minstrel's lay,
For thee, of Bothwell's house the stay,
The shelter of her exiled line,
615 E'en in this prison-house of thine,
I'll wail for Alpine's honored Pine!

"What groans shall yonder valleys fill!
What shrieks of grief shall rend yon hill!
What tears of burning rage shall thrill,
When mourns thy tribe thy battles done,   620
Thy fall before the race was won,
Thy sword ungirt ere set of sun!
There breathes not clansman of thy line,
But would have given his life for thine.
O, woe for Alpine's honored Pine!   625

"Sad was thy lot on mortal stage! —
The captive thrush may brook the cage,
The prisoned eagle dies for rage.
Brave spirit, do not scorn my strain!
And, when its notes awake again,   630
Even she, so long beloved in vain,
Shall with my harp her voice combine,
And mix her woe and tears with mine,
To wail Clan-Alpine's honored Pine."

XXIII

Ellen the while, with bursting heart,   635
Remained in lordly bower apart,
Where played, with many-colored gleams,
Through storied pane the rising beams.
In vain on gilded roof they fall,
And lightened up a tapestried wall,   640
And for her use a menial train
A rich collation spread in vain.
The banquet proud, the chamber gay,
Scarce drew one curious glance astray;

645   Or if she looked, 't was but to say,
  With better omen dawned the day
  In that lone isle, where waved on high
  The dun-deer's hide for canopy;
  Where oft her noble father shared
650   The simple meal her care prepared,
  While Lufra, crouching by her side,
  Her station claimed with jealous pride,
  And Douglas, bent on woodland game,
  Spoke of the chase to Malcolm Græme,
655   Whose answer, oft at random made,
  The wandering of his thoughts betrayed.
  Those who such simple joys have known
  Are taught to prize them when they're gone.
  But sudden, see, she lifts her head,
660   The window seeks with cautious tread.
  What distant music has the power
  To win her in this woeful hour?
  'T was from a turret that o'erhung
  Her latticed bower, the strain was sung.

XXIV

Lay of the Imprisoned Huntsman

665   "My hawk is tired of perch and hood,
  My idle greyhound loathes his food,
  My horse is weary of his stall,
  And I am sick of captive thrall.
  I wish I were as I have been,
670   Hunting the hart in forest green,
  With bended bow and bloodhound free,
  For that's the life is meet for me.

"I hate to learn the ebb of time
From yon dull steeple's drowsy chime,
Or mark it as the sunbeams crawl,   675
Inch after inch, along the wall.
The lark was wont my matins ring,
The sable rook my vespers sing;
These towers, although a king's they be,
Have not a hall of joy for me.   680

"No more at dawning morn I rise,
And sun myself in Ellen's eyes,
Drive the fleet deer the forest through,
And homeward wend with evening dew;
A blithesome welcome blithely meet,   685
And lay my trophies at her feet,
While fled the eve on wing of glee, —
That life is lost to love and me!"

XXV

The heart-sick lay was hardly said,
The listener had not turned her head,   690
It trickled still, the starting tear,
When light a footstep struck her ear,
And Snowdoun's graceful Knight was near.
She turned the hastier, lest again
The prisoner should renew his strain.
"O welcome, brave Fitz-James!" she said;   695
"How may an almost orphan maid
Pay the deep debt — " "O say not so!
To me no gratitude you owe.

700   Not mine, alas! the boon to give,
       And bid thy noble father live;
       I can but be thy guide, sweet maid,
       With Scotland's King thy suit to aid.
       No tyrant he, though ire and pride
705   May lay his better mood aside.
       Come, Ellen, come! 't is more than time,
       He holds his court at morning prime."
       With beating heart, and bosom wrung,
       As to a brother's arm she clung.
710   Gently he dried the falling tear,
       And gently whispered hope and cheer;
       Her faltering steps half led, half stayed,
       Through gallery fair and high arcade,
       Till at his touch its wings of pride
715   A portal arch unfolded wide.

XXVI

       Within 't was brilliant all and light,
       A thronging scene of figures bright;
       It glowed on Ellen's dazzled sight,
       As when the setting sun has given
720   Ten thousand hues to summer even,
       And from their tissue fancy frames
       Aerial knights and fairy dames.
       Still by Fitz-James her footing stayed;
       A few faint steps she forward made,
725   Then slow her drooping head she raised,
       And fearful round the presence gazed;
       For him she sought who owned this state,
       The dreaded Prince whose will was fate! —

She gazed on many a princely port
Might well have ruled a royal court;   730
On many a splendid garb she gazed, —
Then turned bewildered and amazed,
For all stood bare; and in the room
Fitz-James alone wore cap and plume.
To him each lady's look was lent,   735
On him each courtier's eye was bent;
Midst furs and silks and jewels sheen,
He stood, in simple Lincoln green
The centre of the glittering ring, —
And Snowdoun's Knight is Scotland's King!   740

XXVII

As wreath of snow on mountain-breast
Slides from the rock that gave it rest,
Poor Ellen glided from her stay,
And at the Monarch's feet she lay;
No word her choking voice commands, —   745
She showed the ring, — she clasped her hands.
O, not a moment could he brook,
The generous Prince, that suppliant look!
Gently he raised her, — and, the while,
Checked with a glance the circle's smile;   750
Graceful, but grave, her brow he kissed,
And bade her terrors be dismissed: —
"Yes, fair; the wandering poor Fitz-James
The fealty of Scotland claims.
To him thy woes, thy wishes, bring;   755
He will redeem his signet ring.

Ask naught for Douglas; — yester even,
His Prince and he have much forgiven;
Wrong hath he had from slanderous tongue,
760   I, from his rebel kinsmen, wrong.
We would not, to the vulgar crowd,
Yield what they craved with clamor loud;
Calmly we heard and judged his cause,
Our council aided and our laws.
765   I stanched thy father's death-feud stern
With stout De Vaux and gray Glencairn;
And Bothwell's Lord henceforth we own
The friend and bulwark of our throne. —
But, lovely infidel, how now?
770   What clouds thy misbelieving brow?
Lord James of Douglas, lend thine aid;
Thou must confirm this doubting maid."

XXVIII

Then forth the noble Douglas sprung,
And on his neck his daughter hung.
775   The Monarch drank, that happy hour,
The sweetest, holiest draught of Power, —
When it can say with godlike voice,
Arise, sad Virtue, and rejoice!
Yet would not James the general eye
780   On nature's raptures long should pry;
He stepped between — "Nay, Douglas, nay,
Steal not my proselyte away!
The riddle 't is my right to read,
That brought this happy chance to speed.   .

Yes, Ellen, when disguised I stray　785
In life's more low but happier way,
'T is under name which veils my power,
Nor falsely veils, — for Stirling tower
Of yore the name of Snowdoun claims,
And Normans call me James Fitz-James.　790
Thus watch I o'er insulted laws,
Thus learn to right the injured cause."
Then, in a tone apart and low, —
"Ah, little traitress! none must know
What idle dream, what lighter thought,　795
What vanity full dearly bought,
Joined to thine eye's dark witchcraft, drew
My spell-bound steps to Benvenue
In dangerous hour, and all but gave
Thy Monarch's life to mountain glaive!"　800
Aloud he spoke: "Thou still dost hold
That little talisman of gold,
Pledge of my faith, Fitz-James's ring, —
What seeks fair Ellen of the King?"

XXIX

Full well the conscious maiden guessed　805
He probed the weakness of her breast;
But with that consciousness there came
A lightening of her fears for Græme,
And more she deemed the Monarch's ire
Kindled 'gainst him who for her sire　810
Rebellious broadsword boldly drew;
And, to her generous feeling true,
She craved the grace of Roderick Dhu.

"Forbear thy suit; — the King of kings

815　　Alone can stay life's parting wings.
　　　I know his heart, I know his hand,
　　　Have shared his cheer, and proved his brand; —
　　　My fairest earldom would I give
　　　To bid Clan-Alpine's Chieftain live! —

820　　Hast thou no other boon to crave?
　　　No other captive friend to save?"
　　　Blushing, she turned her from the King,
　　　And to the Douglas gave the ring,
　　　As if she wished her sire to speak

825　　The suit that stained her glowing cheek.
　　　"Nay, then, my pledge has lost its force,
　　　And stubborn justice holds her course.
　　　Malcolm, come forth!" — and, at the word,
　　　Down kneeled the Græme to Scotland's Lord.

830　　"For thee, rash youth, no suppliant sues,
　　　From thee may Vengeance claim her dues,
　　　Who, nurtured underneath our smile,
　　　Hast paid our care by treacherous wile,
　　　And sought amid thy faithful clan

835　　A refuge for an outlawed man,
　　　Dishonoring thus thy loyal name. —
　　　Fetters and warder for the Græme!"
　　　His chain of gold the King unstrung,
　　　The links o'er Malcolm's neck he flung,

840　　Then gently drew the glittering band,
　　　And laid the clasp on Ellen's hand.

Harp of the North, farewell!　The hills grow dark,
　　On purple peaks a deeper shade descending;

In twilight copse the glow-worm lights her spark,
   The deer, half seen, are to the covert wending.   845
   Resume thy wizard elm! the fountain lending,
And the wild breeze, thy wilder minstrelsy;
   Thy numbers sweet with nature's vespers blending,
With distant echo from the fold and lea,
And herd-boy's evening pipe, and hum of housing bee. 850

Yet, once again, farewell, thou Minstrel Harp!
   Yet, once again, forgive my feeble sway,
And little reck I of the censure sharp
   May idly cavil at an idle lay.
   Much have I owed thy strains on life's long way,   855
Through secret woes the world has never known,
   When on the weary night dawned wearier day,
And bitterer was the grief devoured alone. —
That I o'erlive such woes, Enchantress! is thine own.

Hark! as my lingering footsteps slow retire,   860
   Some Spirit of the Air has waked thy string!
'T is now a seraph bold, with touch of fire,
   'T is now the brush of Fairy's frolic wing.
   Receding now, the dying numbers ring
Fainter and fainter down the rugged dell;   865
   And now the mountain breezes scarcely bring
A wandering witch-note of the distant spell —
And now, 't is silent all! — Enchantress, fare thee well!

APPENDIX

NOTES

The scene of the poem is laid chiefly in the vicinity of Loch Katrine, in the western highlands of Perthshire. The time of action includes six days, and the transactions of each day occupy a canto.

CANTO FIRST: THE CHASE

LINE 1. The introduction to the first canto is introductory to the whole poem and corresponds to the conclusion of the last canto, to which the student should turn before proceeding to read the chase.

Harp of the North: the spirit of Highland poetry. The harper was a member of each Highland family of pretension. He had neither books nor manuscripts. Making up his song as he went along or reciting from memory, or both, the bard sang to the accompaniment of his harp at the fireside, at festivals, and at feasts.

A generation or so before Scott's day the clan system of the Highlands was broken up. With the downfall of the chief, there was no longer a patron, a home, a place, for the minstrel. The trusted family friend, the singer, the reciter of poetry, the living repository of tribal lore, the teller of tales, the author, librarian and library in one, simply disappeared. Extemporization and the handing down of songs and tales, as a calling, came to an end.

Of written poetry, of print, there was none. Burns had spoken for the Lowlands, Scott, himself, had collected the ballads of the Border and had given the world *The Lay of the Last Minstrel*, as well as *Marmion*, but no northern poet, collector, or translator, had arisen. Highland mountains, waters, glens, and themes were waiting for McDonald, Black, and Stevenson. A considerable amount of verse and tradition, much of it valuable, no doubt, was lost already to literature. Scott thought it high time to begin gathering Highland material. No wonder he wrote in plaintive strain, "that mouldering long hast hung."

2. Witch-elm: the broad-leafed mountain elm, having drooping branches. A *t* has crept into the word through a mistake in the meaning. The correct *wich* or *wych* is an Anglo-Saxon word meaning *pliant, drooping*, or *pendulous*. The term appears with inserted *t* in *witch-alder* and in *witch-hazel*. It might be used instead of *weeping* to form *wych-willow*.

Wich is akin to *weak, wicker, wicket*, and even to *wicked*, but it has no relationship to *witch*, implying magical power. Scott evidently had the idea of magic in mind. He returns to the notion of sorcery in vi, 846.

Saint Fillan's spring. Saint Fillan was an abbot of the seventh century. Two springs were sacred to his memory. One was at the outlet of Loch Earn. The other was situated thirty miles to the westward. The waters of the latter were reputed to have miraculous power to cure insanity. If a crazy person were dipped thoroughly in the spring and left on the sward in the open over night, all had been done that could be done. If the patient expired, it was for the best. If he survived the ordeal, credit was given to the marvelous properties of the spring.

> " Thence to Saint Fillan's blessed well,
>   Whose springs can frenzied dreams dispel,
>   And the crazed brain restore." — *Marmion*, i, 29.

Robert Bruce had faith in Saint Fillan. A relic of this saint was carried by the victorious Scots at the battle of Bannockburn.

10. Caledon: a shortened form of *Caledonia*. About 80 A.D. the Romans, under Agricola, constructed a line of defense running from the lower Clyde eastward across the Lowlands to the Firth of Forth. The dwellers beyond this " Wall of Agricola," armed with bow, small shield, and short pointless sword, were known to the Romans as Caledonians, and the region as Caledonia. These Caledonians, known later as Picts, appear to be the ancestors of the Highlanders. From all accounts they much resembled the followers of Roderick Dhu.

14. **Each according pause**: a pause in the singing filled in with the harmonious tones of the harp. *According* applies also and more appropriately to the music which fills the interval. See i, 622 and 623.

28. " Walter Scott is out and away the king of the romantics. *The Lady of the Lake* has no indisputable claim to be a poem, beyond the inherent fitness and desirability of the tale. It is just such a story as a man would make up for himself, walking, in the best of health and temper, through just such scenes as it is laid in. Hence it is that a charm dwells undefinable among those slovenly verses, as the unseen cuckoo fills the mountains with his note ; hence, even after we have flung the book aside, the scenery and adventures remain present to the mind, a new and green possession, not unworthy of that beautiful name, *The Lady of the Lake*, or the direct romantic opening, — one of the most spirited and poetical in literature, — ' The stag at eve had drunk his fill.' " — Robert Louis Stevenson.

31. **Glenartney** : the valley of the Artney. *Glen* is a genuine Gaelic word meaning a narrow valley. It may be applied to a ravine or canyon or possibly to a vale of modest extent. *Strath* is the corresponding word of wider extent. Just as the Artney empties into the Earn River so Glenartney opens into Strath Earn. See map.

32. **Beacon red**. Allusion is made to signal fires lighted to give warning of forays. The American Indians are still expert in signaling by means of peak fires and smoke rings or spirals produced with the aid of blankets.

> And soon a score of fires, I ween,
> From height, and hill, and cliff, were seen,
> Each with warlike tidings fraught ;
> Each from each the signal caught."
>   — *Lay of the Last Minstrel*, iii, 379–382.

33. In the Gaelic tongue *ben* signifies mountain. **Benvoirlich** is the same as *Mt. Voirlich*. See map.

34. Scott is an expert in securing " apt alliteration's artful aid." In this and following lines we find " bloodhound's . . . bay," " resounded . . . rocky," " faint . . . farther," " hoof . . . horn," and many other instances of alliteration. In line 62, we have " hark . . . whoop . . . halloo."

45. **Beamed frontlet** : antlered forehead. In huntsman's phrase the beam is the main trunk which bears the prongs.

53. It is thought that *m* is silent in **Uam-Var**. Pronounce ū′ȧ-vär.

The verse of the poem consists regularly of eight syllables, accented on the even syllables. To close the stanza, however, line 53 is accented on the first, third, and fourth, instead of on the second and fourth syllables. Note also line 73. By way of an exercise it would be well for the student to look through a few pages for similar variations in the meter. One should not try to read metrically, however. Read smoothly, according to the sense, avoiding sing-song tones, and the meter will care for itself.

54. **Opening** : a sporting term used to describe the chorus of baying when the hounds first see the game.

64. **Fled the roe** . . . **cowered the doe**. Scott was an ardent sportsman and a keen observer. He uses *roe* and *doe* as well as *stag* advisedly. Three distinct kinds or species of deer are known in the Highlands. In order of size they are :

    a. The red-deer. The male is a hart, the female is a hind. A well-developed hart, of about five years, is known to huntsmen as a stag. The stag is a magnificent " Monarch of the Glen," standing four feet high at the shoulders and carrying branched antlers three feet long. The antlers are shed annually. With successive renewals the number of prongs increases. A stag of ten tosses a pair of antlers having ten prongs. The corresponding animal of North America is the wapiti, less correctly known as an elk.

b. The fallow-deer. *Fallow* is an old English word, meaning pale yellow. The fallow-deer wears a pale yellowish jacket brightened by spots of white in rows running lengthwise of the body. The male is called a buck, the female is called a doe. This deer is well domesticated in parks and game preserves. The fallow-deer has palmate antlers and in other ways differs from our white-tail or Virginia deer to which, however, it corresponds in size and economic importance.

c. The roe-deer. This is the smallest of Old World deer. It stands but a trifle over two feet shoulder height and weighs only fifty or sixty pounds. The roe-buck has straight upright antlers about a foot long pronged at the tip.

Scott's verse is accurate. Like the Virginia deer, the doe skulks in a covert, but the timid roe, like its distant cousin, the fleet-footed pronghorn, or so-called antelope, of the western plains, takes alarm quickly and loses no time in lighting out for another neighborhood.

> " While doe, and roe, and red-deer good
>   Have bounded by, through gay green-wood."
>   — *Marmion*, introduction to canto ii.

66. **Cairn** : usually a monumental heap of stones ; here a mountain crag.

68. **Beyond her piercing ken** : out of sight. *Ken* is an old Scandinavian word ordinarily meaning knowledge. In early days the Scandinavians overran and occupied considerable portions of Scotland. Many Lowland words are of Scandinavian origin. Family names ending in *son* — Anderson, Thompson, Williamson, and the like — indicate Scandinavian ancestry. The inhabitants of certain Scottish villages, particularly weaving and fishing villages, look not a little like Norwegians.

71. Linn : a pool, especially one into which a cataract pours. The word may also mean a waterfall or even the ravine or precipice of a waterfall. Here it is synonymous with *gorge* and is used to fill out the verse, prolong the echo, and to rhyme with *din*. Often spelled *lyn*, as in *Brooklyn, Roslyn*, etc. See *Bracklinn*, ii, 270 and vi, 488.

79. High in his pathway hung the sun. The description of various flowers in bloom, fresh foliage, and mention of the summer solstice, in iv, 722, locate the time as near the longest day in the year or late in June. The chase started promptly at sunrise. The poet cannot mean that the forenoon has been spent in reaching Uam-Var.

84. Shrewdly : severely, keenly.

" The air bites shrewdly ; it is very cold."
— *Hamlet*, I, iv, 1.

91. Moss : a peat bog, an open, swampy expanse.

94. The run from the southern shoulder of Uam-Var southward across the valley of the river Teith, and westward over the divide into the valley of the Forth and upward as far as Lochard, would have been a good twenty miles ; that to Loch Achray was about two thirds as far. See map.

95. Wept : drooped like a weeping willow.

Loch, the Gaelic word for lake, should be pronounced to rhyme with the German word *hoch*.

108. Twice that day. Editors have had needless difficulty with this passage. The stag crossed the big bend of the Teith traveling westward. This course caused him to swim the river twice and brought him out on the north bank of the Teith somewhere below Loch Vennachar.

112. Brigg of Turk. *Brigg* or *brig* is a Lowland word meaning bridge. Burns uses the word repeatedly in a spirited poem, *The Brigs of Ayr*. The Brigg of Turk spans a small stream which comes down from Glenfinlas and empties into the water which carries the overflow of Loch Achray into

Vennachar. The tourist naturally pauses here to enjoy the
shade and pluck a bit of moss from the coping of the bridge.
The chase is supposed to have taken place four hundred years
ago, three hundred years before *The Lady of the Lake* was
written, three centuries before ever a road was built to the
shores of Katrine. It is to be feared, therefore, that the gray
masonry of the Brigg never beheld the stag and the lone
horseman with his two dogs.

115. Scourge and steel : whip and spur.

117. Embossed : flecked with foam from the mouth ; a
huntsman's term.

130. Stock : stump.

131. Note that **Hunter** is capitalized. The reason will
appear later. The **mountain** is Benvenue. See map.

137. Death-wound. " When the stag turned to bay, the
ancient hunter had the perilous task of going in upon, and
killing or disabling, the desperate animal. At certain times
of the year this was held particularly dangerous, a wound received from a stag's horn being then deemed poisonous, and
more dangerous than one from the tusks of a boar. . . . At
all times, however, the task was dangerous, and to be adven-
tured upon wisely and warily, either by getting behind the
stag while he was gazing on the hounds, or by watching an
opportunity to gallop roundly in upon him, and kill him with
the sword." — Scott, *Notes*.

" If thou be hurt with hart, it brings thee to thy bier,
  But barber's hand will boar's hurt heal, therefore thou need'st
    not fear." — *An old saying*.

138. Whinyard : a short sword or hunting knife. See
falchion, i, 318 and 466.

145. The **Trosachs** : literally, the bristling; a rugged,
craggy glen through which the outlet of Loch Katrine finds its
way to Loch Achray. In a wider sense the term is applied to
the region between Vennachar and Loch Katrine.

147. Couched : hid.

163. Banks of Seine. James V visited France in 1536. The next spring he married Margaret, the daughter of Francis I. After her death he married Mary of Guise.

166. Woe worth the chase : woe be to the chase ; a mild way of saying, " Cursed be the day."

180. The plot of the poem requires Fitz-James to struggle forward to Ellen's Isle. Otherwise, he would be expected to turn back over the way he came.

183. " I had also read a great deal, seen much, and heard more, of that romantic country where I was in the habit of spending some time every autumn ; and the scenery of Loch Katrine was connected with the recollection of many a dear friend and merry expedition of former days." — Scott's *Introduction*.

Scott had spent two or three of his vacations in this part of Perthshire. His descriptions of the scenery created a furore. People set out in all sorts of conveyances, on horseback, and on foot, to see the Trosachs. From that day to this the stream of tourists has never ceased. Leaving Edinburgh in the morning, tourists may go by rail to Stirling, then by rail to Callander, and by tally-ho along the northern shore of Vennachar, over the Brigg of Turk and past Loch Achray, through the Trosachs to Loch Katrine ; travelers then go up Loch Katrine in a lake steamer and over a pass, by stage again, to Loch Lomond; then down Loch Lomond in a steamer to its foot, where a train is in waiting for Glasgow, — all in a single day, if must be. There are several hotels on the way. At last account, automobiles were prohibited.

184–263. " Perhaps the art of landscape painting in poetry has never been displayed in higher perfection than in these stanzas, to which rigid criticism might possibly object that the picture is somewhat too minute, and that the contemplation of it detains the traveler somewhat too long from the main purpose of his pilgrimage, but which it would be an act of the greatest injustice to break into fragments and present by piecemeal. Not so the magnificent scene which bursts upon the bewildered hunter as he emerges at length from the dell, and commands at one view the beautiful expanse of Loch Katrine." — *The Critical Review* (August, 1820).

" He sees everything with a painter's eye. Whatever he represents has a character of individuality, and is drawn with an accuracy and minuteness of discrimination which we are not accustomed to expect from mere verbal description. Much of this, no doubt, is the result of genius, but the liveliest fancy can only call forth those images which are already stored up in the memory. It is because Mr. Scott usually delineates those objects with which he is perfectly familiar that his touch is so easy, correct, and animated. The rocks, the ravines, and the torrents which he exhibits are not the imperfect sketches of a hurried traveler, but the finished studies of a resident artist. The figures which are painted with the landscape are painted with the same fidelity. The boldness of feature, the lightness and compactness of form, the wildness of air, and the careless ease of attitude of those mountaineers are as congenial to their native Highlands as the birch and the pine which darken their glens, the sedge which fringes their lakes, or the heath which waves over their moors." — *Quarterly Review* (May, 1810).

The lesson to the student is that he should write of what he himself has seen and known.

196. The tower . . . Shinar's plain : the tower of Babel. " And they said, Go to, let us build us a city and a tower whose top may reach unto the heavens." — *Genesis*, 11, 4.

202. Pagod : a sacred tower peculiar to India, China, and Burma; that is to say, to the Far East. The pagoda is from three to thirteen stories high — always an odd number. Each successive story is narrower than the story on which it rests, thus giving the structure a pyramidal form. Each story is surrounded by a balcony. Walls, verandas, cornices, and eaves rise tier after tier and are decorated richly with carvings and paintings.

203. " In Scott's narrative poems the scenery is accessory and subordinate.   It is a picturesque background to his figures, a landscape through which the action rushes like a torrent, catching a hint of color perhaps from rock or tree, but never any image so distinct that it tempts us aside to reverie or meditation." — James Russell Lowell.

204. Stanza xii might well begin with this line.   The subject matter changes here from surface features to vegetation.

208. Dewdrop sheen : shining dewdrop.

218. Foxglove and nightshade : two common flowers, called also *digitalis* and *belladonna*.   They are used in medicine for the heart and the eye respectively.   The foxglove bears a long spike of beautiful flowers which are admired in Scandinavia as fox-bells and in Germany as finger-hats or thimbles.   The nightshade is related to the familiar tomato but is a rank poison.   The deadly nature of the nightshade and the beauty of the foxglove are Scott's justification for calling them " emblems of punishment and pride."

256. Lest this description might seem overdrawn, Scott appended this note in a later edition : " Until the present road was made through the romantic pass which I have presumptuously attempted to describe in the preceding stanzas, there was no mode of issuing out of the defile called the Trosachs, excepting by a sort of ladder, composed of the branches and roots of trees."

281. Churchman : one holding high office in the church.

297. To drop a bead : to slide a bead along the string of a rosary in order to keep count of prayers said.   The original meaning of *bead* is prayer.

305. Scott first wrote :

> " And hollow trunk of some old tree
> My chamber for the night must be."

319. His horn he wound. The *Century Dictionary* condemns this use of *wound*. The correct form is *winded*, meaning that he blew a blast on his horn. *Wound* is part of another verb. As written, the line states that the hunter twisted his horn. Tennyson may be quoted in support of proper usage:

" Gawain raised a bugle hanging from his neck and winded it."

" Then Robin clapped his horn to his lips and winded a blast that went echoing sweetly down the forest paths." — Howard Pyle.

See line 500 for the use of *winded* for *wound*.

331. The present shore hardly corresponds to the poet's **silver strand.** The water now stands several feet above the old beach and laves nothing but rocks and brushwood. The prosaic truth is that the outlet of Loch Katrine has been walled up to create an enormous lake reservoir from which the municipality of Glasgow draws its water supply. The island is only a bow-shot from the shore.

344. A Nymph, a Naiad, or a Grace : in Grecian mythology, inferior divinities. They were imagined as eternally young. They danced attendance on the deities of higher rank and had the power of foretelling events and of inspiring mortals. They were identified with certain objects, localities, and families. If a tree were cut down or if a spring dried up, the corresponding nymph perished. The nymphs of the mountains were called *oreads;* those of the sea, *neriads;* the *dryads* were nymphs of the woods and trees, the *naiads* were nymphs of the rivers, springs, and brooks. Venus was attended by the three Graces, dispensers of beauty, brightness, and joy.

356. Harebell : the common bluebell of Scotland; quite common in America. The blue corollas, bells, about one inch in diameter hang from pedicels so slender that some florists who ought to know better call these flowers hairbells.

360. For **dear,** Rolfe suggests that Scott probably wrote *clear,* and that the compositor easily mistook *cl* for *d. Clear* seems more appropriate, unless the reader bear in mind Ellen's affection for her father, whom she is calling.

363. Notice the triple rhyme.

Snood : a maiden's hair ribbon. At marriage the snood was exchanged for the *curch* or *kerchief*. Another name for the marriage cap or hood is the *coif*, allied to *coiffure*. See iii, 114, 485, 487, and 495.

404. To prune : to smooth.

438. Couch was pulled. Heather was gathered for a bed.

440. Ptarmigan : the rock-ptarmigan, a kind of grouse. In winter its plumage, like the fur of our " rabbits," turns white and protects its owner amid the snow fields. The common species, known as the Scotch ptarmigan, red-grouse, moor-fowl, moor-hen, etc., retains the favorite grayish brown grouse colors the year around.

Heath-cock : a black grouse known also as the black-cock. The male is a stately bird with " jetty wing." Its tail is parted and turns with a curl to right and left. The grouse of Scotland are related closely to the prairie-hens and other species of American grouse. This grouse nested in the glens of Abbotsford.

441. Mere : lake. The word is of the Scottish and English Borders rather than of a land of glens. Compare *Windermere*, *Grasmere*, etc.

442. Evening cheer. As head of the clan, Roderick would have of the best so far as forays and willing gillies could provide, and yet we must wonder what Dame Margaret had to offer. Fifty years before Columbus set sail, there were no potatoes in Europe, let alone any in the Highlands. Scanty oat and barley fields may have been reinforced by meal taken from Lowland farms or by an unguarded cheese. There were no cows on Ellen's Isle. Milk may have been had from Duncraggan or Strathgartney, but it could not be fresh. Coffee was out of the question. Fitz-James was not asked whether he would have sugar and cream in his tea. Perhaps the

hospitable mistress of the mansion pressed him to have more
fish, more fowl, and without doubt gillies had backed French
wine in from some seaport, but tobacco was known only to
the American Indian.

   458. Allan-bane : a minstrel of the highest order, endowed
with second sight.   If the student will follow Allan-bane
through the poem he may acquire a clear idea of the importance
which the Highlander attached to the minstrel — especially
if endowed with second sight.   To be a master, the seer must
possess the ability to see persons not present, to witness events
which are happening elsewhere, and to describe events which
have not yet happened.   In *Waverley* Scott permits Donald
Bean (bane) to lament the loss of his old minstrel, "Duncan
with the Cap."   His son Malcolm is "nothing equal to his
father.   He told us the other day we were to see a great
gentleman riding on a horse and there came nobody that whole
day but Shemus Beg, the blind harper with his dog.   Another
time he advertised us of a wedding and it proved to be a
funeral ; and on the creagh (foray), when he told us we should
bring home a hundred head of horned cattle, we grippit nothing
but a fat baille of Perth."

   The belief in second sight was widespread.   The Roman
consulted an augur for favorable signs and portents before
engaging in battle ; and the Greek commander declined to
leave his anchorage before the oracle had been consulted.   Nor
is the belief in second sight altogether abated.   If newspaper
accounts may be trusted, the finance minister of France, as
late as 1925, summoned an American seeress to Paris and
to Washington that he might consult her as to the outcome of
negotiations which he proposed to undertake with the United
States relative to the settlement of war debts.

   464. Lincoln green : a strong green woolen cloth worn
by foresters and huntsmen.   A superior quality of this cloth
was woven at Lincoln.   The reader of Pyle's *Robin Hood* will
recall that Little John was sent to Hugh Langshanks, the
draper, to buy "twenty-score yards of fair cloth of Lincoln
green " for the band.

478. Emprise : enterprise.

487–489. In the verbs **flew** and **ply** we have a change of tense not allowable in prose.

489. While working on this poem Scott took opportunity one day to read the first canto to an intelligent farmer friend, with whom he often went hunting. " His reception of my recitation," says Scott, " was rather singular. He placed his hand across his brow, and listened with great attention through the whole account of the stag-hunt, till the dogs threw themselves into the lake to follow their master, who embarks with Ellen Douglas. He then started up with a sudden exclamation, struck his hand on the table, and declared, in a voice of censure calculated for the occasion, that the dogs must have been totally ruined by being permitted to take to the water after so severe a chase."

492. Rocky isle. " It is a little island, but very famous in Romance land as ' Ellen's Isle ' ; for Ellen . . . was the name of the Lady of the Lake. . . . It is mostly composed of dark gray rocks, mottled with pale and gray lichen, peeping out here and there amid trees that mantle them, — chiefly light, graceful birches, intermingled with red-berried mountain ashes and a few dark green spiry pines. . . . A more poetic, romantic retreat could hardly be imagined ; it is unique. It is completely hidden, not only by the trees, but also by an undergrowth of beautiful and abundant ferns and the loveliest of heather." — Hunnewell, *Land of Scott.*

500. Winded. Scott is addicted to this form of the verb. It occurs frequently in his prose, as in *Old Mortality :* " The moon broke as the leading files of the column attained a hill up which the road winded." And again, " Along the foot of the high and broken bank winded the public road." A more modern verse would run :

" That wound amid the tangled screen."

Recall i, 319 for an incorrect use of *wound.*

504. Here, for retreat. " The Celtic chieftains . . . had usually, in the most retired spot of their domain, some place of retreat . . . a tower, a cavern, or a rustic hut in a strong and secluded situation. One of these last gave refuge to the unfortunate Charles Edward, in his perilous wanderings after the battle of Culloden." — Scott, *Notes*.

525. Idæan vine : seemingly a translation of the latter part of *Vaccinium vitis Idaea*, which is the botanical name of a common whortleberry closely akin to the American blueberry. Now the whortleberry is a low shrub not over knee-high. *Vitis* is the Latin name of the grape. Evidently Scott was led astray by a clumsy botanical name and meant the common grapevine.

544. When Scott in after years built his home at Abbotsford, the most striking feature was an immense hallway or main entrance fitted up as a museum of warlike antiquities. The plan may have been in his mind when he wrote these lines.

548. Arrows store : arrows in plenty or, as we say, arrows a plenty. " Throngs of knights . . . with store of ladies," says Milton, in *L'Allegro*, 169. See also vi, 124 and 539.

553. Bison : the wild ox or auroch of Europe. It is related closely to the American bison, incorrectly called a buffalo.

573. Ferragus or Ascabart : two legendary sons of Anak. One was forty feet tall ; the other, thirty. These worthies figure prominently in early romance, but it seems a bit forced to have Ellen mention them. Goliath would have been more natural.

580, 581. Scott first wrote :

> " To whom, though now remote her claim,
> 　　Young Ellen gave a mother's name."

The mistress is Ellen's aunt. Ellen gave her a mother's due, though it was more than the degree of kinship could claim. Turn to ii, 248–255 for a statement of relationship.

585. " The Highlanders, who carried hospitality to a punctilious excess, are said to have considered it as churlish to ask a stranger his name or lineage before he had taken refreshment. Feuds were so frequent among them, that a contrary rule would in many cases have produced the discovery of some circumstance which might have excluded the guest from the benefit of the assistance he stood in need of." — Scott.

591. Snowdoun : Stirling Castle.

James Fitz-James : James the son of James. This James was the fifth James in a line of six. His grandson, James VI, became James I of England.

596. God wot : God knows. *Wot* is an out-of-date verb. It is interesting to know, however, that the root is retained in the expression *to wit* and in a number of words such as *wit*, *witty*, *witless*, *witness*, and even in *witch* in the sense of a crone who knows a thing or two.

598. If any particular **Lord Moray** is meant, probably it is James Stewart, a natural son of James IV, and brother of James V.

602. Require : request.

616. Observe the alliteration. **Weird** : skilled in witchcraft.

Down : a hill of moderate elevation and rounded outline. *Down* is current in southern England. *Dun* and *dune* are the northern forms of the word.

642. Bittern : a wading bird of the heron family. The bittern is about two feet in length, with brownish plumage streaked and mottled, and a hollow booming cry. The American bittern is a similar bird inhabiting grassy swamps everywhere. It is an adept at escaping observation by means of standing, bill up, rigid and motionless, for all the world like a clump of dead grass. The American bittern is known from its call as a " stake-driver," " thunder-pumper," etc.

655. Ye : a nominative used instead of an objective for the sake of rhyme.

657. Reveille. Pronounce to rhyme with *assail ye.* A morning bugle call to rouse huntsmen and soldiers. In the

U. S. army the reveille, pronounced *rev'a lee*, follows the first call at an interval of six minutes and is an imperative summons to line up on the parade ground.

720. The birch-trees wept in fragrant balm. The poet has fallen into an exquisite error. A quotation from *Waverley*, chapter xvi, is interesting : " The cool and yet mild air of the summer night refreshed Waverley . . . and the perfume which it wafted from the birch-trees bathed in the evening dew was exquisitely fragrant."

In a footnote added in the edition of 1830, Scott admits that the fragrant birch is not the cut-leafed weeping birch but a woolly-leafed birch more common in the Lowlands. For his day and generation Scott was well informed in natural history. In this particular instance, however, he has combined two differing birches into a hybrid tree just as Holmes united two distinct mollusks to create *The Chambered Nautilus*.

721. Aspens : poplars. The leaf of the aspen hangs on a thin pedicel so delicately flexible sidewise that the blade tips from side to side with the slightest breath of air. This is quite as true of American aspens. On a sultry day when leaves of other trees are quiet the poplar leaves rock and quiver and twinkle in a self-conscious way as though an invisible hand were tapping the tree. When aspens sleep, the air is calm indeed.

745. As an example of the change brought about by Scott and others in the spirit of poetry, the altogether delightful, informal, natural lines of this stanza may be compared with the elevated and beautiful but dignified, awesome, morbid lines of Young. In the latter a tripping phrase would be as much out of place as a pun in the description of a thunderstorm.

> " Night, sable goddess, from her ebon throne,
>   In rayless majesty, now stretches forth her
>   Leaden scepter o'er a slumbering world.
>   Silence how dead ! and darkness how profound !

> Nor eye, nor listening ear, an object finds ;
> Creation sleeps. 'T is as the general pulse
> Of life stood still, and nature made a pause,
> An awful pause, prophetic of her end."

Each canto is supposed to occupy a day. The first canto runs overtime. It begins with yester eve when the stag drank his fill and continues till the morrow's morn when the heath-cock crew on Benvenue — two nights and a day.

EXERCISES

1. Sketch an outline map locating the geographical names which appear in this canto.

2. List the birds, the plants, the four-footed animals, the weapons, and the colors.

3. Index words now out of date.

4. Draw up a list of ten pictures which might serve to illustrate this canto.

5. Write a paragraph on :

  a. A pleasant surprise.
  b. Somewhat disappointing.
  c. An exaggeration.

6. Write another paragraph on one of the following themes:

  a. A moonlit night.
  b. Many are called but few are chosen.
  c. A courteous reception.
  d. Second sight.

7. Rewrite stanza xx in plain prose.

8. Collect the lines of this canto which contain mention of an echo.

9. Classify the persons of the canto as principal characters and secondary characters.

10. Classify the events that happened in this canto as principal incidents and secondary incidents.

CANTO SECOND : THE ISLAND

LINE **17. Speed** : success ; good luck. This is the meaning in the proverb, " The more haste, the less speed." Swiftness is a derived idea, for which see " Speed, Malise, speed," iii, 300.

29. The reference is to Ellen's father, unjustly outlawed. See 142. The old minstrel shrewdly hopes the Hunter may have influence at court.

35. Hap : happening, event, chance, fortune, luck. *Hap* carries with it, in and of itself, no idea of misfortune, rather the opposite. The thought of Allan-bane is, " If you see the Douglas, remember what *happened* to you in this lonely isle, and repay our hospitality by soothing a wanderer's woe." *Hap* appears in *happy, happiness, happen, haply, hapless, happily,* and should not be confounded with *misfortune,* for which we have *mishap*. Thus Scott :

> " 'T is true that mortals cannot tell
> What waits them in the distant dell ;
> But be it hap or be it harm,
> We tread the pathway arm in arm."
> — *Bridal of Triermain.*

109. " The ancient and powerful family of Graham (which, for metrical reasons, is here spelled after the Scottish pronunciation) held extensive possessions in the counties of Dumbarton and Stirling. Few families can boast of more historical renown, having claim to three of the most remarkable characters in the Scottish annals." — Scott, *Notes.*

The three notable Grahams are Wallace's comrade, Sir John the Græme, who fell at Falkirk in 1298 ; the Marquis of Montrose, sung by Aytoun ; and Claverhouse, Viscount of Dundee, the hero of *Old Mortality.*

141. Bothwell's bannered hall. " The picturesque ruins of Bothwell Castle stand on the banks of the Clyde, about nine miles above Glasgow. Some parts of the walls are 14

feet thick and 60 feet in height.   They are covered with ivy,
wild roses, and wall-flowers." — Rolfe.

159. From Tweed to Spey : from one end of the land to
the other. The Scriptural expression is, " From Dan to
Beersheba."   Burns put it :

> " Hear, Land o' Cakes and brither Scots
>   Frae Maidenkirk to John o' Groats," etc.

The Spey is a river in the northern part of Inverness shire.
In point of volume the Spey is the second river in Scotland.
See 206 and note.

166–171. What comparisons are made ?

169. Give the wind : bend to the storm, give way to the
wind, yield to the wind, bow before it. Notice that *wind*
rhymes with *resigned*. This pronunciation is archaic, but
Scott has plenty of good company.

> " Lo, the poor Indian ! whose untutored mind
>   Sees God in clouds, or hears Him in the wind."
>   — Pope, *Essay on Man*, epistle i, 99.

200. The Bleeding Heart (of Robert Bruce) was the device
emblazoned on the banners of the Douglas family. It was
worn as a badge by their retainers and followers. The story
runs that on his deathbed Bruce bequeathed his heart to his
stanch friend James, the Douglas, to be carried in war against
the Saracen.

In company with the king of Leon and Castile, James
joined battle with the Moslems of Granada. Being hard
pressed, he flung the silver casket containing the heart of
Bruce far into the ranks of the enemy, crying,

> " Onward as thou wert wont, noble heart,
>   Douglas will follow thee."

Douglas was slain, but his body and the precious casket were
recovered. Douglas was laid with his ancestors and the
heart of Bruce was deposited in Melrose Abbey.

206. Strathspey, a lively country dance, named from Strath Spey, or the valley of the Spey.   See 159 and note.

> " Warlocks and witches in a dance,
>   Nae new cotillion brent frae France,
>   But hornpipes, jigs, strathspeys and reels,
>   Put life and mettle in their heels."
>   — Burns, *Tam O' Shanter.*

221. Holy-Rood : the royal palace in Edinburgh.   It was a serious offense to draw a weapon in the king's presence or even in the grounds connected with his residence.

235. Guerdon : reward.

236. Ellen's mother, Lady Douglas, and Roderick's mother, the Lady Margaret of the poem, were sisters.   The marriage of first cousins is forbidden by the canons of the Roman Catholic Church.   In rare cases only, a dispensation may be obtained from the Pope.

In references to church and other religious matters, it should be held in mind that, save as pagan rites and superstitions lingered, the entire population of Scotland, Highland and Lowland, adhered to the Roman Catholic Church.   John Knox and Presbyterianism were still a hundred years away.

251. Ellen's father is yet living.   Look up the meaning of **orphan.**   Compare iii, 437 and 440.

260. Maronnon's cell : a convent near the eastern end of Loch Lomond.   Ellen is determined to become a nun before she will wed Roderick.   See v, 534–545 for her father's choice of a refuge for Ellen.   Convents were protected by all the power of the Church.   No impious hand might force the gate of a convent.

270. Bracklinn : a beautiful waterfall in the Keltie, a mile from Callander.   The Keltie leaps from ledge to ledge down a huge rocky stairway fifty feet in height.   A footbridge affords a satisfactory view.

272. Chafe his blood : warm his blood, rouse his temper. The original meaning of *chafe* is heat.   See note on iii, 643.

274. Claymore : a Gaelic word signifying great sword.

277–286. Compare 419–428.   Also iv, 548–553 and v, 128–169.

306. Tine-man. " Archibald, the third Earl of Douglas, was so unfortunate in all his enterprises, that he acquired the epithet of ' tine-man ' because he *tined*, or lost, his followers in every battle which he fought." — Scott, *Notes*.

319. Beltane game :   May-day sports.   *Beltane* is a Gaelic word designating an ancient worship of the sun or of fire.   Once a year the Celts put out their domestic fires, kindled a huge bonfire on a hill, and carried back live coals and brands to their hearths.   In this way they secured pure fire fresh from the sun-god.   No doubt there was shouting and dancing and we know not what wild orgies.   Under the influence of Christianity the Highlanders retained the holiday with its original name, but changed the form of its celebration.

327.   Scott's **canna** is probably a sedge that grows in shallow water around the edges of lakes and produces a large tuft of cottony bristles represented in the United States by several species called cotton grass.

351. Chanters.   The chanter is the tube of the bagpipe, the flute on which the performer plays with his fingers.

362. Gathering : the name of the tune.   Scott quotes Dr. Beattie : " A pibroch is a species of tune, peculiar, I think, to the Highlands and Western Isles of Scotland.   It is performed on a bagpipe, and differs totally from all other music.   Its rhythm is so irregular, and its notes, especially in the quick movement, so mixed and huddled together, that a stranger finds it impossible to reconcile his ear to it, so as to perceive its modulation.   Some of these pibrochs, being intended to represent a battle, begin with a grave motion, resembling a march ; then gradually quicken into the onset ; run off with noisy confusion, and turbulent rapidity, to imitate the conflict and pursuit ; then swell into a few flourishes of triumphant joy ; and perhaps close with the wild and slow wailings of a funeral procession."

392. Burden bore : joined in the chorus. This is the usual meaning. In i, 17 *burden* means theme or subject.

400. The ever-green Pine : the emblem of Clan-Alpine.

405. Bourgeon : to bud, put forth a sprout, blossom. A poetic word.

408. Roderigh Vich Alpine dhu : Black Roderick, son of Alpine.

431. The allusion is to Ellen. Compare 212.

497. Look up the battle of Otterburn, and read the ballad of *Chevy Chase*. The Percy Pennon, taken in that battle by Douglas's ancestor, was now a family trophy carried on triumphal occasions.

504. Waned crescent. The crescent is a new moon in its first quarter or, less properly, an old or waning moon. The crescent was the heraldic device of the Scotts of Buccleuch. It was borne on the banner of Sir Walter Scott of Buccleuch in a skirmish with the followers of the house of Douglas in 1526. Our poet's relatives were trying to take the young king from Angus, the head of the Douglas clan. They were unsuccessful, hence the term, *waned crescent*.

506. Blantyre : a priory, situated on a lofty cliff, rising sheer from the Clyde directly opposite Bothwell Castle.

525. Unhooded. While searching for game the falcon's head was covered with a hood. When game was flushed, the hood was lifted and the falcon took flight.

527. Fabled Goddess of the wood : Diana, the huntress ; Artemis of the Greeks ; sister of Apollo. In art Diana is represented as a maiden of majestic bearing armed with bow and quiver and accompanied by hounds.

548. Ben Lomond. This is at once the most celebrated and the highest of the mountains mentioned in the poem. Altitude, 3192 feet. Rolfe quotes, without comment on Malcolm's wind, the following couplet scratched by some visitor on a window pane in an old inn at Tarbet a hundred years ago :

" Trust not at first a quick adventurous pace ;
Six miles its top points gradual from its base."

577. Royal ward. Malcolm's father is dead. According to
feudal law Malcolm is under the guardianship of the king until
he comes of age. Unless he obeys the king, he is likely to
lose his father's lands and the chieftainship of the Græmes.

582. Douglas' sake. Ordinarily, as here, Scott forms
the possessive of *Douglas, James, pass, Glenfinlas,* and other
nouns ending in *s* by the addition of an apostrophe only.
Occasionally, when in need of an additional syllable to fill
out the line, he adds an apostrophe and *s* and expects the
reader to pronounce accordingly. Note *Douglas's command,*
ii, 828 ; *King James's mood,* v, 876 ; *The pass's jaws,* v, 58.

588. Compare i, 586–589 and ii, 318–322.

616. Tamed the Border-side. Roderick relates the fate
which lately befell the chiefs of the Border and charges the
king with an intent to visit the Trosachs on a similar mission.
" In 1529 James V made a convention at Edinburgh for
the purpose of considering the best mode of quelling the Border
robbers. He assembled a flying army of ten thousand men,
consisting of his principal nobility and their followers, who
were directed to bring their hawks and dogs with them, that
the monarch might refresh himself with sport during the
intervals of military execution. With this array he swept
through Ettrick Forest, where he hanged over the gate of his
own castle Piers Cockburn of Henderland, who had prepared,
according to tradition, a feast for his reception. . . . But the
most noted victim of justice, during that expedition, was John
Armstrong of Gilnockie, famous in Scottish song, who, con-
fiding in his own supposed innocence, met the King with a
retinue of thirty-six persons, all of whom were hanged at
Carlenrig, near the source of the Teviot." — Scott, *Notes.*

623. Meggat's mead : Meggat meadow. The Meggat is
an unimportant upland stream flowing into the Yarrow. The
Yarrow flows into the Ettrick. The Ettrick and the Teviot
are branches of the Tweed.

628. Sheep-walk. James V is credited with keeping ten thousand sheep on his own account in Ettrick Forest. No wonder he wanted sheep stealing stopped.

The region of the Tweed is still famous for the production of mutton and wool. The Tweed gave name to a weave of famous Scotch woolens.

638. Streight: strait, a tight place, a difficulty. The line signifies, " Give me your counsel in the difficulty that I show," — a meaning in accord with Douglas's reply (649), as if in response to a request for his opinion.

678. The Links of Forth: the windings of the Forth below Stirling.

> " Old Stirling's towers arose in light,
> 　　And twined in links of silver bright
> 　　Her winding river lay."
> 　　　　　　— *The Lord of the Isles*, VI, xix.

By association, grassy plots along streams became known as links and still later Scottish sportsmen coined the term *golf-links.*

679. Stirling's porch: the gate-way of Stirling Castle.

699. Startler: one who is startled. This is a peculiar use of the word. The ordinary meaning is one who startles, just as *killer* means one who kills, not one who is killed.

757. Checkered shroud: his plaid. Originally, and here, merely a garment or a piece of cloth.

763. The Græme. Malcolm is a gallant young chap, but he does not appear to advantage. He is a trifle out of place at Ellen's elbow. He overtaxes the hospitality even of a Highland home and nothing becomes him more than his leaving it. In the final scene of the poem, he wins his " fetters and warder," to be sure, but we feel that he has not had a fair chance to show the metal of which he is made. Scott wrote a friend in a half humorous, half apologetic, vein : " You must know this Malcolm Græme was a great plague to me from the beginning. You ladies can hardly comprehend how very stupid lovers are to everybody but mistresses. I gave him that dip in the lake by way of making him do something ; but wet or dry I could make nothing of him. His insignificance is the greatest defect among many others in the poem ; but the canvas was not broad enough to include him, considering I had to group the king, Roderick, and Douglas."

775. This roof. " The Highlander had no scruple about shedding the blood of an enemy ; but he had high notions of the duty of observing faith to allies and hospitality to guests." — Macaulay, *History of England*.

801. Addressed to Malcolm. " Hardihood was in every respect so essential to the character of a Highlander, that the reproach of effeminacy was the most bitter that could be thrown upon him." — Scott.

808. Strength : stronghold, a place of defense.

" Of forayers, who, with headlong force,
    Down from that strength had spurr'd their horse."
                    — *Marmion*, introduction to canto iii.

809. Henchman : originally, a horseman or hostler and, later, a confidential servant, a right-hand man. Scott even says a sort of secretary. In iii, 284, Roderick employs Malise as a messenger and again in iv, 18, Malise returns from scouting. At Highland feasts henchmen stood each at his master's back to see that due honor was paid.

828. Douglas's. The meter requires three syllables.

867. Cormorant : a dark-colored, voracious fishing bird, inhabiting rocky sea coasts. The cormorant, like the pelican, has a fish sac under the bill. The common species is about as large as the Canadian wild goose.

" As with his wings aslant,
    Sails the fierce cormorant,
    Seeking some rocky haunt."
            — Longfellow, *Skeleton in Armour*.

EXERCISES

1. Rewrite stanza xxviii in plain narrative prose.
2. Themes :

   a. Malcolm's account of his visit to Ellen.
   b. Dame Margaret, mother and matchmaker.
   c. The approach of the fleet.
   d. The taming of the Border.

3. Identify the following :

   a. The swimmer. *mal.*   f. The rosebud.
   b. Thy stately form. *Dou.* g. Good friend.
   c. An exile. *Doug.*   h. Flattering bard. *look up*
   d. The struggling foes.   i. The dame.
   e. Undaunted homicide. *Dol j.* An hero's eye. *Doug.*

4. Locate :

   a. Ben Lomond.   f. Glen Fruin.
   b. Bannered hall.   g. Menteith.
   c. A lodge.   h. The flame.
   d. Yarrow braes.   i. Glenfinlas' shade.
   e. The lonely isle.   j. A Lennox foray.

CANTO THIRD : THE GATHERING

LINE **6. How few**, etc.   How few await the tide !

18. Fiery Cross. " When a chieftain designed to summon his clan upon any sudden or important emergency, he slew a goat, and making a cross of any light wood, seared its extremities in the fire, and extinguished them in the blood of the animal. . . . It was delivered to a swift and trusty messenger, who ran full speed with it to the next hamlet, where he presented it to the principal person, with a single word, implying the place of rendezvous. He who received the symbol was bound to send it forward, with equal dispatch, to the next village ; and thus it passed with incredible celerity through all the district which owed allegiance to the chief. . . . At sight of the Fiery Cross, every man, from sixteen years old to sixty, capable of bearing arms, was obliged instantly to repair, in his best arms and accoutrements, to the place of rendezvous. He who failed to appear suffered the extremities of fire and sword, which were emblematically denounced to the disobedient by the bloody and burnt marks upon this warlike signal. . . . During the civil war of 1745-46, the Fiery Cross often made its circuit; and upon one occasion it passed through the district of Breadalbane, a tract of thirty-two miles, in three hours." — Scott, *Notes*.

19–40. Commenting on this passage, Ruskin says: " It has no form in it at all except in one word, but wholly composes its imagery either of color, or of that delicate half-believed life which we have seen to be so important an element in modern landscape." — *Modern Painters*, iii, chapter xvi, paragraph 44. See also iii, 458–461, for use of color instead of form.

37. See note on *mavis* and *merle*, iv, 262.

39. Cushat dove: one of three British wild pigeons. It is known also as the *ring-dove* and the *wood-pigeon*. Its note is less plaintive than that of the American mourning dove. The dove is the emblem of innocence, gentleness, and affection. Note the contrast, which is exceedingly effective.

46. Impatient. What is impatient?

62. Rowan (rō′ăn): the mountain ash; a familiar dooryard tree with abundant white flowers succeeded by bright red berries. It is distantly related to the crab-apple but has the leaves of an ash.

71–73. With *danger* as the subject, convert these lines into a prose sentence.

76. Druid: a member of an ancient dark and gloomy Celtic priesthood. In the day of Julius Cæsar the Druids were influential in the British Isles and in those parts of Gaul which were occupied by the Celts. These priests are thought to have had a little learning. They practiced mystic rites in dark groves and offered human sacrifices. They venerated the oak and the mistletoe.   They were secretive, fanatic, and so opposed to change, particularly to the Roman occupation, that they were hunted down and destroyed by the Roman generals.   Brian is pictured as a representative of Druidism.

91. Brian's birth.   Scott states in a note that he follows a local legend concerning the birth of the founder of the church of Kilmalie.   He leaves open the question whether Brian was an impostor or a fanatic.   Mortals of supposed unnatural origin are not uncommon among primitive peoples.   Greek, Roman, and Gothic, as well as Druidic, mythologies are full of them.

94.   It has been claimed that the gruesome details of an ancient field of strife are in bad taste, even though they are pictured by a powerful genius.

104. Fieldfare: a reddish-brown thrush with speckled breast.   *Fare* means run or go.   The fieldfare is a bird of the open.   The merle and the mavis are copsewood birds.

138. Sable-lettered page: an old English or black letter script used by the monks in preparing manuscripts.   " Lettered page " is correct.   Each page, before the day of print, was executed by the hand of a learned monk.   Many of these books, now preserved with pious care in the libraries of Europe, are marvelously beautiful specimens of handiwork.

154. River Demon.   " The River Demon, or River-horse, for it is that form which he commonly assumes, is the Kelpie of the Lowlands, an evil and malicious spirit, delighting to forbode and to witness calamity.   He frequents most Highland lakes and rivers." — Scott, *Notes*.

161. Mankind: accented on first syllable.   Authority for this accent may be found in Shakespeare's and Milton's writings.

168.   " Most great families in the Highlands were supposed to have a tutelar, or rather a domestic, spirit attached to them, who took an interest in their prosperity, and intimated, by its wailings, any approaching disaster.   The **Ben-**

Shie implies the female fairy whose lamentations were often supposed to precede the death of a chieftain of particular families. When she is visible, it is in the form of an old woman, with a blue mantle and streaming hair." — Scott, *Notes*.

171. Shingly: gravelly, pebbly. It seems natural to connect *shingly* with a shore or hillside covered with thin pieces of stone or flat pebbles, such as boys skip on the water. *Shingly*, however, has no connection with the flatness of shingles or tiles or any other roofing material. Drop out an *h* which has crept in and we have a Norwegian word akin to *sing*. *Shingly*, then, has reference to sound, not shape. A shingly hillside or shore is covered with coarse gravel or small stones and was so termed originally because it gave forth a crunching or ringing sound under foot. *Noisy* is the thought.

189. Cubit's length: about 18 inches; the distance from the elbow to the end of the middle finger. The cross was light and small, easily carried.

191. Inch-Calliach. *Inch* means island, *Calliach* (pronounced kăl'yăk) means nuns or old women.

"The Isle of Nuns, or of Old Women, is a most beautiful island at the lower extremity of Loch Lomond. The church belonging to the former nunnery was long used as the place of worship for the parish of Buchanan, but scarce any vestiges of it now remain. The burial ground continues to be used, and contains the family places of sepulture of several neighboring clans. The monuments of the lairds of MacGregor, and of other families, claiming a descent from the old Scottish King Alpine, are most remarkable." — Scott.

212. Strook: struck; an obsolete past tense of *strike;* used by Milton and by Pope.

214–217. The repetition of the rhyme has been thought to give the effect of successive waves rolling up on the shore.

237. Volumed flame: rolling flames. Before scribes learned to cut into pages and to bind, volumes were rolls of paper, in shape not unlike rolls of wall paper.

243. Goshawk: literally, a " goose " hawk; a large hawk akin to the chicken hawk of America. Like the falcon, the goshawk was tamed and trained to strike game. The falcon aims to soar up and pounce down on its prey, the goshawk pursues in a direct line.

245. Rolfe quotes Taylor: " The whole of this stanza is very impressive; the mingling of the children's curses is the climax of horror. Note the meaning of the triple curse. The cross is of ancestral yew — the defaulter is cut off from communion with his clan; it is seared in the fire — the fire shall destroy his dwelling; it is dipped in blood — his heart's blood is to be shed."

253. Coir-Uriskin. " This is a very steep and most romantic hollow in the mountain of Benvenue, overhanging the southeastern extremity of Loch Katrine. . . . A dale in so wild a situation, and amid a people whose genius bordered on the romantic, did not remain without appropriate deities. The name literally implies the Corri, or Den, of the Wild or Shaggy Men. . . . Tradition has ascribed to the *Urisk*, who gives name to the cavern, a figure between a goat and a man; in short, however much the classical reader may be startled, precisely that of the Grecian satyr. . . . It must be owned that the *Coir*, or Den, does not, in its present state, meet our ideas of a subterraneous grotto or cave, being only a small and narrow cavity among huge fragments of rocks rudely piled together." — Scott, *Notes*.

255. Beala-nam-bo: " the pass of the cattle." The foraging expeditions returning from Loch Lomond came in to Loch Katrine through this pass. See 664.

275. Make **hearth** rhyme with *earth*.

297. Three fathom wide: about eighteen feet. As the boat is yet in motion, the length of the leap is not to be taken too literally. George Washington left a record a trifle better than twenty-two feet.

300. Dun deer's hide: buskins, moccasins. "We go a hunting," writes a Highlander to Henry VIII, " and after that we have slain red deer, we flay off the skin by and by, and setting of our bare foot on the inside thereof, for want of cunning shoemakers, by your grace's pardon, we play the cobblers, compassing and measuring so much thereof as shall reach up to our ankles . . . and stretching it up with a strong thong of the same above our said ankles. So, and it please your noble grace, we make our shoes."

> " The hunted deer's undressed hide
> Their hairy buskins well supplied."
>
> — *Marmion*, v, 5.

332. Changed cheer: with a changed look, an altered countenance. For "sweat of thy brow," Wycliffe says, " sweat of thy cheer." The meter requires three syllables to conform with *swarthy smith*.

349. Duncraggan: a hamlet at the mouth of Glenfinlas, about a mile above the Brigg of Turk.

369. Coronach. " The *coronach* of the Highlanders was a wild expression of lamentation poured forth by the mourners over the body of a departed friend. When the words were articulate, they expressed the praises of the deceased, and the loss the clan would sustain by his death. The coronach has for some years past been superseded at funerals by the use of the bag-pipe; and that also is, like many other Highland peculiarities, falling into disuse, unless in remote districts." — Scott, *Notes*.

A *wake*, or sitting up with the body of the dead, is still practised by Celtic people, particularly the Irish.

386. Correi: a hillside frequented by game.

394. Stumah: Duncan's hound. The name is Celtic, signifying faithful. Compare *Fido*.

452. " Inspection of the provincial map of Perthshire, or any large map of Scotland, will trace the progress of the signal through the small district of lakes and mountains. . . . The first stage of the Fiery Cross is to Duncraggan, a place near the Brigg of Turk, where a short stream divides Loch Achray from Loch Vennachar. From thence, it passes towards Callander, and then, turning to the left up the pass of Leny, is consigned to Norman at the Chapel of Saint Bride, which stood on a small and romantic knoll in the middle of the valley, called Strath-Ire. Tombea and Arnandave, or Ardmandave, are names of places in the vicinity. The alarm is then supposed to pass along the Lake of Lubnaig, and through the various glens in the district of Balquidder, including the neighboring tracts of Glenfinlas and Strath-Gartney."— Scott, *Notes*.

528. Supplies the Teith: not literally. Lubnaig's lake supplies the Leny which in turn empties into the Teith. See map.

530. "Hope deferred maketh the heart sick." — *Proverbs*, xiii, 12.

541. Brae: the slope of a hill; related, it may be, to *brow*.

546. Bracken: a tall, coarse, dark-colored fern.

569. Scott refers to the shepherd custom in his own day of setting out fires in the late autumn or early spring to burn off the dead herbage, in order to have green pasturage unmixed with the dried growth of a previous year. These hill fires swept over a wide extent and were a magnificent spectacle, especially in the night.

570. Balquidder: a village near the eastern end of Loch Voil. The last home and the burial place of Rob Roy.

575. *Beacon lights* and *signal fires* were employed to rally the forces of the Border. It would be interesting to compare modern methods of mobilizing an army.

As an instance of similar enterprise, the carrying of the news of Lincoln's election by the Pony Express from St. Joseph on the Missouri to Sacramento in eight days may be mentioned. The total distance of 1966 miles was divided into 190 stations from fifteen to twenty-five miles apart. For several years, despite hostile Indians, four hundred station men, four hundred and twenty of the fleetest, toughest horses that money could buy, and eighty expert riders, including Buffalo Bill, kept the mail bags going at break-neck speed. Perhaps some day the Pony Express may take the place of the Fiery Cross in a great American poem.

590. Each Highland warrior brought his own weapons, food, and clothing. A Highland army could be put into the field and into action in a marvelously short time, but for want of steady food supplies it could not be held together long. Modern nations provide arms, uniform, and rations. The question of food was put crisply by Napoleon: An army crawls on its belly.

601. After sending out the Fiery Cross, Roderick and his scouts go west " with anxious eye " to make sure that no rising in the upper Forth and Loch Lomond district may imperil Ellen and her father in Coir-Uriskin. Inasmuch as Roderick does not intrude on his way back, we must add this to the list of the unhappy chieftain's unselfish, chivalrous acts.

643. Chafed with the lake: chafed the lake; blew over its surface and made it rough. *To make warm* is the original meaning, retained in *chafing-dish;* then comes *to warm by rubbing* and, finally, *to fret*. *To chafe* a thing, therefore, means *to fret* it, to wear it, not to warm it. Compare *chauffer*.

672. A single page, to bear his sword. According to Scott the regular attendants attached to a Highland chief were: (1) the *henchman;* (2) the *bard;* (3) the *bladier*, or spokesman; (4) the *gillie-more*, or sword-bearer; (5) a *gillie*, who bore the chief across the fords; (6) a *gillie* to lead the horse; (7) a *baggageman;* (8) a *piper;* (9) a *piper's gillie* to carry the bagpipe.

713. *Ave Maria*. Hail Mary, the opening words of a Latin hymn addressed to the Virgin Mary. The construction of the hymn should be noted. It consists of three stanzas. Each stanza is composed of two quatrains, making six quatrains in all. The even-numbered lines of the first, second, and third quatrains rhyme with the odd-numbered lines of the fourth, fifth, and sixth quatrains, respectively. Thus there are but two rhymes in the hymn.   Twelve lines rhyme with *mild* and twelve rhyme with *prayer*.

Aside from the opening words the prayer bears no particular resemblance to the Latin hymn.   Ellen's prayer is one of supplication, of request, not of praise.

724. Down of eider.   The eider is a large duck frequenting the coasts of the North Atlantic.   There are several species. At an early day the inhabitants of the Western Isles of Scotland attached importance to the flesh and eggs of the eider. The Esquimaux still do so.   These ducks line their nests with an incredible quantity of soft, short, elastic, downy feathers plucked from their own breasts.

747–752. Roderick's words as quoted hardly harmonize with his attitude as indicated by *muttered, sullen,* and *flung.*

EXERCISES

1. Sketch a map and indicate by a red line the course of the Fiery Cross.

2. Themes:
   a. The superstitions of the canto.
   b. Mary's wedding.
   c. The state of Roderick's mind.
   d. The atmosphere of this compared with previous cantos.
   e. The best scene for a painter.
   f. The worship of the Druids.
   g. Roman auguries.
   h. The Highland call to arms, — its advantages and disadvantages.

3. Write fifty words on the comparison made in connection with:

   a. Their answer hoarse.
   b. Duncraggan's huts.
   c. Lance's point a glimmer made.
   d. A harder task to prove.
   e. Our flower was in flushing.

4. Write suitable titles or headings for a score of the stanzas.

5. Write a brief note of explanation of:

    a. Her chalice reared.

    b. His impatient blade.

    c. The joyous wolf.

    d. Teith's young waters.

    e. No tie but to his clan.

6. Identify:

    a. The sickening victim.

    b. The henchman on the prow.

    c. The sapling bough.

    d. A cruel pledge.

CANTO FOURTH: THE PROPHECY

LINE **36**. **Boune**: prepared, ready; used to fill the line and rhyme with *Doune*. See v, 466 for a fitting use of the word.

63. The Taghairm (tăg'ĕrm). "The Highlanders, like all rude people, had various superstitious modes of inquiring into futurity. One of the most noted was the *Taghairm*, mentioned in the text. A person was wrapped up in the skin of a newly-slain bullock, and deposited beside a waterfall, or at the bottom of a precipice, or in some other strange, wild, and unusual situation, where the scenery around him suggested nothing but objects of horror. In this situation, he revolved in his mind the question proposed; and whatever was impressed upon him by his exalted imagination, passed for the inspiration of the disembodied spirits, who haunt these desolate recesses." — Scott, *Notes*.

66–78. Ah! well the gallant brute, etc. "I know not," writes Scott, "if it be worth observing that this passage is taken almost literally from the mouth of an old Highland kern, or Ketteran, as they were called. He used to narrate the merry doings of the good old time when he was follower of Rob Roy MacGregor. This leader, on one occasion, thought

proper to make a descent upon the lower part of the Loch
Lomond district, and summoned all the heritors and farmers
to meet at the Kirk of Drymen, to pay him black-mail; *i.e.*,
tribute for forbearance and protection. As this invitation
was supported by a band of thirty or forty stout fellows, only
one gentleman, an ancestor, if I mistake not, of the present
Mr. Grahame of Gartmore, ventured to decline compliance.
Rob Roy instantly swept his land of all he could drive away,
and among the spoil was a bull of the old Scottish wild breed,
whose ferocity occasioned great plague to the Ketterans.
' But ere we had reached the Row of Dennan,' said the old
man, ' a child might have scratched his ears.' "

74. Beal 'maha: " the pass of the plain."

77. Dennan's Row. See Rowardennan, on the eastern
shore of Loch Lomond, now the boat landing for Ben
Lomond. The circumstance is historical.

79. That bull. A white bull was an unusual sacrifice.
The native cattle of the Highlands were an undersized, shaggy,
hardy, long-horned, black breed from which, however, the
famous Galloways have been brought up.

83. Verge: edge, face. Pronounce to rhyme with *targe*.

84. Hero's Targe: a cataract in Glenfinlas, a short distance
above Duncraggan. Tourists particularly interested in the
scenes of the poem leave the main road at Brigg of Turk
and go up the valley through Duncraggan to Hero's Targe
and back again.

90. The **wizard** is the same Brian who prepared the fiery
cross.

98. broke: cut up, quartered, dressed.

99. " ' There is a little gristle,' says Turbervile, ' which is upon
the spoone of the brisket, which we call the raven's bone; and
I have seen in some places a raven so wont and accustomed to
it, that she would never fail to croak and cry for it all the time
you were in breaking up of the deer, and would not depart
till she had it.' " — Scott, *Notes.*

In Jonson's *Sad Shepherd*, Marian tells Robin Hood of the breaking of a deer,

> " Now o'er head sat a raven,
> On a sere bow, a grown, great bird, and hoarse,
> Who, all the while the deer was breaking up,
> So croaked and cried for 't, as all the huntsmen
> Especially old Scathlock, thought it ominous."

150-165. Locate the Braes of Doune, Loch Earn, and Benledi. Roderick's forces lie in Lanrick Mead. If reinforced by the clansmen from Loch Earn, he proposes to take position on the southern slopes of Benledi, otherwise he will retire into the Trosachs.

153. Sable pale. In heraldry, a broad perpendicular stripe of black occupying the middle of the shield. *Pale* is akin to *pole* and *palisade*.

174. Stance: standing, position, foundation.

177. targe: shortened form of *target* to rhyme with *charge*. " A round target of light wood, covered with strong leather and studded with brass or iron, was a necessary part of a Highlander's equipment. In charging regular troops they received the thrust of the bayonet in this buckler, twisted it aside, and used the broadsword against the encumbered soldier. In the civil war of 1745 most of the front rank of the clans were thus armed." — Scott, *Notes*.

181. Chieftain's glance. Roderick still has a care for Ellen.

198. Red streamers of the north: aurora borealis, northern lights. The farther north we travel, the more brilliant they are.

> " And red and bright the streamers light
> Were dancing in the glowing north.
> He knew by the streamers that shot so bright
> That spirits were riding the northern light."
> — *Lay of the Last Minstrel*, ii, 86.

" Or like the borealis race
  That flit ere you can point their place."
                              — *Tam O'Shanter.*

222. Thou saidst. When did he say so?

223. Trowed: believed.

231. Cambus-kenneth's fane: an abbey on the east bank
of the Forth a mile below Stirling. James III was buried
here. *Fane* means a holy place, a sanctuary, a church.

250. Sooth: true.

260. One can hardly wonder that Scott represents Ellen
as not heeding; for the ballad of Alice Brand creates an impatient feeling in the mind of even an ordinary reader. The
interest in the story is now too intense for a lengthy song
entirely English in its character and as much out of keeping
here as the coronach over Duncan's bier was in keeping with
the circumstances of its introduction.

262. The mavis and merle: two celebrated songsters.
The merle is a large black thrush. It is the British blackbird, but should not be confused with the American blackbird. Our red-winged blackbird is related to the bobolink,
the oriole, and the meadow-lark. He is a fine fellow, bravely
togged out, but he has little music in him. The British blackbird belongs to a musical family and has a fine mellow voice.
The mavis is known also as the songthrush and the throstle;
it ranks with the nightingale and the skylark among old world
singers. Both the mavis and the merle are copsewood musi-
cians. They have been favorites of the poets from Chaucer
on.

Although this is not an article on ornithology, it is interesting to know that of a hundred thrushes no species is found
on both sides of the Atlantic. Led astray possibly by the
term *blackbird*, the poet Longfellow introduces the merle into
the society of the jay, oriole, and blue-bird in Connecticut:

" It was the season when all through the land
  The merle and mavis build."

277. Vest of pall: vestments, garments. Pall is a rich cloth, usually of silk, much worn by ladies, the nobility, and by ecclesiastics in the middle ages.

285. Vair: the fur of small animals, particularly of the gray squirrel. Vair was accounted suitable trimming for " vests of pall." Cinderella's slipper was made of this material and should have been called a " vair-slipper, " not a glass-slipper.

291. Own Richard here follows the meter and accent of *lot be hard*. It is well in a case like this to slur a trifle.

298. Woned: dwelt.

306. Fatal green. The elves were reputed to wear green habits, and were offended if mortal ventured to put on green clothing. Green was a favorite color in Ireland. It was considered unlucky in Scotland and particularly unlucky, not to say fatal, to the whole clan of Graham.

330. Kindly blood: kindred blood, the blood of a kinsman, the blood of one's own kind. In *Hamlet* we have " More than kin and less than kind."

355. 'Twixt life and death. A belief was long prevalent among Europeans that living persons, both babes and adults, but babes in particular, were snatched away and adopted by the fairies.

357. Wist I: if I knew.

358. Sign: to make the mark of the cross.

371. Dunfermline: an old town, containing a castle and an abbey, situated 17 miles northwest of Edinburgh. It was long the residence of the Scottish kings. Robert Bruce was buried in the abbey. It has been called the " Westminster of Scotland."

387. Bank and bourne: bank and stream. *Bourne* is the same as *burn* and should be pronounced to rhyme with *return*. Skeat fails to find any justification for relating this word to

bourne meaning boundary or limit.   *Bourne* (burn) meaning
stream or brook appears in names connected with rivers as
Westbourne, Bournemouth, Melbourne, etc.

392. Augur scathe: foretell harm, injury, mischief.

403–404. This couplet suggests a parallel passage from
Julius Cæsar:

> "Set honor in one eye and death i' the other,
>   And I will look on both indifferently;
>   For let the gods so speed me as I love
>   The name of honor more than I fear death."

411. Scott wrote first, "By Cambusmore my horses wait,"
and then he thought better of it and moved the horses nearer
so that Ellen might not have so far to walk.

464. This ring. A king's ring was a letter of authority
none might dispute.   Queen Elizabeth sent Raleigh her ring.
Compare *Genesis*, xli, 41: "And Pharaoh said unto Joseph,
See, I have set thee over all the land of Egypt.   And Pharaoh
took off his ring from his hand and put it upon Joseph's hand."

504. Female form. In a letter to a friend Scott wrote:
"I wish I could give you an idea of the original, whom I really
saw in the Pass of Glencoe many years ago.   It is one of the
wildest and most tremendous passes in the Highlands, winding through huge masses of rock without a pile of verdure,
and between mountains that seem rent asunder by an earthquake.   This poor woman had placed herself in the wildest
attitude imaginable, upon the very top of one of these huge
fragments; she had scarce any covering but a tattered plaid,
which left her arms, legs, and neck bare to the weather.   Her
long, shaggy, black hair was streaming backwards in the
wind, and exposed a face rather wild and wasted than ugly,
and bearing a very peculiar expression of frenzy.   She had a
handful of eagle's feathers in her hand."

506. Weeds: garments, clothing.   We retain the word
in *widow's weeds.*

> " His russet weeds were brown as heath
> 　　That crowns the upland fell,
> And the hair of his head was frizzly red
> 　　As the purple heather-bell."
> 　　　　　　— Leyden, *The Cout of Keeldar*.

511. Gaudy broom. A patch of broom in blossom presents an expanse of vivid yellow.

531. Allan, etc. " The Allan and the Devan," wrote Lockhart, " are two beautiful streams — the latter celebrated in the poetry of Burns — which descend from the hills of Perthshire into the great carse, or plain, of Stirling."

555. Maudlin: an English pronunciation of *Magdalene*.

559. Pitched a bar: replaced in modern sports by *throwing a hammer*.

567. Batten: feed, fatten.

590–605. The stag wears a suit of Lincoln green. Who is the wounded doe? Who are the hunters? **A stag of ten** is a stag with ten branches on his antlers.

624. Compare v, 200.

642. Daggled: wet, — a Scandinavian word. A milder term than *draggled*.

> " The warrior's very plume, I say,
> 　　Was daggled by the dashing spray."
> 　　　　　— *Lay of the Last Minstrel*, i, 29.

658. Compare 553.

713. Scott uses **brown** advisedly. The time is midsummer. Owing to the high latitude of Perthshire the summer day is much longer than in any part of the United States. The evening twilight is prolonged into a drowsy gloom that hardly grows black before the morning twilight comes. One can make out to read until a very late hour.

760. See i, 589 and ii, 588.

798. Purpled. Those who have given attention to the matter say that the drier the atmosphere, the bluer forest-clad mountains appear to be and that moist air produces a purple effect.

EXERCISES

1. Themes:

    a. The fulfillment of the Taghairm.

    b. The ballad of Alice Brand.

    c. Suggestions for tableaux.

    d. The hour at which this and preceding cantos close.

    e. Portions of canto founded on fact.

    f. The climax of Ellen's misfortune.

2. Explanatory notes:

    a. In mid-air stayed.

    b. The Lowland tongue.

    c. His dainty fare.

    d. Pledge may rest secure.

    e. That fatal bait.

3. Locate:

    a. That steepy glade.

    b. Dunfermline gray.

    c. Stirling gate.

    d. Devan's tides.

    e. Coilantogle's ford.

4. Identify:

    a. The brave foemen.   *Rod.*

    b. The fierce avenger.

    c. A wounded doe.   *Murdo*

    d. Yon wily kern.

    e. The kind youth.

    f. The gallant brute.

    g. A wakeful sentinel.

    h. The fateful answer.

    i. A messenger of doubt.

5. Write lines 734–760 in the form of a dialogue:
> *Roderick.* Thy name and purpose! Saxon, stand!
> *Fitz-James.* A stranger.
> *Roderick.* What dost thou require?
> *Fitz-James.* Rest, etc.

CANTO FIFTH: THE COMBAT

LINE **10. Sheen**: shining, bright.

15. By: an expressive little word. The soldiers hurry through their morning prayers to make an end of the matter.

122-127. Through the death of his royal father on Flodden Field, James became king while still a mere boy. While not making himself known to Roderick, yet he is speaking of his own youth and of the disorder which prevailed before he was old enough to assert himself. See note on ii, 616.

126. Mewed: caged, shut up, confined like a falcon in its mew.

165. Shall with strong hand, etc. "So far, indeed, was a foray from being held disgraceful, that a young chief was always expected to show his talents for command so soon as he assumed it, by leading his clan on a successful enterprise of this nature, either against a neighboring sept (clan), for which constant feuds usually furnished an apology, or against the Sassenach, Saxons, or Lowlanders, for which no apology was necessary. The Gael, great traditional historians, never forgot that the Lowlands had, at some remote period, been the property of their Celtic forefathers, which furnished an ample vindication of all the ravages that they could make on the unfortunate districts which lay within their reach." — Scott, *Notes*.

180. Even as a spy. Roderick, whom Scott would represent as frank and courteous, here contradicts himself; for in his conference with Brian, iv, 140–149, the chieftain meets a disclosure of the augury by saying that he had already arranged his plans for bringing Fitz-James into ambush to be slain.

183. Fitz-James refrains from telling his vow to revenge Blanche of Devan.

196. This is the most dramatic situation in the poem. " In all Scott's poetry, this is his master stroke," says one critic.

The incident is drawn from an actual occurrence in Inverness-shire. An English officer with a small escort, carrying money with which to pay the garrison at Inverness, was delayed over night at a miserable little inn.

At nightfall an intelligent, well-dressed Highlander came in and the officer insisted on sharing with him the best supper that the inn could set up. The stranger accepted with evident reluctance, but later entered into an agreeable conversation and betrayed an intimate knowledge of the country. Finally, in response to the officer's frank disclosure of his errand and his fear of being robbed by John Gunn, a noted freebooter of that region, the Highlander accepted, though with evident hesitation, a pressing invitation to act as a guide.

In the morning, accordingly, they set out and while passing through a solitary and dreary glen the talk came around again to the subject of John Gunn. " Would you like to see him? " asked the guide, and, without waiting for an answer, whistled shrilly. The English officer and his small force were surrounded in a twinkling by a large number of well-armed Highlanders. Resistance was out of the question. " Stranger," said the guide, " I am that very John Gunn by whom you feared, and not without cause, to be intercepted: for I came to the inn last night for the express purpose of learning your route, that I and my followers might ease you of your charge by the road. But I am incapable of betraying the trust you have reposed in me and, having convinced you that you were in my power, I can only dismiss you unplundered and uninjured." He then directed the officer on his journey and disappeared with his men as suddenly as they had presented themselves.

A similar situation is recounted by Kipling in *The Ballad*

of East and West. Kipling has done nothing any better. The *Ballad* should be read at this point without fail.

198. Wild: adjective. The signal, wild as the scream of the curlew, flew from crag to crag. The curlew is a large snipe with a long bill curving downward.

246. Mother Earth. The allusion is to Cadmus. According to Greek mythology, Cadmus slew a dragon and sowed its teeth in a furrow. Up sprang a host of armed men.

298. See map. Name the three parent lakes.

301. A series of slight ridges and lines of depression are yet seen, marking, it may be, the position of an old Roman camp, fortified after the manner described in Cæsar's *Gallic War*.

303. Eagle wings. An eagle with wings unfurled and a thunderbolt clutched in the talons of one foot was the ensign of the Roman legion.

329. Prophet bred: Brian. See iii, 91 and iv, 124.

344. Strengths: strongholds, fastnesses. Note the quotation from *Marmion* on page 230 for a similar use of the word.

347. " The two principal figures are contrasted with uncommon felicity. Fitz-James . . . is gay, amorous, fickle, intrepid, impetuous, affectionate, courteous, graceful, and dignified. Roderick is gloomy, vindictive, arrogant, undaunted, but constant in his affections and true to his engagements; the whole passage in which these persons are placed in opposition, from their first meeting to their final conflict, is conceived and written with a sublimity which has been rarely equalled." — *Quarterly Review,* 1810.

356. Carpet knight: one who prefers the palace to a battlefield. When before did Roderick accuse an opponent of effeminacy?

364. Ruth: pity, compassion; akin to *rue,* meaning to regret.

383. Trained abroad: in France, where James spent some time, and, no doubt, took pains to become an up-to-date young man. In France shield and broadsword had already given way to the rapier which, later, was followed by the smallsword — in turn succeeded by the pistol and to-day by the revolver.

388. Unequal war. The nub of the fight is this: the sword and buckler, ferocity, sheer strength, and lawlessness of antiquity were matched with the slender rapier, the guarded temper, skill, and respect for law and order of modernity. We may regret to see a tower of strength fall but it was always so. David slew Goliath, Fitz-James overcame Roderick. Skill is the master of power.

395. As firm rock. The ability of a skilled fencer to catch or ward off downright blows is marvelous, but he requires rather more agility and freedom of movement than is possessed by a rock.

462. Fairer freight: Ellen.

468. Bayard is the horse of Fitz-James. In 453 we must understand that one leads a palfrey and the other leads Bayard.

469. De Vaux. In *The Bridal of Triermain*, iii, 1, Scott makes *brave De Vaux* rhyme with *plundered flocks*.

470. Scott was a fine horseman. Instead of drawing on his imagination, he here describes a favorite horse of his own.

" I took uncommon pains to verify the accuracy of the local circumstances of this story. I recollect, in particular, that to ascertain whether I was telling a probable tale, I went into Perthshire, to see whether King James could actually have ridden from the banks of Lake Vennachar to Stirling Castle within the time supposed in the poem, and had the pleasure to satisfy myself that it was quite practicable." — Scott, *Introduction*.

We can readily imagine Scott going at a mad gallop from Coilantogle ford to Stirling. Locate the places named. They were the homes of friends whom Scott had visited again and again. Compare this ride with Browning's *How They*

Brought the Good News from Ghent to Aix.   Read, also, Long-fellow's *Paul Revere's Ride*.

503. Bulwark of the North.   Stirling Castle is situated on an impregnable crag near the only passable ford in the Forth, short of its head waters.

Roman legions, Highland forayers, the followers of Bruce, the Covenanters, the troops of Claverhouse, Cromwell's soldiers, the hasty forces of the Pretender, and the determined armies of British monarchs surged back and forth for centuries under the mighty rock of Stirling.

504. Stirling.   " The glory of Scotland . . . who does not know its noble rock, rising the monarch of the landscape, its majestic and picturesque towers, its amphitheatre of mountain and the windings of its marvellous river : and who that has once seen the sun descending here, in all the blaze of its beauty beyond the purple hills of the west, can ever forget the plain of Sterling, the endless charm of this wonderful scene, the wealth, the splendor, the variety, the majesty of all which here lies between earth and heaven." — Fullarton, *Gazetteer of Scotland*.

" That night we struck the Allan Water and followed it down ; and coming to the edge of the hills saw the whole Carse of Stirling flat as a pancake, with the town and castle on a hill in the midst of it, and the moon shining on the Links of Forth." — Stevenson, *Kidnapped*.

525. Saint Serle : an obscure saint or else a saint invented to rhyme with *Earl*.

544. Bride of Heaven : a nun.

550.   Stirling was a royal residence during the earlier reign of the Stuart family.   William, Earl of Douglas, although a royal guest under safe conduct, was stabbed in an apartment of the castle by the hand of King James II.

551. Fatal mound : a slight eminence northeast of the castle but within the castle wall.   Here the royal headsmen executed state offenders.

558. Franciscan steeple: the Grayfriars Church, built by
Fitz-James's father. It still stands. James VI was crowned here,
with John Knox to preach the coronation sermon.

562. Morrice-dancers. *Morrice* is thought to be a perver-
sion of *Moorish*. According to this notion the morrice-dancers
came from Spain, where a somewhat similar dance is called
the fandango. The British morrice-dancers combined the
dance with May-day and burlesque festivities requiring a
comedy company for an exhibition. *The Abbot*, chapter xix,
contains an extended and lively description of these revelries.

The student would do well at this point to read *The Fair
Maid of Perth*. It is rich in description of Highland customs
and festivities. There is nothing in all Scott's writings more
graphic than the death of MacIan, the sweep of the funeral
flotilla down Loch Tay, the services of burial, and the feast
held to induct his son into the chieftainship. A Highland
feud combat, — thirty wielders of the broadsword on each
side, — gives the reader an adequate idea of courage and
fidelity to clan; the market which raiders found for their
hides in the leather-working city of Perth demonstrates the
intercourse between the tradesmen and the hillmen; and the
mummeries and festivals of that "fair city" throw light on
the sports held in the city of Stirling as described in this canto.

586. Shame: bashfulness or else consciousness of some
prank or escapade of the kind for which James was noted.

611. In a note to *The Fair Maid of Perth* Scott quotes a
local antiquary who thus describes the attire of a morrice-
dancer once worn in the presence of a visiting monarch and
now preserved entire among the treasures of Perth:

"This curious vestment is made of fawn-colored silk, in the
form of a tunic with trappings of green and red satin.
There accompany it *two hundred fifty-two* small circular
bells, formed into twenty-one sets of twelve bells each, upon
pieces of leather, made to fasten to various parts of the
body. What is most remarkable about these bells is the
perfect intonation of each set. . . . These concords are
maintained not only in each set but also in the intervals

between the various sets. The performer could thus produce, if not a *tune* at least a pleasing and musical chime, according as he regulated with skill the movements of his body."

614–618. Merely actors, of course, not the merry tenants of Sherwood Forest. In *Ivanhoe*, written ten years later, Scott brings Robin Hood and his archers to the siege of Front-de-Bœuf's castle.

615. Quarterstaff: a stout cudgel about the length of a man. The quarterstaff was a favorite weapon in the hands of Little John and the other members of Robin Hood's band.

630. Wight: a chap, a fellow.

641. A golden ring. "The usual prize of a wrestling match was a ram and a ring, but the animal would have embarrassed my story." — Scott.

648. Bar. See iv, 559.

653. A rood: a rod; variously estimated at from 5½ to 8 yards.

660. Ladies' Rock: a safe rock half way down the cliff whence the ladies viewed the sports. It was not necessary to build bleachers.

730. Baron: the Douglas.

758. With flint: with stones.

790. Widow's mate. Woman's mate would be more accurate, but less poetic, less expressive, less piquant.

819. The following remarks of Coriolanus, act i, scene 1, show that Shakespeare's opinion of the "fool multitude" is even harsher than Scott's:

"What's the matter, you dissentious rogues,
    That, rubbing the poor itch of your opinion,
    Make yourselves scabs? . . .
    What would you have, you curs,
    That like not peace nor war. . . .
    He that trusts to you,

Where he should find you lions, finds you hares,
Where foxes, geese: You are no surer, no,
Than is the coal of fire upon the ice,
Or hailstone in the sun. . . .
Who deserves greatness, deserves your hate.
　　　. . . He that depends
Upon your favours swims with fins of lead
And hews down oaks with rushes. Hang ye! Trust ye?
With every minute you do change a mind
And call him noble that was now your hate,
Him vile that was your garland."

832. Fantastic as a woman's mood. Compare *Marmion*,
vi, 902: "O woman, in our hours of ease," *et seq.*

887. Referring to the assassination.

EXERCISES

1. Select passages particularly worth memorizing.
2. Themes:
   a. A comparison of cantos iv and v.
   b. Scott's choice of adjectives.
   c. Martial Faith and Courtesy's bright star.
   d. The evolution of weapons used in personal combat.
   e. Had Fitz-James fallen.
   f. The sympathies of Ellen and Malcolm had they witnessed the combat.
   g. Douglas as king.
3. Explanatory notes:
   a. Gained not the length of horseman's lance.
   b. My pass hangs in my belt.
   c. Albany held borrowed truncheon.
   d. These loose banditti.
   e. Pointed to his dagger blade.
4. Identify:
   a. This ruthless man.
   b. The foremost foeman.
   c. The struggling foe.

d. The dark gray man.

e. The bride of Heaven.

CANTO SIXTH: THE GUARD–ROOM

This canto does not seem to have a fitting name. Would not " The Castle" be more appropriate?

LINE 3. **Caitiff**: literally, a captive; hence, a wretched or unfortunate person. Here the term means one bound to a life of toil.

4. " In the sweat of thy face shalt thou eat bread." — *Genesis*, iii, 19.

15. **Gyve**: more frequently used in the plural. Gyves are fetters, particularly for the legs. In a technical sense debtors were not imprisoned for debt, but up to the day of Dickens a debtor might be ordered, in the name of the king, to pay that which he owed. If he failed to comply, he might be thrown into jail for disobedience to the royal command, that is to say, for contempt of court.

47. **Adventurers**: soldiers like John of Brent. Up to this time the Scottish monarchs had depended on the nobility and barons for soldiers. These men in turn called their vassals, the occupiers of their lands, into the field. James V introduced the policy of hiring adventurers for a wage. The adventurers, or soldiers of fortune, differed from the Hessians employed by King George during the war of the American Revolution. The former served as individuals and received each his own pay while the latter were rented out in a body by their prince.

60. **Halberd**: a combination of pike and battle ax. The halberd was about a foot taller than a man.

88. **Buxom.** The original meaning is *like a bow;* hence bending, pliant, yielding, companionable, lively.

90. The *Soldier's Song* is not to be taken too seriously. It is in keeping with the convivial, devil-may-care spirit of a band of hirelings whose trade is the carrying of arms. In this sense it is the most successful song in the entire poem.

Scott himself, while noted for jollity, was ever reverent and always chivalrous.

It is interesting to know that this particular bit of verse was a favorite of the poet, Robert Browning. Lord Jeffrey, the reviewer, says, " The greatest blemish in the poem is the ribaldry and dull vulgarity which is put into mouths of the soldiery in the guard-room."

Poule: Paul.

92. Black-jack: a large drinking cup or flagon of black leather.

93. Seven deadly sins: pride, idleness, gluttony, lust, avarice, envy, wrath.

95. Upsees: a Dutch tipling term; drink deeply, take a good drink.

100. Gillian: a lass or wench. The term appears in an abbreviated form in " Jack and Gill." *Gillian* is not a term of respect.

103. Placket and pot: petticoat and drinking cup; hence, " woman and wine."

111. Bertram is come from Mar's army at the Trosachs.

128. Wax: grow. Compare the German *wachsen*, also the Scriptural mustard seed which " grew and waxed a great tree." — *Luke*, xiii, 19.

170. Needwood: a royal forest in Staffordshire. Without doubt John of Brent had broken some severe Norman game laws; — in other words had taken the king's deer and had fled to save his life. A chapter from Pyle's *Robin Hood* would add interest here.

221. Hest: behest, command.

233. Compare the **vacant purse** with the *mingled braid*, iv, 683. It was a custom of chivalry for a man to wear conspicuously a lady's glove, flower, knot of ribbons, or other favor as a token of loyalty to her. Modern usage with reference to wearing rings, pins, field colors, and the like, is quite different.

295. Leech: physician, healer.

306. Prore: prow.

319. Roderick's first inquiry is for Ellen's safety.

347. O'er Dermid's race: over the clan of the Campbells. The Campbells and the MacGregors were hereditary enemies. The Campbells finally got the better of their enemies to such an extent that the very use of the name MacGregor was forbidden by law. Scott had a strain of Campbell blood in him, but he was not in the habit of referring to it.

369. Note that this stanza is all a part of Allan's improvised account of the battle.

Battle of Beal' an Duine: a wonderful, an overpowering, description. In these pacific days we may question whether a view of any battle array is worth ten years of peaceful life, but Scott is certainly at his best. Premonitions appear early in the poem. Rumor, a darkening of the sky, rumblings, flashes, and now the war cloud bursts.

Enthusiasts declare this to be the greatest battle scene in literature. Though the conflict is too restricted, too brief to be compared with great battles, much may be said in support of this opinion. The actual grip at arms is brought on more clearly, more swiftly, more fatefully, and the conflict is fought more vividly than the Battle of Flodden Field. The question, from whatever angle it be approached, is too great, however, to be settled by a say-so.

Of Allan-bane's rank there can be no doubt. He is crowned for all time as the king of the minstrel race. The white-haired Harper not only surpasses the minstrel "infirm and old" of the *Lay,* but he surpasses all other minstrels. Scott handles the situation with art. He does not tax the reader's credulity by drawing on Allan's power of seeing events as they happen elsewhere; he represents Old Fidelity as an eye-witness moving along the shoulder of a lofty lookout; he leaves the reader free to concentrate on Allan's intense off-hand picture of the conflict.

This extemporaneous recital was fresh in Macaulay's mind when he wrote the oft quoted statement: "The arts of poetry and rhetoric may be carried near to absolute perfection and may exercise a mighty influence on the public mind in an age in which books are wholly or almost wholly unknown."

395. The northern shore of Achray.

404. barded. Protected by armor; used of horses. Cf. *The Lay of the Last Minstrel*, i, 311 :

> " Above the foaming tide, I ween,
> Scarce half the charger's neck was seen;
> For he was barded from counter to tail,
> And the rider was armed complete in mail."

452. Tinchel. " A circle of sportsmen, who, by surrounding a great space, and gradually narrowing, brought immense quantities of deer together, which usually made desperate efforts to break through the *Tinchel*." — Scott, *Notes.*

539. Bonnet-pieces: handsome gold pieces. They bore the head of James V wearing a bonnet or Scotch cap in place of the usual crown. A justifiable device of the king to render himself popular. These pieces were coined in the king's own mint from Clydesdale gold.

542-543. It would seem that these lines might be transposed to advantage. When there is no reason for the contrary, it is better to have the horse before the cart.

565. Duncraggan's widowed dame: Duncan's widow. Stanza xviii of the third canto should be read at this point to refresh the memory. The deed ascribed to this intrepid woman actually occurred a century or two later when a soldier of Cromwell's invading force attempted to reach the island and met his doom at the hand of a Highland woman.

638. Storied pane. Stained glass windows adorned with celebrated scenes and memorial figures.

> " Can storied urn or animated bust
> Back to its mansion call the fleeting breath? "
>
> — Gray's *Elegy.*

> " And storied windows richly dight
> Casting a dim religious light."
>
> — *Il Penseroso*, 159, 160.

665. Tired of perch and hood: weary of idleness. See note on ii, 525.

740. Scott has guarded the identity of Fitz-James with care, not desiring the reader to know, before reaching this point, that *the Hunter* is the king of Scotland. The student would do well to return to the first mention of the horseman who rode foremost and alone, i, 113. Follow the Hunter and Stranger through the several cantos to the present moment, and note how delightfully the poet almost reveals, yet guards, the secret of the poem, quite as a novelist guards his plot.

Scott himself, in the same note in which he describes the farmer sportsman's fear lest the heated dogs should be ruined by cold water, continues: " Another of his remarks gave me less pleasure. He detected the identity of the King with the wandering knight, Fitz-James, when he winds his bugle to summon his attendants (v, 445). This discovery, as Mr. Pepys says of the rent in his camlet cloak, was but a trifle, yet it troubled me; and I was at a good deal of pains to efface any marks by which I thought my secret could be traced before the conclusion, when I relied on it with the same hope of producing effect with which the Irish post-boy is said to reserve a ' trot for the avenue.' "

785. " This poem, the action of which lay among scenes so beautiful and so deeply imprinted on my recollections, was a labor of love, and it was no less so to recall the manners and incidents introduced. The frequent custom of James IV, and particularly of James V, to walk through their kingdom in disguise, afforded me the hint of an incident which never fails to be interesting if managed with the slightest address or dexterity." — Scott, *Introduction*.

846. See opening of canto i.

849. Fold and lea: sheepfold and meadow.

868. Scott's ear for music was said to be strangely deficient, but he imitates the dying cadences of the harp exquisitely.

EXERCISES

I

1. Select a narrative stanza and turn it into prose.

2. Select a descriptive stanza or passage and rewrite it in prose.

3. Point out the means employed to create an impression of swiftness in the progress of the Fiery Cross.

4. Describe the minor plot in canto iii.

5. Tell a story of Roderick Dhu's recovery, and subsequent life.

II

Draw comparisons between:

1. The Boat Song and the Coronach.
2. The *Battle of Beal' an Duine* and *Flodden Field*.
3. The targe and sword and the rapier.
4. The Highlands and the Border.
5. Roderick Dhu and Rob Roy.
6. The Trosachs and Stirling — as strongholds.

III

1. Name the most surprising moment in each canto.
2. Name the hour at which each canto opens and closes.
3. Name the instances of Highland hospitality.
4. List Scott's synonyms for *sword*.
5. List the flowers of the poem; the birds.

IV

Who are:
1. The sapling bough. *angus*
2. That woman void of fear.
3. A stag of ten. *James Fitz*
4. Heart broken boy. *Rod*
5. Snowdoun's knight. *James Fitz James*
6. The aged minstrel. *aller*
7. Beardless boy. *Mal.*
8. Mine honored friend.
9. The noble stem. *Duncan*
10. The rosebud. *Ellen*

V

Whose words are these and to whom do they apply?
1. Yon woodsman gray. *James Fitz*
2. A darksome man.
3. Your lances down. *Rod.*
4. Feeble hand.
5. A noble friend or foe.
6. Sad was thy lot.
7. Fling in the picture of the fight.
8. Well the gallant brute I knew.
9. Stand, or thou diest.
10. I hold the first who strikes my foe.

VI

Locate name of speaker and circumstance in the following:
1. O, it out beggars all I lost.
2. Woe worth the chase, woe worth the day.
3. The toils are pitched, the stakes are set. *Blanch*
4. Thy counsel in the streight I show.
5. Good is thine augury and fair.

6. Thou art gone and forever.
7. My hawk is tired of perch and hood.
8.   Farewell to thee
    Pattern of old fidelity.
9. Get thee an ape and trudge the land.
10. Come one, come all.   This rock shall fly
    From its firm base as soon as I.
11. I 'll dream no more.   By manly mind
    Not even in sleep is will resigned.

VII

Resolutions for debate.
1. That Roderick deserved a better fate.
2. That James V served the Border-men right.
3. That Scott overdraws the picture of the Trosachs.
4. That Scott's narrative surpasses his description.
5. That Malcolm is not interesting.
6. That *The Lady of the Lake* is a girl's poem.

A FINAL EXAMINATION

TIME: TWO HOURS.   ANSWER ANY TEN.

1. State conditions which favored a popular·reception of the poem.

2. Sketch a map of the Forth river, its lakes and tributaries.

3. Describe the personal appearance and character of one personage.

4. Describe, very briefly, one of the surprises of the poem.

5. Name the cantos in order, with a minor character in each.

6. Quote ten lines — not necessarily consecutive.

7. Who are:

> A graceful dame.
> A wounded doe.
> A fairer freight.
> The orphan heir.
> John of Brent.

8. Describe an instance of Highland hospitality, highly creditable.

9. Explain in few words:

> The deer is broke.
> Slackened bow.
> Snooded maiden.
> Shroud of sentient clay.
> No other favor will I wear.
> He gave his counsel to the wind.

10. State circumstances:

> Come, loiterer, come.
> Speed, Malise, speed.
> This signet shall secure thy way.
> Whistle or whoop and thou shalt die.

11. Supply the rest of the comparison:

> Like wild ducks crouching in the fen.
> Like castle girdled with its moat.
> Like bloodhounds now they search me out.
> As the mist slumbering on yon hill.
> As on descended angel gazed.

THE STORY OF THE POEM

The Publication of the Poem. — The popularity of *The Lay of the Last Minstrel* and of *Marmion* encouraged Scott to undertake this poem. He seems to have had some doubt whether he could keep up his reputation, but ventured and with success. In June, 1810, *The Lady of the Lake* came from the press of John Ballantyne and Company of Edinburgh.

Its Wonderful Reception. — Mr. Cadell, a well-known publisher, wrote: "I do not recollect that any of all the author's works was ever looked for with more intense anxiety, or that any one of them created a more extraordinary sensation when it did appear. The whole country rang with the praises of the poet — crowds set off to view the scenery of Loch Katrine, till then comparatively unknown; and as the book came out just before the season for excursions, every house and inn in that neighborhood was crammed with a constant succession of visitors."

In addition to the greeting due a work of genius, a special reason for the enthusiastic reception accorded a Highland poem by a British public may be found in the attitude of that public at this particular time toward the Highlands. Macaulay puts the case in a nutshell: "As long as there were Gaelic marauders, they had been regarded by the Saxon population as hateful vermin who ought to be exterminated without mercy; as soon as the extermination had been accomplished, . . . as soon as cattle were as safe in the Perthshire passes as they were in Smithfield [London cattle market], the freebooter was exalted into a hero of romance. As long as the Gaelic dress was worn, the Saxons had pronounced it hideous, ridiculous, nay, indecent. Soon after it had been prohibited, they discovered it was the most graceful drapery in Europe."

With people in this frame of mind, a semi-historical poem depicting the scenery of a section of the Highlands, and the customs, superstitions, hospitality, and bravery of its inhabitants, coming from the most gifted pen of the day, could not fail to capture the reading public. From its first appearance *The Lady of the Lake* was received with an enthusiasm comparable to the excitement which stirred the United States when *Uncle Tom's Cabin* came out.

Scott's Happy Choice of Scene. — Two quotations from the author's introduction to *The Lady of the Lake* are given here to indicate what led Scott to make Perthshire the scene of his forthcoming poem.

" The ancient manners, the habits and customs of the aboriginal race by whom the Highlands of Scotland were inhabited, had always appeared to me peculiarly adapted to poetry. The change in their manners, too, had taken place almost within my own time, or at least I had learned many particulars concerning the ancient state of the Highlands from the old men of the last generation. I had always thought the old Scottish Gael highly adapted for poetical composition. The feuds and political dissensions which, half a century earlier, would have rendered the richer and wealthier part of the kingdom indisposed to countenance a poem, the scene of which was laid in the Highlands, were now sunk in the generous compassion which the English, more than any other nation, feel for the misfortunes of an honorable foe. . . .

" I had also read a great deal, seen much, and heard more, of that romantic country where I was in the habit of spending some time every autumn; and the scenery of Loch Katrine was connected with the recollection of many a dear friend and merry expedition of former days. This poem, the action of which lay among scenes so beautiful and so deeply imprinted on my recollections, was a labor of love, and it was no less so to recall the manners and incidents introduced.". . .

THE GEOGRAPHY OF SCOTLAND

Guide-posts. — To get a notion of the geography of Scotland, it is a good plan to locate first of all the city of Glasgow on the Clyde, and Edinburgh on the Firth of Forth. These cities are only forty miles apart, a fact which gives

THE RIVERS TWEED AND ETTRICK

us a good idea of Scottish distances. Locate also Dunbar, a seaport twenty miles east of Edinburgh, and Aberdeen a hundred miles up the eastern coast.

Main Divisions. — Scotland is divided into three physical, three occupational, three literary regions, — the Border, the Lowlands, and the Highlands. The Border lies south of a line drawn southeasterly from Dunbar through the sources of the Clyde to the coast of southern Ayrshire. The Highlands lie north of a line drawn also in a southeasterly direction from Aberdeen to the Forth of Clyde. The Lowlands lie between the lines thus drawn.

The Border, so called because it lies next to England, is a rolling, in part mountainous region. There are mountains rising to an elevation of from 2000 to 3000 feet, but the surface for the most part consists of rounded hills well adapted to grazing and sheep raising. The Nith, the Annan, the Esk, the Liddel, shape their courses to the Forth of Solway; the Ettrick, the Yarrow, and the Teviot hasten to join the Tweed on its way to the North Sea.

The Lowlands are neither low nor flat. Two rivers of importance run parallel but in opposite directions. The Clyde rises in the Border and flows northwesterly into the Firth of Clyde. The Forth rises in the Highlands and flows southeasterly into the Firth of Forth. At their nearest approach these streams are not over twenty miles apart. The Lowlands are well adapted to dairying and to mixed agriculture. Iron and coal abound. Mining, manufacturing, commerce, and learning got an early start here. Though the Lowlands comprise but a sixth of the area of the entire country, this region is the Scotland of early history, the Scotland of Wallace, of Bruce, of the Douglas, the Scotland of Queen Mary and of the six kings called James.

The Highlands are different. The elevation is not great. Ben Nevis, the highest peak, rises only 4406 feet above sea level. There are beautiful glens and fertile valleys but the country is rough. Enormous rock-masses, granitic and slaty ridges, and rolling moors, are tumbled together seemingly without system.

In many mountainous regions like Switzerland, there are long river valleys, connected by mountain passes which

give access to the interior.   But in the Highlands there are
no natural gateways; long valleys and communicating
waters are wanting.

The stupendous irregularity of the surface and the lack
of roads and bridges rendered it impracticable to feed an
invading army or to get anywhere with it.   Nowhere else
in Europe is there a more natural refuge for a hard pressed

BRIGG OF TURK, TROSACHS

race.   Into this fastness the Picts, known later as the
Highlanders, came and, suiting their mode of living to the
character of the country, resisted change for thirty-five
generations.

With this picture of the country itself in our minds, let
us turn to a study of the people who inhabited it.   In 1753
the poet Goldsmith, unfair but candid, said, " An unfruitful
country, with hills all brown with heath, and valleys scarce
able to feed a rabbit."

THE HIGHLANDERS

Race and Language. — The Highlanders are a fragment of the great Celtic race which once occupied the better part of western Europe. They were driven by successive waves of Teutonic invaders to seek refuge in strongholds along the Atlantic.

They spoke and to a degree yet speak the *Gaelic* language, which is akin to the *Erse* of Ireland and to the *Manx* of the Isle of Man. The arts of poetry and rhetoric appear to have been cultivated to a high degree by their minstrels, but only in an oral way. At the time of the supposed Roderick Dhu, no Gaelic books or even writings were known.

Home Comforts. — Those who are familiar with the frontier cabin, the sod house, or the tar-paper shack of the American pioneer are not shocked by a description of the Highland hut, but pictures of Highland housekeeping are not inviting. Undoubtedly Scott idealizes Highland conditions.

Dislike for Work. — Macaulay describes the Highlanders as showing a " disposition to throw on the weaker sex the heaviest part of manual labor, which is characteristic of savages. . . . Nor did the women repine at their hard lot. In their view, it was quite fit that a man . . . should take his ease except when he was fighting, hunting, or marauding. To mention his name in connection with commerce or with any mechanical art was an insult. Agriculture was indeed less despised. Yet a high-born warrior was much more becomingly employed in plundering the land of others than in tilling his own. . . . His inordinate pride of birth and his contempt for labor and trade were indeed great weaknesses, and had done far more than the inclemency of the air and the sterility of the soil to keep his country poor and rude."

Religion. — The monks of the Catholic church made a heroic effort to convert the Highlanders. They built chapels, founded monasteries, and established convents. Whatever degree of light and learning, or of protection to the innocent, was carried into the wilderness was due to early, persistent, zealous missionary effort. Even so the religion of the greater part of the Highlands was a rude mixture of aggressive Christianity and lingering paganism.

Scott recognizes and indeed points out this condition clearly in *The Lady of the Lake*. A mere list of the superstitions is instructive: the ordeal of the hide, the sword leaping from its scabbard, the foretelling events, the ordeal of Saint Fillan's spring, Brian's unnatural birth, the Ben-Shie, the croaking raven, the men of peace, and other more or less primitive beliefs indicate that Scott had made a close study of these matters.

Forays. — Scott has dealt more fully with raids and cattle droving in his novels and in his poems of the Border. The attitude of Roderick, canto v, stanza vii, is the typical mountaineer's view, the view of the Cheyenne war chief. Macaulay summarizes: " His predatory habits were most pernicious to the commonwealth; yet those erred greatly who imagined that he bore any resemblance to villains who, in rich and well-governed communities, live by stealing. When he drove before him the herds of Lowland farmers up the pass which led to his native glen, he no more considered himself as a thief than the Raleighs and the Drakes considered themselves as thieves when they divided the cargoes of Spanish galleons. He was a warrior seizing the lawful prize of war, of war never intermitted during the thirty-five generations which had passed away since the Teutonic invaders had driven the children of the soil to the mountains."

Garb. — The bagpipe, the plaid, and the bonnet are fixed in the mind of the public as peculiar to the mountaineer. The color of the plaid or tartan varied. No two clans wore the same tartan. A Glengarry bonnet can be told as far as it can be seen, from a MacGregor.

Scott writing for his little grandson says: "The dress of these mountaineers was also different from that of the Low-landers. They wore a plaid, or mantle of frieze, or of striped stuff called tartan, one end of which being wrapped round the waist, formed a short petticoat, which descended to the knee, while the rest was folded round them like a sort of cloak. They had buskins made of raw hide; and those who could get a bonnet, had that covering for their heads, though many never wore one during their whole lives, but had only their own shaggy hair tied back by a leathern strap."

Arms. — A student of antiquities can tell from the point of an arrow the stage of development attained by its maker. The stone ax may have been used in the Isle of Man centu-ries after it had disappeared from the Isles of Greece, but wherever found it indicates a certain stage of advancement or backwardness. The bow and arrow, the shield and sword, and the rapier came into use in the order named. Of the Highlanders Scott says: "They went always armed, carrying bows and arrows, large swords, which they wielded with both hands, called claymores, pole-axes, and daggers for close fight. For defense, they had a round wooden shield, or target, stuck full of nails; and their great men had shirts of mail, not unlike to the flannel shirts now worn, only composed of links of iron, instead of threads of worsted; but the common men were so far from desiring armor, that they sometimes threw their plaids away, and fought in their shirts, which they wore very long and large, after the Irish fashion."

Government. — The inhabitants of the Border were divided into great families such as the Kers, the Homes, the Scotts, and the like, the heads of which commanded the allegiance of their followers to the last breath of life. An even more intensified neighborhood spirit prevailed in the Highlands. " This part of the Scottish nation," says Scott,

IN THE TROSACHS

" was divided into clans, that is, tribes. The persons composing each of these clans believed themselves all to be descended, at some distant period, from the same common ancestor, whose name they usually bore. Thus, one tribe was called MacDonald, which signifies the sons of Donald; another MacGregor, or the sons of Gregor; MacNeil, the sons of Neil, and so on. Every one of these tribes had its own separate chief, or commander, whom they supposed to be the immediate representative of the great father of the tribe from whom they were all descended. To this chief they paid the most unlimited obedience, and willingly followed his commands in peace or war; not caring although, in doing so, they transgressed the laws of the king, or went into rebellion against the king himself. Each tribe lived in a valley, or district of the mountains, separated from the others; and they often made war upon and fought desperately with each other."

To this Macaulay adds: " Had an observer studied the character of the Highlanders he would have found that the people had no love for their country or for their king; that they had no attachment to any commonwealth larger than the clan or to any magistrate superior to the chief. . . . Their intense attachment to their own tribe and their own patriarch, though politically a great evil, partook of the nature of virtue. . . . There must be some elevation of soul in a man who loves the society of which he is a member and the leader whom he follows with a love stronger than the love of life."

THE HISTORICAL BACKGROUND

Fitz-James and the Douglas. — Of the various characters in *The Lady of the Lake*, Fitz-James and the Douglas are historical. The disguised Fitz-James represents James V of Scotland, the son of James IV who fell on Flodden Field. His mother was a sister of the much married Henry VIII of England. He was the husband of Mary of Guise and the father of Mary Queen of Scots. He was but a year and a half old when his father died.

The regency was much fought over. First his mother, then an uncle, controlled the boy. Then the Douglas, Earl of Angus, who had married the widow, got possession of young James, surrounded him with a picked guard of one hundred men, and held him a virtual prisoner until he was twenty-six years old. One night when vigilance was relaxed, James dressed himself as a groom and went to the stables under pretext of getting horses ready for an early hunt the next morning. Mounting and riding out without arousing suspicion, the young prince, who was supposed to be abed, galloped all night with two trusty servants from Falkland to Stirling.

" At daylight he reached the bridge of Stirling, which was the only mode of passing the river Forth, except by boats. It was defended by gates, which the King, after passing through them, ordered to be closed, and directed the passage to be watched. He was a weary man when he reached Stirling castle, where he was joyfully received by the governor, whom his mother had placed in that strong fortress. The draw-bridges were raised, the portcullises dropt, guards set, and every measure of defence and precaution resorted to.   But the King was so much afraid of again falling into the hands of the Douglases, that, tired as he was, he would not go to sleep until the keys of the castle were placed in his own keeping, and laid underneath his pillow." — *Tales of a Grandfather.*

Free from the Douglas. — In Stirling he was safe from the Douglases.   On pain of death he forbade any of the name to come within twelve miles of the Castle.   Here he called the Estates (parliament) together and caused a decree of perpetual banishment to be declared against the Douglas and his kinsmen.   But in *The Lady of the Lake* James relents and becomes reconciled to old Archibald Douglas, the father of Ellen.

James's Rule. — As soon as James was seated firmly, he began to institute reforms.   An early project to which Roderick refers in scathing terms (ii, 615) was the reduction of the Border to some degree of order.   By hanging and other repressive measures James made the rearing of sheep and cattle a peaceful occupation.   He established the Court of Sessions (supreme court), of which Scott became clerk three hundred years later.   He caused a search for precious metals to be instituted.   Lead was found in abundance and also the Clydesdale gold from which the " bonnet pieces " were coined.

Death of James. — James was a brave, active monarch and did much for Scotland.   Toward the end of his short reign he got into trouble with England.   His military operations miscarried and he fell into melancholy.   He died, of a broken heart, Scott says, in 1542 at the early age of 31, when his daughter, Mary Queen of Scots, was but seven days old.

LIFE OF WALTER SCOTT

Ancestry. — Walter Scott was born in Edinburgh, August 15, 1771 — less than four years before the battle of Bunker Hill.

Though born in Edinburgh, he was a Border lad. His father was the only Scott to leave the Border for city life.

On his mother's side Walter sprang from the Rutherfords and the Swintons, — Border men all. On his father's side the ancestral tree struck its roots deep in Border soil with branches, seemingly, in every valley, — Scotts, literally, all over the Border.

Childhood. — While still a youngster he contracted infantile paralysis. On the advice of one grandfather, Dr. Rutherford of Edinburgh University, wee Walter was sent to live in the country with his other grandfather, the respected sheep-farmer at "Sandy Knowe."

One of his earliest memories is of lying on the floor while his grandfather tried to beguile him to crawl. Among other remedies employed was the ordeal of the hide. As often as a sheep was killed Walter was stripped and wrapped in the warm, reeking pelt, — somewhat on the principle of a hot mud-bath.

With the best of care the child improved but, as a matter of fact, never recovered the entire use of his right leg. Scott went through life with a noticeable limp and often sought the aid of a cane or the shoulder of a companion. He was so robust and so active by nature, however, that he became an expert horseman, and was foremost at the hunt or in spearing salmon.

Sandy Knowe was the earliest home Walter could remember and proved to be not only the home of his childhood but his vacation home for many a year. A better home he could not have had. He was a household pet, and to partially satisfy his insatiable appetite for stories, his grandmother told him of warlocks and witches; of giants, and fairies and kings; told him tales of forays and fights; and repeated ballads and songs till he knew them by heart. Often he was taken out to the pasture where he lay on the grass watching the sheep nibble, while he extracted from the shepherd the last word of shepherd lore or gossip. Then, again, an aunt, Janet Scott, read to him. He seems to have kept some one busy entertaining him most of the time.

"Sandy Knowe," says Washington Irving: "was favorable both for story-teller and listener. It commanded a wide view over all the Border country, with its feudal towers, its haunted glens, and wizard streams. As the old shepherd told his tales he could point out the very scene of the action."

In the introduction to the third canto of *Marmion*, Scott has paid generous and grateful tribute to the early and moulding influence of Sandy Knowe and its kindly people. His words remind one, in a way, of the fireside scene in Whittier's *Snowbound*.

> "Thus while I ape the measure wild
>   Of tales that charmed me yet a child,
>   Rude though they be, still with the chime
>   Return the thoughts of early time;
>   And feelings, roused in life's first day,
>   Glow in the line and prompt the lay."

Health. — Every effort was made to cure Walter's lameness. Aunt Janet deserves a halo. When a sacrifice was to be made she was the heroine of the play. We find her sojourning with Walter at Bath for the sake of the springs and again at the seashore for the salt water bathing.

At both places Walter found more than healing waters. At Bath he was taken to see *As You Like It*. An early start for a four year old. In those days children were to be seen and not heard. Walter petrified his aunt Janet, delighted his uncle, Captain Robert Scott, and, no doubt, scandalized the audience by expressing his glee or otherwise as the play progressed.

At Prestonpans, at the age of eight, he made the acquaintance of a retired soldier, who " had pitched his tent " in that village. The veteran took the utmost satisfaction in narrating his campaign experiences. He took deep offense and withdrew his affections, however, when Walter's perverse and teasing assertion that General Burgoyne would lose his way in the American wilderness came true. This Captain Dalgetty is the original of the soldier of that name so prominent in *The Legend of Montrose*.

Home Life. — From Prestonpans Walter went to his father's house, which " continued to be my most established place of residence until my marriage in 1797." Walter was one of twelve children, not all of whom grew up.

Not enough has been made of his mother. The lad inherited literary talent from his mother rather than from his father: from the scholarly Rutherfords rather than from the Border Scotts. A passage from the *Autobiography* gives a glimpse of the home life and his mother's influence.

" I felt the change, from being a single indulged brat to becoming a member of a large family, very severely; for, under the gentle government of my kind grandmother, who was meekness itself, and of my aunt, who, though of an higher temper, was exceedingly attached to me, I had acquired a degree of license which could not be permitted in a large family. I had sense enough, however, to bend my temper to my new circumstances; but, such was the agony which I internally experienced, that I have guarded against nothing more, in the education of my own family, than against their acquiring habits of self-willed caprice and domination. I found much consolation, during this period of mortification, in the partiality of my mother. She joined to a light and happy temper of mind a strong turn to study poetry and works of imagination.

" My lameness and my solitary habits had made me a tolerable reader, and my hours of leisure were usually spent in reading aloud to my mother Pope's translation of Homer, which, excepting a few traditionary ballads, was the first poetry which I perused. My mother had good natural taste and great feeling: she used to make me pause upon those passages which expressed generous and worthy sentiments, and, if she could not divert me from those which were descriptive of battle and tumult, she contrived at least to divide my attention between them. My own enthusiasm, however, was chiefly awakened by the wonderful and the terrible — the common taste of children, but in which I have remained a child even unto this day."

High School. — Walter's education was now undertaken in earnest. He entered the Edinburgh High School, and applied himself with varying degrees of success. He is said to have balked at Greek, but he put in five years at Latin. The first years were burdensome drill work, but in the remaining two years Walter began to distinguish himself by felicitous translations of Virgil and other Latin poets.

Though not a part of the school course, " my acquaintance with English literature was gradually extending itself. In the intervals of my school hours I had always perused with avidity such books of history or poetry or voyages and travels as chance presented to me, — not forgetting the usual, or rather ten times the usual, quantity of fairy tales, eastern stories, romances, etc. These studies were totally unregulated and undirected. My tutor thought it almost a sin to open a profane play or poem; and my mother, besides that she might be in some degree trammeled by the religious scruples which he suggested, had no longer the opportunity to hear me read poetry as formerly. I found, however, in her dressing room (where I slept at one time) some odd volumes of Shakespeare; nor can I easily forget the rapture with which I sate up in my shirt reading them by the light of a fire in her apartment, until the bustle of the family rising from supper warned me it was time to creep back to my bed, where I was supposed to have been safely deposited since nine o'clock."

Playtimes. — These school days were not occupied wholly with literature. Border blood showed itself. Though Walter was lame he was active and led a following of lads, now to climb Arthur's Seat, hear stories, and look down on Edinburgh, or else to head a raid against the town boys between whom and the school an altogether delightful and not infrequently bloody feud existed. Says Scott:

" Among my companions, my good-nature and a flow of ready imagination rendered me very popular. Boys are uncommonly just in their feelings, and at least equally generous. My lameness, and the efforts that I made to supply that disadvantage, by making up in address, what I lacked in activity, engaged the latter principle in my favor; and in winter play hours, when hard exercise was impossible, my tales used to assemble an admiring audience round Luckie Brown's fireside, and happy was he who could sit next to the inexhaustible narrator. I was also, though often negligent of my own task, always ready to assist my friends, and hence I had a little party of staunch partizans and adherents, stout of hand and heart, though somewhat dull of head, the very tools for raising a hero to eminence. So on the whole I made a brighter figure in the yards than in the class."

More Poor Health. — At this time Walter's health gave the family further concern, so he discontinued his work in the high school and went to live again with Aunt Janet. Her new home was in Kelso, one of the most beautiful villages in Scotland. In after days Scott declared he owed much to the picturesque scenery of the vicinity. Here he became acquainted with the Ballantyne boys of whom we shall hear later.

Walter read everything he could lay his hands on. He had already made a collection of ballads largely in manuscript. At Aunt Janet's he came across Percy's *Reliques of Ancient Poetry*. He writes:

" I remember well the spot where I read these volumes for the first time. It was beneath a huge platanus tree, in the ruins of what had been intended for an old-fashioned arbor. . . . The summer day sped onward so fast, that, notwithstanding the sharp appetite of thirteen, I forgot the hour of dinner, was sought for with anxiety, and was still found entranced in my intellectual banquet. To read and to remember was in this instance the same thing, and henceforth I overwhelmed my schoolfellows, and all who would hearken to me, with tragical recitations from the ballads of Bishop Percy. The first time, too, I could scrape a few shillings together, which were not common occurrences with me, I bought unto myself a copy of these beloved volumes; nor do I believe I ever read a book half so frequently or with half the enthusiasm."

University Life. — From 1783 to 1786 Walter attended the University of Edinburgh. Here, as in the high school, he followed his own bent. He read omnivorously, particularly poetry and history dealing with medieval Europe. Demonology and witchcraft seem to have had a peculiar attraction for him.

Apprenticeship. — On May 15, 1786 — the date is of interest because he seems so young, only fifteen years old — Walter signed articles of apprenticeship for five years under penalty of forty pounds and entered his father's law office. As this apprenticeship preceded the day of the typewriter, a considerable portion of his time was spent in copying legal papers — as high as one hundred twenty sheets in a day, he tells us. For a Border lad this work was distasteful and was exchanged on the slightest pretext for a hike. No wonder, for Edinburgh was, and still is, a compact city with most enticing surroundings.

Legal Training. — In the office Scott acquired perforce method, accuracy, and skill in despatching business. But aside from delightful pen pictures of this or that advocate and clear drawings of court scenes, his writings are free from legal proceedings and bear out the assertion that he took little interest in the law. In the meantime, however, under constant spur from his father, Scott attended law lectures at the University and was admitted to the bar in 1792. He practised law in a desultory manner for fourteen years.

Liddesdale Raids. — The young advocate's start in life cannot have been as difficult as the experience which greets many a lawyer. He appears to have remained in his father's office and in his father's home. The spectres of rent and board and the expense of a law library cannot have haunted him.

During the early years of his " practice " Scott took seven successive annual vacation trips, " Liddesdale Raids," he called them, into the Border country. With a lawyer friend, a Mr. Shortreed, as a guide, he ransacked the old moss-trooping valley of the Liddel to perfection. They rode on horseback, of course, Border fashion, for there were neither wheels nor roads in the valley. There were no inns, but an Edinburgh advocate was not an everyday visitor. The travelers were made welcome at the shepherd's hut and at the minister's manse.

We are indebted to Judge Shortreed for an account of the " raids." We read of mosses, moors, dark bridle-paths, hospitality, songs, the lilt of " Dick o' the Cow "; of dogs, horses, and sheep; of devilled ducks and salmon; of punch, and of a wooden punch bowl called " Wisdom." A Dr. Elliot, parish minister, supplied a large bundle of ballads in manuscript which helped out in the preparation later of Scott's *Minstrelsy of the Scottish Border;* another Elliot, won by the way Scott had of making friends with the retinue of dogs in the farmyard, served later as the original of Dandie Dinmont in *Guy Mannering.*

" Oh, what pleasant days," wrote Shortreed, " and then a' the nonsense we had cost us naething. We never put hand in pocket for a week on end. Toll-bars there were none — and indeed, I think our haill charges were a feed o' corn to our horses in the gangin' and comin' at Riccortoun mill. . . . Sic an endless fund o' humor and drollery as he then had wi' him! Never ten yards but we were either laughing or roaring and singing. Whenever we stopped, how brawlie he suited himsel' to everybody. He aye did as the lave did; never made himsel' the great man, or took ony airs in the company. I've seen him in a' moods in these jaunts, grave and gay, daft and serious, but he was aye the gentleman. . . . He was *makin' himsel'* a' the time, but he didna ken maybe what he was about till years had passed; at first he thought o' little, I dare say, but the queerness and the fun."

Scott's father thought about it enough for two. In very desperation and bitterness of heart he reproached his son for his vagabondage with, " I greatly doubt, sir, you were born for nae better than just a gangrel scrape gut " (wandering fiddler).

For a picture of this anxious, excellent father with all his limitations and of affectionate, rollicking Walter with all his shortcomings, turn to the portraits of Alan Fairford and his father, Saunders, in *Red Gauntlet*.

Marriage. — In keeping with Scott's character, his domestic life ran happily. His one romance was not successful. One evening, during a genuine Scottish downpour, Scott loaned his umbrella and lost his heart to a charming young lady at the door of Greyfriars Church. For some years Scott hoped to marry her but the families on both sides thought the young people not suited in point of rank. The lady married a title, one of Scott's personal friends. Scott admitted, even when well on in years, that in his opinion she had spoiled a match which should have been made.

However, he returned the same summer from a raid into Wordsworth's country with a favorable opinion of a Miss Carpenter, the lovely daughter of a French refugee. Scott's family objected to her nationality, but the young people were married shortly (1797) and set up housekeeping at Lasswade on the Esk, six miles from Edinburgh.

Ashestiel. — In 1799 Scott was appointed Sheriff (county judge) of Selkirkshire; this led the family to a brother's house, Ashestiel, in that shire. The best of Scott's poetical work was done here. The view from his door is thus described in the introduction to the first canto of *Marmion*:

> "Late, gazing down the steepy linn,
> That hems our little garden in,
> Low in its dark and narrow glen,
> You scarce the rivulet might ken,
> So thick the tangled greenwood grew,
> So feeble trilled the streamlet through;

Now, murmuring hoarse, and frequent seen
Through bush and briar, no longer green,
An angry brook, it sweeps the glade,
Brawls over rock and wild cascade,
And, foaming brown with doubled speed,
Hurries its waters to the Tweed."

Abbotsford. — Mr. and Mrs. Scott lived happily at
Ashestiel with their "four hardy imps," but Scott had set

ABBOTSFORD AND THE RIVER TWEED

his heart on building up an estate of his own. He fixed on
an old farm down the Tweed about six miles, in the vicinity
of Melrose Abbey and in full view of the Cheviot Hills.
Catching a happy inspiration from a near-by ford across
which the monks of Melrose must have waded to and fro,

THE LIBRARY AT ABBOTSFORD

he called his new place Abbotsford. To Abbotsford accordingly, in 1812, he moved with twenty-five cart-loads of furniture, antiquities, and trumpery, not forgetting his dogs, his pigs, his horses, his poultry, his fishing-tackle, his guns, and the family.

Abbotsford was not particularly attractive to begin with. The old farmhouse faced a muddy duckpond, and was flanked by a kail yard on one side and by stables on the other, but the place had the making of what Scott wanted. As the years went by he bought tract after tract of adjacent land. He set out extensive plantations of young trees which he took the greatest delight in trimming with his own hand. Winding roads, bridle-paths, footways, game coverts, gardens, flower beds, hedges, seats, arbors, and grounds were laid out with skill.

The farmhouse gave way to a mansion of dark gray granite to which successive additions, towers, and turrets, gave the effect of a feudal castle. Despite massive walls and deep windows the interior was made cosy and attractive. Broad, low windows overlooked inviting views of the Tweed and of the lawn.

Scott's library was notable, but the feature of the house in which the owner took particular pride was a spacious entrance hall adorned with arms and armor, antiquities, and trophies of the chase — a veritable museum. This entry way resembled the entrance to the island home of Roderick Dhu, described years before (i, 544–559).

In all, Scott is said to have spent three hundred and eighty thousand dollars on Abbotsford — easily equivalent in purchasing power to a million dollars in our day.

Scott desired to establish a family of which he would be regarded as the head, but none of his children long survived him. Abbotsford is now in the hands of wealthy relatives. The apartments and grounds are kept as Scott left them,

and are shown with the greatest kindness to the tourist
and literary pilgrim.

Irving's Visit. — In the summer of 1817 Washington Irving visited Scott. He has left a pleasing picture of the
family life at Abbotsford:

" The noise of my chaise had disturbed the quiet of the
establishment. Out sallied the master of the castle, a black

THE ARMORY AT ABBOTSFORD

greyhound, and leaping on one of the blocks of stone, began
a furious barking. This alarm brought out the whole garrison of dogs, all open-mouthed and vociferous. In a little
while the lord of the castle himself made his appearance. I
knew him at once by the likenesses that had been published
of him. He came limping up the gravel walk, aiding himself
by a stout walking staff, but moving rapidly and with vigor.
By his side jogged along a large iron-gray stag hound, of

most grave demeanor, who took no part in the clamor of the canine rabble, but seemed to consider himself bound, for the dignity of the house, to give me a courteous reception.

" Before Scott reached the gate, he called out in a hearty tone welcoming me to Abbotsford, and asking news of Campbell. Arrived at the door of the chaise, he grasped me warmly by the hand: ' Come, drive down, drive down to the house,' said he, ' ye're just in time for breakfast, and afterward ye shall see all the wonders of the Abbey.'

" I would have excused myself on the plea of having already made my breakfast. ' Hut, man,' cried he, ' a ride in the morning in this keen air of the Scotch hills is warrant enough for a second breakfast.'

" I was accordingly whirled to the portal of the cottage, and, in a few moments, found myself seated at the breakfast table. There was no one present but the family, which consisted of Mrs. Scott; her eldest daughter, Sophia, then a fine girl about seventeen; Miss Anne Scott, two or three years younger; Walter, a well grown stripling; and Charles, a lively boy, eleven or twelve years of age.

" I soon felt myself quite at home, and my heart in a glow, with the cordial welcome I experienced. I had thought to make a mere morning visit, but found I was not to be let off so lightly. ' You must not think our neighborhood is to be read in a morning like a newspaper,' said Scott; ' it takes several days of study for an observant traveller that has a relish for old-world trumpery. After breakfast you shall make your visit to Melrose Abbey; I shall not be able to accompany you, as I have some household affairs to attend to; but I will put you in charge of my son Charles, who is very learned in all ways touching the old ruin and the neighborhood it stands in. . . . When you come back, I'll take you out on a ramble about the neighborhood. To-morrow we will take a look at the Yarrow, and the next day we will drive over to Dryburgh Abbey, which is a fine old ruin, well worth your seeing.' In a word, before Scott had got through with his plan, I found myself committed for a visit of several days, and it seemed as if a little realm of romance was suddenly open before me."

Working Hours. — Ere he left Ashestiel Scott ordered his life with system. Six o'clock found him throwing off page

THE BRAES OF YARROW

after page with untiring rapidity. He breakfasted at nine, by which time he had done enough " to break the neck of the day's work." Back to his desk again and by noon he was his " own man." Afternoons were spent on horseback, or with a hunting neighbor, or with fishing tackle, or with a salmon spear or with Tom Purdie trimming trees, or else in showing visitors the Tweed, Melrose Abbey, and the braes of Yarrow.

Speaking of his literary methods Scott put the matter

this way: "I lie simmering over things for an hour or so before I get up — and there's the time I am dressing to overhaul my half-sleeping, half-waking *projet de chapitre*, and, when I get the paper before me, it commonly runs off pretty easily. Besides, I often take a doze in the plantations, and while Tom marks out a dyke or a drain as I have directed, one's fancy may be running to its ain riggs in some other world."

Scott's Senses were peculiarly unequal. His hearing was none too good, and his sense of smell was deficient. It was a matter of remark that his sense of taste was blunted. But his eyesight was keen, and added to his popularity in the hunting. "It was him that commonly saw the hare sitting," said his little son.

Scott was keenly sensitive to melody in words and rhythm in verse, but he had no ear for music. The beauty of a landscape or the associations of a ruined castle worked on his emotions until he was almost speechless, but try his best and he could not make a drawing to illustrate his notes.

Professional Courtesy. — Scott was a writer of unfailing courtesy. He was a contemporary of Burns, Burke, Wordsworth, Coleridge, Campbell, Carlyle, Macaulay, Byron, Moore, Shelley, Keats, De Quincey, and of the Americans, Poe, Irving, and Cooper. He admired and was admired by the leading writers of Germany and of France, but did not lose his poise. He edited the works of Dryden, of Swift, and of others less noted, in a wholesome, appreciative way. He wrote review articles without number and compiled a faithful history of Scotland for *Gardner's Encyclopedia*. Even though he had not written his major poems or the Waverley Novels, he would have been a man of literary note. His day was marked by undignified literary quarrels, but he took no part in them. Nearing the end and looking back over his life he wrote:

" It only remains for me to say that, during my short preeminence of popularity, I faithfully observed the rules of moderation which I had resolved to follow before I began my course as a man of letters. If a man is determined to make a noise in the world, he is sure to encounter abuse and ridicule, as he who gallops furiously through a village must reckon on being followed by the curs in full cry. Experienced persons know that in stretching to flog the latter, the rider is very apt to catch a bad fall; nor is an attempt to chastise a malignant critic attended with less danger to the author. On this principle, I let parody, burlesque, and squibs find their own level; and while the latter hissed most fiercely, I was cautious never to catch them up, as schoolboys do, to throw them back against the naughty boy who fired them off, wisely remembering that they are in such cases apt to explode in the handling. Let me add that my reign (since Byron has so called it) was marked by some instances of good-nature as well as patience. I never refused a literary person of merit such services in smoothing his way to the public as were in my power; and I had the advantage — rather an uncommon one with our irritable race — to enjoy general favor without incurring permanent ill-will, so far as is known to me, among any of my contemporaries."

Literary Origin. — Scott inherited a rare, a new combination of ancestral traits. He was born into a family of intelligence with means to care for his health and to give him a fitting education. He came to maturity at a time when literary material was abundant and was waiting to be used; at a time when each parish contained at least a clergyman and a schoolmaster of education who could supply the material Scott wanted.

Edinburgh was long the residence of royalty, the seat of a noted university, the home of the higher courts, and an active publishing center. In Scott's day, its social atmosphere, with less to distract, was more stimulating, more distinctively intellectual than that of London. Though he *was* a genius, a rare man, a phenomenon, Scott was also, and to a marked degree, the product of his day and of his social surroundings. His success was due to ancestry, environment, and opportunity.

Scope. — Scott was local, not national. Carlyle was a son of Scotland, as crabbed a Scot as ever piled thistles, but his likes and his dislikes were world-wide in their application; Macaulay was a Highlander, the grandson of two Highland parish ministers, but he drove a British quill; Burns was a Lowlander, a plowman poet all his life, but he was Scottish; no one would think of calling him the Lowland poet; but Scott was a Borderman always.

He wrote poetry and prose with equal facility. In chronology his work ranged from the Crusades to his own generation; geographically, his scenes extend from Syria to Inverness; he was intensely patriotic, a member of the local militia, loyal to George III to a fault; for all that, he was a Borderman. This word is the key to Walter Scott, his life, and his activities.

Writings. — The subjoined table of Scott's writings is somewhat condensed. A vast amount of material in the form of magazine articles and labor connected with editions of Swift and other authors is omitted, but the dates show how Scott advanced steadily from one form of writing to another.

I. TRANSLATIONS		1795–1800
II. BALLADS		1800–1819
Eve of St. John	. . . . . .	1800
Border Minstrelsy	. . . .	1802–1803
Cadyow Castle	. . . . .	1802

III. POEMS OF ROMANCE

The Lay of the Last Minstrel . . . 1805
Marmion 1808
The Lady of the Lake 1810
Vision of Don Roderick . . . 1811
Rokeby 1812
The Bridal of Triermain . . . 1813
The Lord of the Isles . . . 1815

IV. WAVERLEY NOVELS

Waverley 1814
Guy Mannering 1815
The Antiquary 1816
The Black Dwarf 1816
Old Mortality 1816
Rob Roy 1818
The Heart of Mid-Lothian . . . 1818
The Bride of Lammermoor . . . 1819
The Legend of Montrose . . . 1819
Ivanhoe 1820
The Monastery 1820
The Abbot 1820
Kenilworth 1821
The Pirate 1822
The Fortunes of Nigel . . . 1822
Peveril of the Peak 1823
Quentin Durward 1823
St. Ronan's Well 1824
Redgauntlet 1824
The Betrothed 1825
The Talisman 1825
Woodstock 1826
The Two Drovers 1827
The Highland Widow . . . 1827
The Surgeon's Daughter . . . 1827

The Fair Maid of Perth 1828
Anne of Geierstein 1829
Count Robert of Paris 1831
Castle Dangerous 1831
V. TALES OF A GRANDFATHER . 1827–30
Life of Napoleon 1827

Verse. — Although Scott's early life was an excellent preparation for his work, he appears to have drifted into authorship on a leisurely tide. He was twenty-four years old before he began to appear in print. He began with translations of German poems. These were accounted good by the few who took the pains to read them. He then tried his prentice hand on ballads which were accounted spirited and well written.

In 1802, at the age of thirty-one, he prepared *The Minstrelsy of the Scottish Border*. This was a collection of the best of the ballads which he had gathered and contained a few original contributions made by himself and friends.

One piece of verse designed for the collection pleased Scott so much and seemed to him to have such possibilities that he kept it out. It grew under his hand by easy transition from a Border ballad into a six-canto metrical romance, which he named *The Lay of the Last Minstrel*.

The collection gave Scott position, the poem made him famous. *Marmion: a Tale of Flodden Field* soon followed and was enormously popular. *The Lady of the Lake* was greeted with sufficient applause to turn the head of an ordinary man. These three, *The Lay of the Last Minstrel*, *Marmion*, and *The Lady of the Lake*, are Scott's notable poetical works.

Other poems followed but they exhibited a marked falling off. They were comparatively poor reading and were a disappointment to his admirers. Byron, too, had sprung into fame over night. Scott realized that through his own decline and the rise of another he had been supplanted hopelessly in popular favor.

Prose. — In the meantime Scott got to work on prose fiction. Falling back on his talent for story telling, he resurrected a partly written manuscript and finished it. In 1814, accordingly, epoch-making *Waverley* was published, but Scott, uncertain of the result, withheld his name. The success of the tale was so pronounced, however, and so immediate, that *Guy Mannering*, *Rob Roy*, and, in fact, a whole procession, led by these worthies, appeared in rapid succession — all under the banner of " The Author of *Waverley*."

Many were in the secret. The pretext of unknown authorship was kept up more in a spirit of fun than otherwise. At more than one banquet, Scott joined in toasting the unknown but evidently talented author of *Waverley*, wishing him all success and a long career.

Finance. — Scott was not a penniless author. His family was well-to-do. His childhood was expensive. As a boy he may have been kept a trifle short of pocket money, but his education and entrance to the law were made easy by parental solicitude. Mrs. Scott had $2500 a year.

For his own income the Selkirkshire appointment brought in $1500 a year, and an appointment as Clerk of Sessions (supreme court) carried ultimately a salary of $4000. He inherited also from an uncle and received a share of his father's property. Altogether he must have had an income of ten thousand dollars a year independently of law and literature. His books sold well and yielded a large income. His official duties required but a part of the day during less than half of the year. So Scott was in position to live the life of a country gentleman.

Disaster. — Scott bought Abbotsford and embarked on vast expenditure. He kept open house, rivalling the expense of a hotel.   He spent money freely on his family. Though he earned large sums and spent royally, no one accused Scott of going beyond his means.

In 1820 George IV made him a baronet, but Sir Walter continued to work hard and to live an outdoor life devoted to his dogs, his horses, his trees, and his neighbors.

In 1826, through no seeming act of his, misfortune came down like an avalanche.   In earlier days Scott had formed a business connection with boyhood friends who published his works under the name of Ballantyne and Co.   This firm was not a brilliant success and was forced to sell the novels to Constable and Co.   The two firms continued to be connected.   London losses carried Constable and Co. down and the Ballantynes went with them.   Scott, at the age of fifty-five, found himself responsible for the debts of his firm to the amount of approximately $600,000.

An ordinary man would have been crushed, but, mindful of Walter who led the Scotts at Otterbourne and of Auld Wat of Hardie, Scott's courage rose to the occasion.   The public was stirred and felt that help should be given.   One gentleman declared that if every man to whom the author of *Waverley* had given a month of pleasure were to send him a sixpence Scott would rise the next morning richer than Rothschild.

Scott declined all compromise.   To the suggestion that he pay all he could and call it quits, he replied, " For this in a court of honor I should deserve to lose my spurs "; to offers of assistance he replied, " Gentlemen, time and I against any two.   Let me take this good ally into company, and I believe I shall be able to pay you every farthing."

In the midst of his distress Lady Scott died and left him to carry on the struggle alone.   At this point he wrote in his journal:

" For myself, I scarce know how I feel — sometimes as

THE MONUMENT TO SCOTT AT EDINBURGH

firm as the Bass Rock, sometimes as weak as the water that breaks on it. I am as alert at thinking and deciding as I ever was in my life. Yet, when I contrast what this place now is with what it has been not long since, I think my heart will break."

However, Scott adopted heroic measures. He dismissed most of his servants, sold his town house, and cut expense in every direction. Like Fitz-James, " he manned himself with dauntless air," and attacked the problem. He finished *The Life of Napoleon Bonaparte*. It brought in $90,000. He wrote *Woodstock*. It yielded $40,000. A new edition of his novels was prepared and 23,000 sets were sold to a public eager to help. In less than two years Scott was able to pay in $200,000 on, not *his* debts, but the debts of his old firm in which he was a silent partner. For a few years his earnings were $50,000 a year. He took out an insurance policy on his life for $110,000 which at death, together with the sale of rights to publish his works, practically wiped out the largest debt ever shouldered by an author.

Failing Health. — Through the pressure of overwork and care, Scott's health finally gave way. His physician thought a winter cruise in the Mediterranean might help. In the autumn of 1831, the government placed a frigate at his disposal. He passed the winter, accordingly, at Rome, Naples, Malta, and other places, but did not mend. His sad heart yearned for the Tweed and his beloved Border hills. " Let us to Abbotsford," was his plea, so in June he turned homeward via Venice and overland. He was carried southward from Edinburgh, on the last stage of the trip. " When, turning himself on his couch, his eye caught at length his own towers, at the distance of a mile, he sprang up with a cry of delight."

Abbotsford, his friends, and his pets gave him renewed strength for a few days only.

The end is best described by Lockhart: " About half-past one p.m., on the 21st of September, Sir Walter breathed his last, in the presence of all his children. It was a beautiful day — so warm, that every window was wide open — and so perfectly still, that the sound of all others most delicious to his ear, the gentle ripple of the Tweed over its pebbles, was distinctly audible as we knelt around the bed, and his eldest son kissed and closed his eyes."

Scott was laid away among the roses of Dryburgh Abbey. Many wreaths have been laid on his bier; none more sincere or more fitting than Carlyle's: ".And so the curtain falls and the strong Walter Scott is with us no more. It can be said of him, when he departed he took a man's life with him. No sounder piece of British manhood was put together in that eighteenth century of Time. Alas, his fine Scotch face, with its shaggy honesty, sagacity and goodness, when we saw it latterly on the Edinburgh streets, was all worn with care, the joy all fled from it: — ploughed deep with labour and sorrow. We shall never forget it; we shall never see it again. Adieu, Sir Walter, pride of all Scotchmen, take our proud and sad farewell."